Tears of Deception

Patrick Pierre

ISBN: 979-8-9857208—7-7

2nd Edition

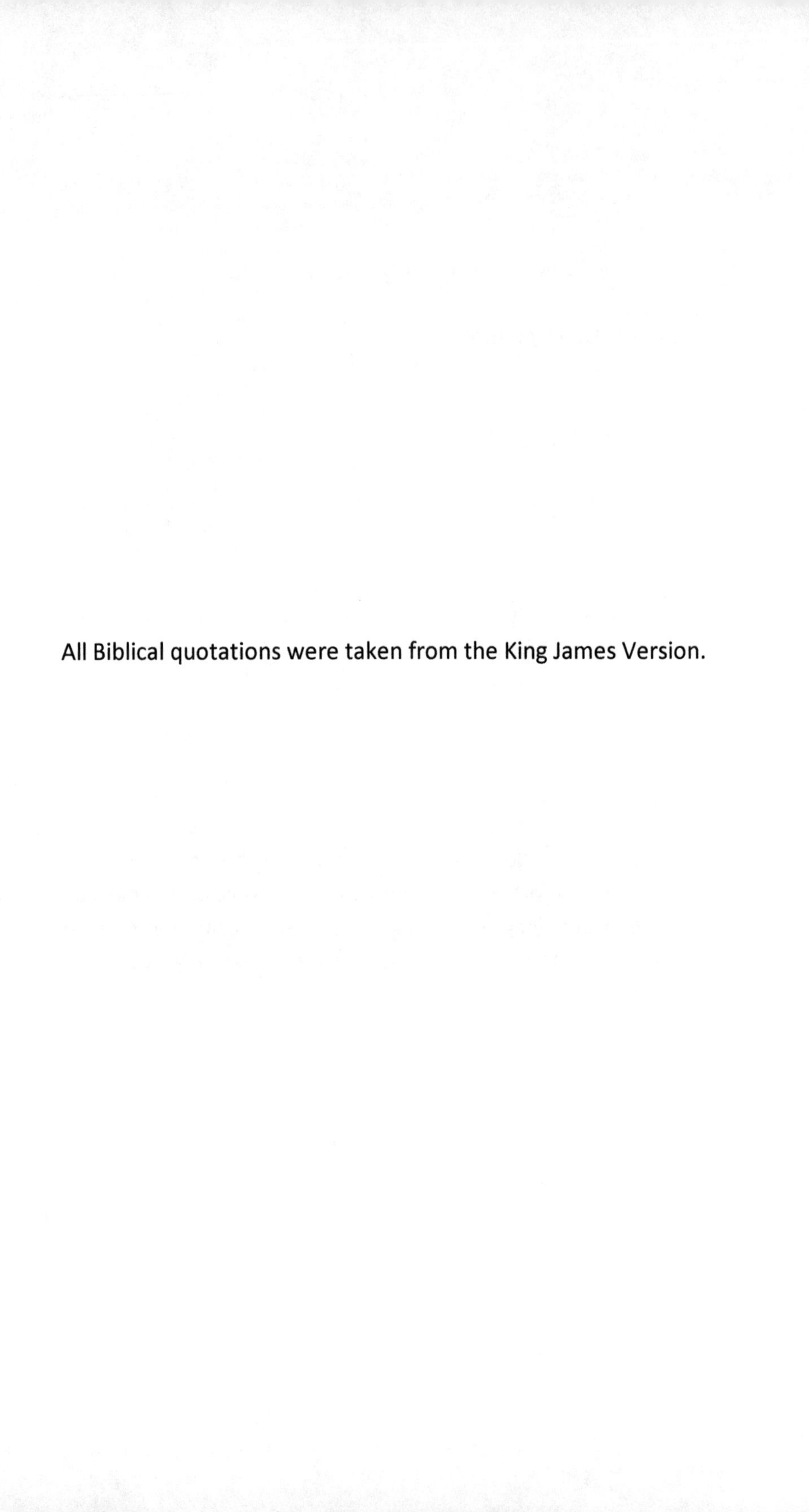

All Biblical quotations were taken from the King James Version.

About the Author

Patrick Pierre was born in Port-au-Prince, Haiti. Some He is the Pastor of Union Baptist Church in Society Hill, South Carolina. He is the author of Sold Out with A Kiss, Stop God Is Talking, The World Is in Turmoil, Animal Quest, The Necessity of Worship, (Worship is not an option, but a requirement), and Audio book of The Necessity of Worship. Patrick Pierre studied and accomplished many things which could be very impressive to others. The greatest accomplishment in his life is the fact that he accepted Jesus Christ as his Lord and Savior. To better introduce himself "Patrick Pierre is a child of God.

Dedication

The Union Baptist Church United Ministry, Society Hill, SC., Church Family, I appreciate your prayers and your support. I love you from the bottom of my heart.

To the most beautiful lady that ever walk on the planet earth, my late mother Ena and the greatest man of my life, my late father Fernand Pierre.

To my Uncle Rodrigue Casimir, I thank you for being my role model.

To all my children, brothers and sisters, nieces and nephews, my love for you is unconditional.

To Deacon William and Pastor Faye Waiters, thank you a million times for your support and encouragement for standing by my side through "thick and thin."

To Jean and Carolle Fleurio, you have shown me what love is all about and I thank you.

To my wonderful sister-in-law, Carolyn Simon, thank you for your patience and your dedication.

To all my critics, respectable job, keep on criticizing me and I still love you. Finally, to all the earthquake victims of my hometown Port-au-Prince, Haiti my prayers will always be with you.

IN MEMORY OF

My Father, Fernand Andre Pierre and my Beautiful Mother, Ena Casimir Pierre,

Uncle Rodrigue Casimir

Father Edner Day,

Mrs. Patricia Diane Pierre,

Mother Grace Fergus,

Trustee Claude Fowler,

Deacon William Bill Waiters,

Mother Marie Swiney,

I Miss You Guys so much and Continue to Rest in Peace

Acknowledgment

My Wife, Joy Roberts Pierre

And

The Union Baptist Church Family.

INTRODUCTION

"Tears of Deception" is based on a story that my father told me. It demonstrates the power of forgiveness and love over vengeance and hate. It is a love story that contains a religious awakening that would allow one to see the mercy of God. Pachouco, in his love life deceptions, quickly recognized the power of prayers because his mother, Faye Esther, was a praying woman. Pachouco understood that God could and will pardon anyone who confesses and repents their sins. He also understood God's capability to look beyond the sinner's fault and saw his needs. Again, this is the power of love, confession, and forgiveness. Pachouco learned a valuable lesson: "Never said never" because God is in control.

Who can say they have never done anything wrong that deserved an eternal voyage to Hell? But thanks be to a Merciful and Powerful God who teaches the way to repentance. Who can cast the first stone at anyone for their unruly behavior toward a Good God Almighty? Remember, we were guilty from birth again. God sent a Savior to redeem us from the grip

of a destroyer and a killer. True repentance to God is all it takes to regain our heavenly citizenship. It's impressive how the Supreme Being rejoices over a sinner man’s confession and true repentance. As a result, He welcomes the sinner man with His Agape Love with open arms. The contrary is this approach to humanity, who feels only his sins have the right to be forgiven by God, and everyone else is beyond forgiveness and on their way to hell. Average believers seem to forget or ignore the purpose of the coming of the Son of man. Here is the fact, "For the Son of man is come to save that which was lost." (Matthew
18:11)

I thank God for His coming.

LOVE

Love is a four-letter word so innocent in its spelling and imperative indeed. Soon it has control over one's heart. It can bring joy, happiness, heartache, and pain. Even though "love is an action word," it has been known to be misunderstood by many. To play with love is to play with fire. Fire does burn. Playing with someone's feelings is like playing with a gun with one bullet in the chamber. A dangerous game like this can bring death. Again, love is a four-letter word that is hazardous as hazardous can be. Who can brag they had never played into the stupidity of love? If so, do not claim the victory yet. Is it a game everyone must play at least once in a lifetime? Madness, some people make this game a part of thei3r lives.There was a man named Pachouco. He was from the beautiful Island of Haiti. He also was a member of the Haitian Elite; therefore, he was not poor. He believed sincerely in honor before love. Pachouco is a man of integrity, a family-oriented person who "feared the Lord and hated evil."

Pachouco left his native country to reside in the United States of America and later became a citizen. The first state Pachouco lived in was New York. There he encountered many difficulties. For example, his brother, Serge Gerard, lived in Brooklyn for many years. He had chosen an American girlfriend for Pachouco even before entering New York. Her name was Loretta. According to Serge Gerard, Loretta was the most beautiful woman Pachouco would ever lay his eyes on, and time will tell.

Serge Gerard sent a few pictures of Loretta to Pachouco to see how he liked her. When Pachouco saw her photographs, he went crazy over her beauty. She reminded him of his mother, Faye Esther. He agreed to enter a long-distance relationship with her. However, there was a problem. Pachouco did not speak English fluently at the time. With the help of a French / English Dictionary and what he learned from the classroom, he put together lovely little letters to win her heart. They could not communicate well on the phone because of the language barrier. Many days, Serge Gerard played the role of translator for both. He is a manipulator knew how to twist conversations. He translated what he thought would make Pachouco eager to meet her.

Pachouco met a few obstacles in his love life at home, which turned his heart toward American women. Pachouco had never dreamed of living in the United States, delighted at home. But those few obstacles he experienced brought him to the conclusion that he would not date nor marry island girls. It is not because they were not good enough, but he had become entrapped with nothing but grief from his last two serious relationships. He had made a promise to his mother and himself. If the second relationship did not work out, she would be an American girl the next time he dated. Serge Gerard, well informed about the sourness of his second engagement and the pledge that he once made, quickly introduced Pachouco to Loretta.

Pachouco had been conversing with her for almost a year now. In one of the translations performed by Serge Gerard, his manipulations led Pachouco to believe that Loretta desired to visit him in Haiti. So happy was Pachouco; he offered to pay for the trip. Serge Gerard became the travel agent, planner, and confident right away. No one knew about this trip in question except the three of them.

Pachouco never knew much about his brother until he arrived in New York ten years later. At that time, he would meet his brother face to face for the first time. Pachouco was too young to remember when his brother left Haiti. Therefore, Pachouco had extraordinarily little remembrance of him. It did not stop him from loving Serge Gerard dearly. Pachouco felt in all his brothers, and he was the only one that stood by his side when deception struck Pachouco's love life the second time.

The greatest weakness Pachouco had was that he honored and deeply respected all his family and friends. He praised them with the highest praise; they cannot do any wrong in his eyesight.

One day, a family friend came from Brooklyn, New York, to visit Pachouco and his mother. Her name was Valada, a beautiful Haitian woman, and a true Friend. She stopped by the house to chat with Faye Esther, Pachouco, and others in the house. Faye Esther loved Serge Gerard and considered him as her biological Son. Faye Esther trusted him with great trust. Of course, she knew that Valada was living near him, so she inquired of Valada how Serge Gerard was doing. Valada started to criticize Serge Gerard's behavior abroad in the presence of everybody, which was "a no, no," as far as Pachouco was concerned. She talked about his oldest brother, whom he loved greatly. He shouted at Valada, "You're lying. We are not going this route."

Why was Pachouco becoming so offended, wondered Valada? She came to warn him of Serge Gerard. Pachouco, with a furious look, thanked Valada for her visitation. He asked her to allow him to figure Serge Gerard out for himself because he hated hearsay. She replied to Pachouco's comment by adding, "Time will tell." She gave him a package sent by Serge Gerard from Loretta, and Valada kissed everybody goodbye. The few things that Pachouco needed to know, relating to his brother, was on the verge of being revealed to him by Valada, but he blew it by failing to listen. Inside the package, Valada had given Pachouco was a letter. Loretta claimed she wanted badly to come to see him in that letter. She acquired her passport and made her reservation. However, something came up, and she had to cancel the trip. Loretta promised to refund him every dime he spent for the voyage. Pachouco got on the phone in a hurry, called his brother, all concerned, and asked him, "why did Loretta cancel the voyage?" He replied to Pachouco, "Are you kidding me? She cannot do that. I'm going to call Loretta. I will get back to you." Later that night, Serge Gerard touched bases with him adopted a sad story that someone broke into her house. They stole everything she ever possessed, even money that did not belong to her. She had to produce ten thousand dollars. According to Serge Gerard again, Loretta's sister, Tenaja Ashanti, loaned her two thousand of the ten thousand dollars lost. He claimed he gave Loretta two thousand more. He suggested Pachouco might contribute the remaining balance of six thousand dollars. Pachouco reminded him of the seven thousand dollars he sent to her for her trip not too long before.

"They stole that too," and he continued, "man trust me," Loretta is in big trouble. If she does not replace the money, I'm afraid she might face prosecution, even jail terms. Little brother, keep everything "on the down-low." Pachouco filled with compassion, replied to his brother, "Let me give it some thought." He said exactly what Serge Gerard expected him to say. Instantly he asked Pachouco, "How long do you need before sending the money to Loretta?"

Pachouco responded “I’m not sure. Besides, I might not be able to send all of it.”

Serge Gerard continued by saying, “Just do your best. At least, she knows you are there for her, Pachouco. However, if I were you, instead of wiring the money to avoid any extra charges, I would entrust it with Valada. However, in five days, Valada will be back in Queens, New York.”

Pachouco never had a problem praising nor bragging on his brother’s genius mind. He never ceased to amaze Pachouco; for this reason, he placed much trust in his oldest brother.

Instead of six thousand dollars, he sent Loretta eight thousand dollars cash in large bills by Valada, who also had a heart for Pachouco, but she kept it far from his knowledge. She knew how he felt about the women from the Island.

ENGAGEMENT

Pachouco and Loretta were engaged. They planned to marry the next day after they met face to face for the first time in New York.

At this point in their relationship, Loretta had already received a dozen pictures of Pachouco while he barely had four pictures of hers. They tried to talk on the phone at least once a week, whenever the translator was available. Pachouco could hardly wait to kiss and marry Loretta. He kept all her pictures underneath his pillow and kissed them goodnight every night.

One Sunday, Pachouco called Serge Gerrard to share the good news of the rededication of his life back to the Lord. His brother answered him without hesitation, saying,

"You and Loretta, I'm convinced, created for each other."

"Wow! Share with me, Big Brother, what brought you to this conclusion?"

He replied, "Pachouco, she did the same thing this morning. Your spirits commune daily." Some people may wonder right now, how someone can say, "He is in love with a woman, he only saw in a picture?" There is one thing relating to life "never say never." Whatever way one chooses to think of love, which is what it is. Love could be manipulative, especially when a third party is involved. To love sometimes is to suffer. One should ask a lover a couple of questions: (1) Can infatuation convert to sincere love? (2) Can platonic love develop into a sexual affair? These were habitual questions often crossing the mind of Pachouco. Even though he was a well-educated man, writer, poet, song composer, Bible commentator, and Christian, Pachouco possessed all this knowledge under his conscious mind. However, his love for Loretta overpowered his mind's eye and blinded him.

Unbelievably, Pachouco had made the first step of being recovered, founded, and deliberated the day he rededicated his life to his God. A spirit of unworthiness to worship God had fallen on Pachouco after being deprived of his religious value by his previous love connection. Now Loretta turned his world upside down." He prayed to God to allow him to meet her face to face. He often thanked his brother for the great feeling he had for Loretta. The burning desire to meet "the apple of his eye, his soul mate," was not according to God but Serge Gerard, the hook-up man. Pachouco catches in the hook like a catfish, which not yet realizes its hooks in the hook of manipulation, fraud, and deceit. So far, what seemed so confusing is that Pachouco never took time out to calculate the costs of these endeavors. Pachouco's mind made up. He was willing to pursue this adventure at any cost. Behind his belief was what his mother called the power of stupidity. Pachouco put all the confidence he possessed in his brother. Since the adventure began, Pachouco became closer and more attached to him, whom Pachouco again had no remembrance of neither seeing nor meeting Serge Gerard before.

It appears at a time, and one can be so blind by the word TRUST until they set themselves up for deceit and a fall. The delightful book of life often reminds all citizens on the planet earth not to put their trust in man. Regardless of the Bible's warning to humanity, "There is a way which seemeth right unto a man, but the end thereof are the ways of death." Proverbs 14:12.

Pachouco learned at an early age that love was strong enough to destroy, to kill sound wisdom, common sense, integrity, and can give birth to stupidity and hatred. Of course, therefore love and hate live next door to each other.

Of what Pachouco learned from his mother, Faye Esther, his brother's past was awe-inspiring. His character was nothing less than enormous and incredible. Serge Gerard loved his family; he enjoyed helping others regardless of who they were. Faye Esther told Pachouco that honesty, integrity, and trustworthiness befitted his daily walk. Pachouco agreed that the two of them shared the same values in life. Pachouco believed in his heart that a man of his brother's caliber usually has excellent taste. The fact that he picked Loretta for Pachouco's wife-to-be increased his love for her. To put the icing on the cake, Serge Gerard accompanied Loretta's pictures with the letter to Pachouco. Photogenically, she was gorgeous, gorgeous enough to drive any man crazy. As mentioned earlier, he kissed those pictures every single night God had created to say goodnight. Fantasy was the world Pachouco was living in daily.

With a significant concern, something about Loretta's pictures triggered Pachouco's love. Loretta and his mother identically resembled one another. Here are two people, living in two unusual parts of the world, two different nationalities, looking so much like twins. When Pachouco compared those pictures of Loretta with the ones Faye Esther had taken when she was about Loretta's age, Pachouco found him unable to distinguish who was who? The similarity of the two influential women in Pachouco's life raised his curiosity to see to meet his mother's twin and his future wife. Every single week, he dreamed about her. The worse reached his heart: he had allowed obsession to dwell in it. Her beauty possessed him. Those pictures of Loretta are black and white, like his mother's photos. Pachouco hoped to receive a series of Loretta's color pictures. He made his request known to Serge Gerard. He is expecting him to translate it to Loretta, who was on the phone. Pachouco also mailed his request to her. She responded that he would have to hurry up and marry her if he needed more pictures. She can hardly wait to be his wife. Once again, Pachouco had no objection. No one knows how hard it is to suffer in silence, except the one that suffers.

Who can accuse Pachouco of falling in love with Loretta for her beauty? Speaking of beauty, Pachouco's mother, Faye Esther, had the countenance of a beautiful angel. Everywhere she went, boys, girls, men, and women recognized her beauty, smile, shape, and outstanding personality. Faye Esther had many admirers back in the day. She was simple; through it all, she was faithful to her husband, Fernand Andre. Most people believed that if she were a citizen of the United States, she could have been Miss. USA. When she was young, someone always wanted to take her photo anywhere she went. Faye Esther's beauty still drove men and women crazy even in her old age.

Goodness! when looking at her photographs, one cannot help thinking she just fell out of a catalog or a magazine for beauty queens. If Loretta had his mother's traits, the way Serge Gerard described her, Loretta was truly a virtuous woman. When his brother portrayed Loretta's countenance and personality to Pachouco, Serge Gerard said, "Pachouco, who can find a virtuous woman?"

Pachouco took the quotation over: "for her price is far above rubies. The heart of her husband doth safely trust in her so that he shall not need spoil." Proverbs 31: 10, 11.

Serge Gerard was an intelligent man. After Pachouco ended the quotation, his brother assured him he had found one in Loretta. Pachouco responded that he blesses to have her as a fiancée and him as a Big Brother.

The love and respect Pachouco had for both were so sincere that he demonstrated it whenever he could interject it into a conversation.

People, not all, may have trouble understanding that a man would marry a woman simply because she looks like his mother or has the characteristics of his mother. Honestly, this is what attracted Pachouco to Loretta. He had a great desire to bring the relationship to the open, and Serge Gerard refused the idea utterly. What was the refusal about? He persuaded Pachouco to keep everyone in the dark about this great love story because people might jeopardize the plan. Pachouco agreed with his oldest brother, but in the back of his intellect, he wanted to know how could this be? His obedience towards his big brother and the trust he placed in him prevailed, a mode of silence set in the mouth of Pachouco.

TIRE-SOME

Pachouco was tired of the translation mess and decided to enroll in an English school to learn the language. He desired to speak fluently to Loretta without an interpreter. Embarrassingly, he was limited in expressing his feelings because of the language barrier. Serge Gerard would have to be the one to translate it to Loretta. He wrote love letters to her twice a week, but it took too long for an answer. He broke the news to his oldest brother about going to school to study English. There was quietness on the other end of the phone. The three-way conversation momentously was a one-way deal. Pachouco thought a bad connection invaded the telephone line. Therefore, he repeated himself once more about his enrollment in English class. Then, both Serge Gerard and Loretta laughed ridiculously hard. Pachouco wanted to know what was so funny.

Serge Gerard replied, Oh, nothing serious, man. "The apple of your eye" "Congratulated you for going to learn English to speak to her. She was flattered."

"Tell Loretta I would do anything to please her."
"Anything, repeated, Serge Gerard. She will never forget those words. On the other hand, Loretta discovered a few bad French words and phrases,

which had the capability to drive Pachouco to sin. She did not mind using French sentences such as: "Je t' aime beaucoup. I love you so much. Jour et nuit Je pense a toi. Day and night and I think about you. Voulez-vous coucher avec moi ce soir mon amour? Do you want to sleep with me tonight, my love?" Whenever Pachouco replied to her in French, she understood not.

She amazed Pachouco every time she used French sentences. Loretta sounded as she was born in a French-speaking country like them. One night, while the trio was on the phone, Loretta decided to flirt again with her fiancé in French by saying to Pachouco, "Voulez-vous coucher avec moi ce soir, mon amour?" Pachouco asked Serge Gerard that night why did Loretta sound accent-free when she spoke French. "Who is her teacher?" Bragging, as usual, Serge Gerard and Pachouco injected, "Serge Gerard was the man who taught her."

Pachouco failed to ignore the tiny bit of French sentences used by Loretta. Phrases can tease any man who loves a woman long distance. Those words started to take root in Pachouco's heart. He should have known, "the flesh is a mess," that could eventually involve him in a mess.

One night, he violated the calling time set by Serge Gerard. He decided to call Loretta after midnight. The set-up hours were from 8:00 am through 11:00 pm. The rate per minute was higher in the daytime. Therefore, they preferred to converse at night. Pachouco wasted much money on the phone just to hear her voice. Again, love has the power to make anyone look foolish, a game everyone would play at least once or twice in life.

Well, Pachouco violated his curfew and called Loretta after midnight. A young woman answered the phone. Her voice reminded him of Loretta. The only difference was that the young woman answered the phone in French. "Yes, may I help you?" It was the English translation. In the background, he heard a male voice that sounded like his brother. Pachouco said, "Loretta, Loretta, can I speak to Loretta." The young woman answered him by saying, "Wrong number," and hung up the phone. Pachouco convinced the voice in the background was Serge Gerard, quickly thought to himself; Serge Gerard would not be at Loretta's house this late. Pachouco did not understand nor hear those two words, "Wrong number." He realized three facts about the English language: 1) it is not an easy language to learn. 2) One can speak it, still having trouble hearing it.

3) One can hear English but still cannot speak it. Pachouco became sure he had dialed a wrong number. He left no room for discouragement to set in.

He kept on learning English. He determined that he would have enough vocabulary to carry on a conversation when the good Lord allowed him to meet her. His goal was to no more prolonged need his brother's translation.

JEOPARDY

Pachouco's savings were in jeopardy. He had to pay Loretta's way to a model school, which he had no problem doing. Besides, being a model was what his mother, Faye Esther, in her younger age, became. Because of this knowledge, he loved the idea of Loretta being enrolling in the modeling school. Again, she demonstrated to Pachouco that she and his mother did think alike. The same traits stories were true. He shared with Serge Gerard his observation of the situation.

Serge Gerard commented, "Loretta never met your mother, not one day in her life. Ignorant of your mother's activities when Faye Esther was her age, coincidently, how Loretta has the desire to accomplish the same goal that your mother reached. It seems clear that Pachouco patterns after Faye Esther. Pachouco, what is going on with this picture?"

Pachouco got happy with Serge Gerard's observation; he laughed so hard, saying at once that "Big Brother, but they also act alike."

Suddenly, he declared to Pachouco, "Baby Brother, that there are mysteries in this relationship. Let me show you a perfect one in all of them. You heard the story right; Andre Fernand, our father, did likewise for Faye Esther. He paid her way to one of the greatest modeling schools in Europe when she was Loretta's age. "History repeated itself" you are doing identically for Loretta, paying for her school and apartment. Little brother, I do not care what you say, "God ordains the love between you and Loretta."

Pachouco responded, "man, you're fantastic. I never thought of it that way. You're right, Andre Fernand, our dad, indeed did that for my mother."

Serge Gerard replied, "You do know Pachouco; good men run in the family. I'm so proud of you, Pachouco."

Serge Gerard was a manipulator from his heart. He carefully studied Pachouco's lifestyle. He knew how crazy Pachouco loved Faye Esther. He had complete knowledge of Pachouco's assets, how much his baby brother is worth, and was well informed on his well-paying job. Serge Gerard believed if Loretta asked Pachouco to do something, nine times out of ten, he would perform it.

Serge Gerard owed Pachouco so much money. How and when would he pay him back remained to be seen. Serge Gerard had claimed that a major financial disaster struck him and his wife, Natacha. They were ready to foreclose on their home. He called on his baby brother for a loan. Pachouco did not mind helping them to save their house. Pachouco loaned him the funds because he often heard his mother say, "when Serge Gerard used to have money, he loaned a helping hand to many people." Pachouco never had the opportunity to speak with Natacha, his sister-in-law. She had a hearing problem. Therefore, she was not able to communicate on the phone, according to her husband. He never spoke to their children because English was the only language they knew. Serge Gerard presented Natacha as the most fabulous wife globally; he placed her in the same category with Loretta and Faye Esther. Pachouco desired to meet his sister-in-law. He started to imagine double dates between the four in the sleepless City.

Regardless of the situation, Pachouco was so happy to help them. In an extraordinary love letter, Loretta expressed to her fiancé her regret for not having money. She explained that if she had money, she would have given it to Serge Gerard for two reasons.

1) Pay Serge for introducing her to the most extraordinary man of her life besides God. "Pachouco, my love, you are my hero," thank God for Serge Gerard. 2) He worries too much about all the money that he owes you, Pachouco. It is beginning to affect his rest at night.

Again, "If I had the money, I would reimburse you for him. He is afraid that not having the cash to pay you back might interfere with your brotherly love toward him."

"Loretta, to be honest with you, my finances are in jeopardy. I tell you what; I give you my word, this day, that my oldest brother, my confidant our best man for our wedding, from this day forward, does not owe me any money. This is a gift, from you and me to him, thousands of dollars. Above were the words he wrote to answer his sweetheart's letter. He added; Loretta makes sure Serge Gerard reads this letter." The sad part about having money is that it mingles family, friends, and enemies together, which makes it difficult for the one with the finances to identify or acknowledge who is fake and honest. That is until the money is gone. Loretta shared the news with Serge Gerard that his outstanding debt owed to his baby brother had been written off. In other words, he no longer had to reimburse Pachouco any money. Happy was Serge Gerard, he called his little brother and pretended regardless, he wanted to pay him back to the penny everything he borrowed from him. Pachouco encouraged him not to worry about the debt and consider it paid in full. He thanked Pachouco for his giving heart. He reminded Serge Gerard to thank Loretta instead of him. She was the one that initiated the idea. Serge Gerard commented, "I should have known you would do anything to please her." He was an exceptionally smooth man, and he had total control over Pachouco and Loretta's love story.

Serge Gerard daily lost control of his drinking, gambling, and drug addictions. Those habits grew worse in him. When the beautiful Valada came to visit Faye Esther and Pachouco, she intended to share with them her great concern over his addictions. Pachouco shut her up before she started. Valada's intention was not to gossip about him. She felt Pachouco could help him if he knew about Serge Gerard's problem. Even though he was an alcoholic, he respected his younger brother enough in this aspect. He would not talk to Pachouco when he drank. He recognized where Pachouco stood in the matter of drinking and gambling. They had this conversation before. Pachouco was a particular character, but his brother was an evil force to be reckoned with. Too bad, Pachouco would be the last person to recognize it.

What had started this belief was one night Serge Gerard luckily made a phone call to Pachouco's mother in Haiti. He inquired about the activities of his little brother. He was familiar with the answer. Someone from Pachouco's neighborhood left not too long ago to reside in Jamaica Queens. She told him how successful Pachouco was. The moment he heard the news from another reliable source, his brain started thinking of a way to befriend Pachouco. Quickly, he developed an interest to play the "Big Brother" role.

Faye Esther was so happy to hear from him; he was her heart. She proudly told him the great accomplishment of his brother as a real estate agent and a surveyor.

"Thank God for answering prayers," responded Serge Gerard. When Pachouco was little, "I prayed daily to God to set a great bond between him and me. Now the hour is here. I'm an American citizen now."

"Congratulations son! Shouted Faye Esther."

"Thank you, continued Serge Gerard. Anyway, the purpose of my calling is to let you know I'm filing legal papers for Pachouco to reside in the US. When he comes, he will be able to file for you."

"My goodness! Thank God for you. We know we can always depend on you." She calls Pachouco, "Your brother Serge Gerard is on the phone. He has some good news for you," uttered his mother. They talked that night for at least five hours. By then, Serge Gerard discovered all he was lacking to make him effective in the role he intended to play. From that day forward, he would play the part of Big Brother. A few days later, Pachouco sent him his birth certificate to begin the paperwork to come to New York and live with him. One fact Pachouco did not know the Department of Homeland Security changed the law. It would take Serge Gerard a good ten years or more before he could bring him to New York legally. He led Pachouco to believe his trip to the states legally would come sooner than later. Pachouco, to make ready for this great transition, had sent Serge Gerard money to open a savings account for him. The promise not to let anyone know, not even Loretta, about the deal; the intention behind the savings was to purchase a home five years after marriage. Pachouco started to sell many of his assets. He wired the funds to Serge Gerard to deposit them in the account to collect interest. In addition to supporting Loretta while in modeling school. The situation became more complicated each day. How can someone who lived in a third-world country have that many possessions, quickly converted into cash, in a heartbeat? Serge Gerard learned that it does not matter how poor a country is. Among the citizens, most would be "poor as a snake;" another group would find itself between the poor and the rich, and the last group would be pure and simply filthy rich.

Life is what it is, life. It never leads anyone to believe it is fair. The surprising aspect, in this case, was that people on the island expected the funds to come from the US to Pachouco in Haiti. However, strangely, it is the other way around. How did Pachouco gain all these possessions from in a country, like his native one? Haiti was once upon a time surnamed "Paradise on Earth." Life over there was beautiful. Many people left their native land to reside in Haiti. Anyone who had his head on his shoulder could have made it at the time in the first free Black republic since 1804.

Pachouco again is a unique character. Serge Gerard had no idea of the dozen trips to the US that had been offered to Pachouco. Of course, Pachouco had money; he turned every single one of them down. Pachouco often said, "the only way he would fly to the United States as if he had a green card in his wallet. Otherwise, he was not going just to visit or live there illegally." Serge Gerard knew about this resolution. He agreed with Pachouco for several reasons. When Pachouco graduated from vocational school, evildoers had not yet contaminated the country politically. Pachouco's riches were fair. It came from his hard labor. Remember, he is a brilliant man. If speaking of his love for Loretta and the things he would do for her, a lot of people wondered where he had lost his common sense. It is so hard for others to understand when people are in love, their visions are blurred, and they cannot see past their nose.

There are other issues concerning the trio. Serge Gerard advised Pachouco to guard the relationship between him and Loretta as a secret. Why, so much secrecy if they claimed they loved each other. Serge Gerard is a thinker; everything he does has a purpose. It is usually whatever he can gain out of the situation. He asked Pachouco again to maintain the engagement with Loretta "on the down-low." Otherwise, the well-being of his baby brother could be at stake. What does that mean? He tried to warn Pachouco of the malefactors, the rootworkers. In their native land, one must choose which side he wanted to be, the Lord's or the devil's side. The reality is, "no one can serve two masters." There are consequences for those who view this system as a fairy tale. Serge Gerard ascertained that Pachouco believed in God. However, he constantly intended to raise the spirit of fear in Pachouco's mind because he had to cover his tracts. He reminiscently brought up the fact of how jealous people are. If they found out he was engaged to marry a foreigner, his envious friends might practice roots and witchcraft to destroy him. The warning did what it sent out to do, play with Pachouco's intelligence. The advice was simple "be careful, Pachouco, you are still living in Haiti."

Everything he mentioned to Pachouco should have been taken into consideration. Serge Gerard's real reason beyond this great observation is not yet discovered. Have patience said a wise man, "the truth will come out sooner or later."

One Sunday evening after Church, Pachouco's Pastor gave him a call. He was worried about Pachouco's slackness in the church. It had been six months since Pachouco graced the Sunday evening services and Wednesday night bible study with his presence. His Pastor knew something was up. Pachouco was a faithful member; his commitment superseded all.

A few months after meeting Loretta, Pachouco's church activities felt the presence of a lack of interest from him. Serge Gerald told him Wednesday night around 7:30 PM and Sunday evening was the best free days for them to communicate. His oldest brother heard from Faye Esther that Pachouco had an admirer at the church. She only attended service on Sunday and Wednesday evenings because of her work schedule. Pachouco pledged never to date another girl from the island. Even though he felt that way his mother sensate his heart seemed fond of that young woman, Carolle was her name. To shift Pachouco's heart away from her entirely, Serge Gerard chose those days to keep him away from the church. Faye Esther's observation was wrong about her son's feelings toward Carolle. Faye Esther thought Pachouco had an eye for Carolle, and she was the only female Pachouco took out twice since his horrible deception happened. After nicely recuperating, they went together to a couple of church functions. Remembered he lost his mind at least a year earlier because of a horrifying crime in which he was an eyewitness. His rebound and recovery from this turmoil brought the family closer than ever. Then, he met Leslie after his ordeal with Minerva ended.

The earlier tragedy struck Pachouco like lightning, making international news, reaching his brothers and sisters' ears abroad. Pachouco had two remarkable incidents covering a few chapters of his life. They were moments not many people on earth could survive. Both tragedies took a toll on him. It drove Pachouco crazy deprived him of his right mentality at least a good year for the first one, another six months following the second drama. He did not know how to cope with the first drama. He thought to himself, concluded the only way out was to turn to God. Pachouco felt like joining the seminary becoming a preacher, and he refused to glare at another woman in a sentimental fashion. A celibacy lifestyle was the favorable option that attracted his heart. Afraid of the occurrence anew of the third analogous situation, he coached himself to hate entering a relationship and avoid falling in love a third time. Pachouco's worse enemy since those tragedies took place was the nightly nightmare he was having. At that point, Pachouco was in the great necessity to live a drama-free life. The question was where he would find such a life. In one of his poems, he wrote he posed a question: “What is love without drama?” He answered it by saying: “nothing, nothing, nothing, the only sure thing he could offer a woman right now.” Who was able to criticize Pachouco, who encountered many obstacles, in his love story? Obstacles that he had trouble understanding. He found himself making some obscene remarks concerning God, who lost control of the universe in his eyesight, for allowing the occurrences of these horrible dramas to get the best out of him. The obscene language from Pachouco was the product of stressful and depressing faculties. He quickly came to his senses realized it could have been worse, but God overlooked his fault and protected him those days.

Before the horror, Pachouco was stress less, painless, and walking in the fullness of God, only enjoying the ups of life. Afterward, suddenly the terrible ordeal entered his life, introducing Pachouco to sleepless and restless nights. The remembrance of the trial alone turned out to be a hard pill to swallow. The inevitable lousy thinking gained control of his “Mind, body, and soul,” refusing to evict. Pains, fears, strange sensations, and the hearing of the gunshots blast moved their headquarters right into his heart.

Pachouco sometimes disliked seeing the day end for the night brought sensate thoughts. Often the following dusk, the disturbing dreams began.

PART II

HOW IT BEGAN

The hour is here to discuss what had happened in Pachouco's life before he met Loretta on the phone. What pressured him to go this route? What could Pachouco have done differently to avoid these two great catastrophes? What life deceptions drove him to seek love refuge, far away from the Island? There were two young women in Pachouco's past. It would be unfair not to discuss them before continuing with Loretta's story. Their names are Minerva and Leslie. In detail, here are the transpiration and the conclusions of the whole Pachouco trial period. How it begins:

Pachouco met a girl named Minerva in June of 1961. She was five, and he was six years old. Both attended the same religious school one grade apart. They caught themselves liking each other. When they reached six and seven years old, they opined that they had something going on as far as love, as they cared for one another. As every opportunity presented itself, they tried to sneak a kiss on the lips. Their novice faculties did not permit them to go further beyond the lips. They loved to "play hide and seek," just to slink some more kisses. When Pachouco and Minerva turned seven and eight years old, Pachouco discovered there was a part of his body that had a greater feeling whenever he embraced her. Now

Pachouco loved that sense; all he had to do to initiate it was to meditate on Minerva, and the organ stretched out. He was ignorant about what to accomplish with it besides urinating.

When she went to his house one evening, they hid behind the door, embracing. Suddenly she felt something hard touching her. Minerva asked Pachouco what he had in his pocket that was so hard. He told her nothing. She felt it again. Immediately, she called him a liar demanded he empty both of his pockets turn them inside out, and he did. She inspected them and found nothing neither suspicious nor harmful. An embarrassed Pachouco, who knew what she was talking about, at this point, had a great desire for the nerve to flatten. Too bad, Pachouco's wish was denied because the nerve in question had a mind of its own. To quit while he could have been his best solution. However, she wanted to kiss some more. One more time, she felt it; she glared at him to enunciate, what in the world was that?

Pachouco was in a desperate move to shut her mouth and to set free her wandering brain. He took her right hand and made her touch his organ.

"Mercy," when she realized what she was tapping on, Minerva quickly remembered what her mother had taught her. She went bizarre slapped Pachouco with everything she had. With her left knee, she struck that complex nerve in a second space; she flattened it with pains. The nerve did not contain a mind of its own. She ran for her life without looking back. Hurtful,

Pachouco cried bitterly. He tried to understand what went wrong. Why, Minerva acted like a wild horse fighting, kicking him for nothing.

What went wrong that evening? Minerva's mother, Mrs. Ema, taught her if she had ever been around a boy or a man who took her hands to make her feel something hard from his pants that meant she was in danger. She needed to start fighting for her life by hurting the hard stuff with her knees. Then run for her life, never speaking with that evil boy or man anymore.

Two years passed Minerva stayed away from Pachouco. Their parents were much-close friends; they knew Pachouco, and Minerva were platonically playing love. They reached a little bit of maturity. They decided to end this bicker; it had been almost three years now. Officially, they became high school sweethearts. They developed a great relationship. Both were academically very smart. They studied and did a lot and other choices together, filled with good manners. Pachouco and Minerva were in love. Whenever they exchanged a kiss since the last incident, he recollected the outcome of that evening. He made sure a chair was nearby to sit down to avoid any physical contact which might trigger his organ to rise. Believe it or not, he was a quick learner. One night, he sat down to kiss her; she pulled him up to stand. He felt again the arising up of his organ. He stuck his behind so far out to avoid body contact to stay clear of the trouble. She pulled him again toward her, and she laughed hysterically. She explained to him the motive of her behavior that evening. What her mother, Mrs. Ema, told her to do to a fresh boy as Pachouco was what once made them cry, turn around, and bring joy in their lives. This was the power of maturity. Pachouco could not stop laughing after knowing why he was abused and beaten by Minerva.

They entered a covenant at the same hour: no premarital sex. Pachouco and Minerva agreed to protect each other sanctity. The moment their desires teamed up with their weaknesses and vulnerability, they wanted to hold fast to the religious values they were taught in school, "sex is for a marri couple to enjoy, as a gift of God." Her goal was to marry him lose her virginity on the honeymoon night.

PACHOUCO & MINERVA

Pachouco and Minerva were Catholics. They attended the same school through kindergarten to high school years. He walked Minerva to and from school every single day God created. He picked her a flower along the way to her house presented it to her daily. Then, they started to walk. He performed this routine of flowers five years straight.

One day, oversleeping, got the best out of Pachouco. He forgot to grab a flower for Minerva. It was a sad day for both. He usually kissed her good morning. He leaned over to kiss her she refused. He pondered in his mind, what did he perpetrate to encourage Minerva to behave like this? They walked to school, and he conversed; she was playing deaf and dumb for the time being. She had not heard a word spoken by Pachouco. On their way back from school, the situation seemed to be worst instead of better. It commenced raining that afternoon. Pachouco took his shirt off from his back. He placed it over her head to keep her hair from being wet. She removed the shirt tossed it at him. Goodness, the sky of Haiti hid, crying for Pachouco. Both were soaking wet. Poor Pachouco, the next day, he popped up with no flower again; two days in a row, he was swimming in hot water.

Love is the easiest thing to be taken for granted, anytime, anywhere, conscientiously, or not.

Pachouco attempted to figure out the reason Minerva showed anger toward him. Unsuccessfully he arrived at nothing. The matter seemed too serious now. Tears were flowing like a river from her eyes. Pachouco is quickly aware he needed help to deal with the issue. Pachouco visited the priest. Every single person in the community recognized their relationship. Everybody knew that Pachouco and Minerva were a perfect couple. They stood tall in their community, a good role model for lovers, young and old.

He went to see Father William, a youth counselor. He explained to the priest the best he could of her attitude regarding him. The tears that she shared were unnecessary. Father William grabbed his two hands and initiated a word of prayer, asking God for clarity. He notified Pachouco; Minerva emotionally had been hurt. "I advise you, Pachouco, to retract the first day to see if there was a behavior change on your part. Had you forgotten to perform a habitual task that immediately impressed her?" Pachouco replied that she should have communicated whatever it was. Father William glimpsed at him answered, "She wanted you to calculate it without her help." Whatever it was, it was imperative to her. Besides, it never took a woman long to become spoiled. Well, uttered Pachouco, "there's only one thing I recalled, but I denied it. If so, she would be upset over petty stuff like this."

"The petty stuff might be your problem insinuated the priest."

"No, it could not be, entered Pachouco. It was a tiny matter." Father William, "I usually picked her a flower from the bushes every morning. I was running late two days in a row; I didn't have the time to pluck Minerva one today or yesterday."

Father William smiled asked Pachouco, "How long have you been giving her flowers from the bushes?"

"About five years, which was nothing for her to be upset."

Pachouco, while arguing the point Father William stopped him and said, "Pachouco, my son, listened closely, never start doing anything for a woman if you do not intend to keep on doing it. If she never asked you to stop, she appreciated it. Nevertheless, if you quit on your own, a real woman will automatically believe you do not love her anymore. Why was there a change? Pachouco, my son, you're taking things for granted."

"No way" applied Pachouco.

With all his wisdom, Father William entered with a soft voice a custom, or a habit changed in the middle of a relationship, has the power to destroy the peace and kill the joy of it. Again, the things one starts in love must continue. If a man kissed a woman every day when he dated her, he would need to kiss her daily when she became his wife. After twenty-five, fifty, or a hundred years of marriage, keep kissing her daily. Because of love, the act performed unto never ends; it grows stronger. Instead of a kiss a day, kiss her up to three times or more daily. This keeps the fire of love burning. Go Pachouco, said Father William. Pick Minerva some flowers, instead of two for two missing days, give her an increase by bringing four flowers from the bushes.

Pachouco thanked Father William. Deep in his heart, he doubted the Priest's advice. But because of respect, he was willing to try it. He doubted seriously that the flowers were the reason she guarded her silence. She knew he plucked them next door to her house. She watched him in the morning breaking them from the branches, and she could have picked them herself if it meant that much to her. Pachouco was on his way to pick her up grabbed five flowers. He explained to Minerva that four flowers were for the missing days and that one was for today; she jumped in his arms kissed him so tenderly.

"Thank God for you, Pachouco, finally realized how much these flowers meant to me because you gave them to me, darling," shouted Minerva.

"I apologize to you, my beautiful angel. I promise not to let that happen anymore."

After arriving in school, he ran to Father William: it worked, Father William, jumping like a kid, "what you advised me to do," it worked. Father William repeated these words to Pachouco, "son, you live, you learn." "Never play with a woman's feelings to avoid living inside a tomb in a graveyard."

Father William had been an immense help to Pachouco and Minerva. The advice he gave them was what minimized the urge for sexual activities between them. Father William encouraged both to remain focused on their well-planned future. Indeed, they were an ideal couple. Most people called them the twins, on some accounts, they dressed alike. Where one was present, the other one was not too far behind. They were members of the same social clubs. They had many things in common. The people of the community personally believed they created for each other. They even conceived the same ideas. It was amazing how two people's hearts communicated. In the picture galleries all over downtown, Pachouco and Minerva's portraits' exposition caught every customer and visitor's eye. They provoked other couples to jealousy involuntarily with their lifestyle as well as their involvement in community services. Pachouco and Minerva had no other choice but to live a careful life in the presence of their peers and of society period. Their presence alone fashioned real love until its lively appearance shined on everyone near them. Their company was always accompanied by the joy of being alive, the pleasure of being in love, and the pleasure of being happy.

Father William often refers to Pachouco and Minerva as one of the most fabulous couples of their era in his biblical counseling class. Their relationship is based on biblical principles.

They brought freedom of love into existence. They fit perfectly well together. They had had challenging moments in their lives also. Especially when their bodies traveled the opposite way of their values, and their religious beliefs were totally against sex before marriage. One night, the urge to have sexual intercourse got their best. They appeared extra romantic. The conservative couple was about to violate their promise: premarital sex had been erased from their vocabulary. Regardless of the swearing Pachouco and Minerva partook of on a Valentine's Day, the pains of sexual intercourse grew to be inevitable. Pachouco and Minerva, so desperate, developed a strong feeling they had to have sex tonight. Unlike Minerva, she took off her clothes. Surprisingly, she stood there naked, reached over for Pachouco, who forgot these words, we cannot do this.

There is a time in love when one of the two

lovers become weak and propose to perform an act far away from their character. When true love is present, the stronger one should decline the proposal for further discussion until both are in their right state.

To have sex with someone intoxicated unconsciously, or to have sex with a virgin who lost control in an enthusiastic moment, is a crime against trust. She took Pachouco's clothes off; they started to romance out of the ordinary. They fashioned their mind to ignore the pledge they had once vowed to themselves.

Minerva's body overheated sexually, craving for his body as she was running out of time. Both virgins acted as if they planned to surrender and bow down at sensual desire. That night, no matter the cost, they felt the need to override their belief. Kissing each other, like kissing, was going out of style and as if there was no border in love.

Pachouco and Minerva stayed in church daily. They dwelled with religious parents. Knowing this fact, where did they learn these passionate moves. They functioned as if they were the ones who created the entire romantic's action. Whatever they imagined seemed to work for them because it appeared enjoyable. Minerva was more aggressive than Pachouco. At this point, she was powerless; her weakness lay down in Pachouco's hands. It was left up to him to take advantage of her or not. Minerva's spirit was set in one tract: "let us make love tonight."

When the hour had arrived for Pachouco to penetrate Minerva at her persistent request, He reasoned to himself, and he recognized the presence of wrongdoing. He decided not to pursue this adventure, which could be costly for their bright future. Besides, Minerva's character did not want to explore a new avenue so dangerous, such as sex.

She kept saying, come on, Pachouco, this will be the last time. She will never ask him to do this again after this night until they get married. Please, Pachouco, please, and tears were dropping from her eyes. Pachouco, sorry from his heart, advised her to wait on the honeymoon night. "Tomorrow is our prom night," uttered Pachouco. "Let us talk it over, following the dance. If necessary, we will discuss it for us to partake in sexual intercourse, and then it might happen."

She looked at him, eyes filled with tears, and said, "Tomorrow will be too late."

Notice that tomorrow will be their prom night. How is that? Pachouco was one grade ahead of Minerva. He decided to flunk a grade so that they could graduate at the same time. Love is known to bring stupidity out of the best. Minerva tried to persuade Pachouco to violate the rule. He stood his ground and declined her offer. They helped each other dress up. Minerva said to him with a heart filled with remorse and shame, "You are not ashamed of me, are you?"

"No," answered Pachouco.

She adds "I wish you understand for real what I am feeling inside. My love for you right now is too strong for me. I do not mind breaking the fundamental social rule; ignore all religious values prohibiting us from sleeping together. I know indeed, sex is for married people to enjoy. To show you how badly I want you, honey, if you would have said to me, let us get married now, I believe deeply in my heart, you would not have received any objection from me. Pachouco, I feel just like a person ready to take a trip to an unknown destination, to an undistinguished world. So unexpected is the journey that the time to say farewell to her family and friends has failed her. Therefore, timelessly, she would depart without a goodbye."

Minerva felt she had been granted twenty-four hours to accomplish her most desirable want as making crazy love to her boyfriend. They agreed to remain faithful until they met again as a demonstration of true love.

"Pachouco, the angels above, had chosen to save us from this mistake. I love you with true love, continue Minerva, the more I look at you, the more I hate not to be the wife or your dream. I know that you love me with all your heart Pachouco. I perceive the love that you possess for me as so strong, too strong for me to ignore. Once upon a time, I spoke to God about us, which may sound like a lunatic. He told me His desire was for you and me to grow old together, as the oldest married couple in the world. God has changed the plan for some reason; the fact that you and I are well acquainted with God's ways, we know He has a reason for everything. Pachouco tomorrow will be our Prom night. Our class has great faith in us. They vote us King and Queen. In my soul, walking by your side tomorrow would be the closest I will ever be to bind close or lasting ties with you. There I will be in my white dress, you in your black tuxedo. We will get out of the limousine after the chauffeur opens the door: You will gently catch me by the arms. Give me my last kiss before escorting me to my last dance." Like a happy virgin bride who goes back to the limousine at the end of the wedding ceremony. With her mindset on the honeymoon, she wonders how tasty intercourse will be on the first try."

Minerva, in her allusion, stares at Pachouco. Her eyes appear to be in a trance. She says Pachouco, "you will never find another girl that loves you the way I do. Nevertheless, "for me, you will always be the first and the last man that ever kisses me. No matter what will occur between us, I want you to live your life Pachouco in the fullness of God. The regret that I have right now, I would have been so proud of myself for losing my virginity to a man who absolutely loves me; there is no doubt about it."

Pachouco has devoted all his attention to Minerva, his handkerchief soaked with tears from their eyes. Finally, she is through expressing her sentiment to him. He aggressively seizes the opportunity to enter a few words in his sweetheart's ears. He begins by saying,

"Tomorrow, after the dance, Minerva, we will debate the sex issue again. To be honest with you, my dear, in the state you are in, right now, if I had agreed to make love to you, God would not be please with either one of us. He would see us as covenant breakers. Besides Minerva, my conscience would deprive me the peace of mind by accusing me of taking advantage of you, my spiritual wife. Do you remember Minerva;

three weeks ago, we renewed our pledge. In the presence of Father William, no premarital sex was our covenant. Minerva, let us wait and see what tomorrow night following the Prom may bring."

"I insist, Pachouco. It will not be tomorrow night for us."

"From what I hear," injected Pachouco, "Are you planning to dump me and break my heart after the night is over?"

"Boy, give me a break, if I had any control over the future, you would stick with me until death does us part."

"Minerva, you are overtired. You are talking out of your mind." I understood that we stayed up late studying exams three weeks straight. It was incredibly stressful for both of us, but it paid off. We graduate with honors. However, the scholarship alone

we receive from the top universities crowns our efforts. You have the right to be tired, Minerva, my love. You deserve to obtain a goodnight's sleep. When tomorrow comes, half of our conversation and half of the things we did earlier will be lost in the land of well resting night. Minerva, believe me, your body is craving a goodnight's sleep. It has been affected and invaded with hallucinations. Minerva, you need not fear tomorrow. It's just another day. A day for me to show you how much I care for you. How much I want to kiss the ground, you walk on. Yes, tomorrow if you allow me to take it back, it's just not another day. I would prefer to say it's just a particular day. Yes, indeed, for you and I to count our blessings. We might run out of numbers, or our limited mathematical skills would not permit us to number them. Still, Minerva, tomorrow will bring us a few steps closer to our blessed future. Unless God changes His ordained plan for us. Daily Minerva, I thank God for preserving us all these years, especially when our flesh declared wars with our sanity. We claim victories tonight over our intellect, over our flesh, over our lust, and over our wants. Minerva, you are my future, you are my sunshine, you are my dream girl, you are the one, my queen, and for you, I live. You are afraid of tomorrow. I cannot wait to meet this unknown day, called tomorrow. One thing I know is for sure you are my tomorrow, and it will not mean anything to me without your presence. Minerva, I thank you for this night, we passed the test, and our purity remains untouchable. This night also is a special one for us. It has placed the seal of approval as far as the capability to protect each other. In a time of weakness, when the flesh is experiencing trouble at every end, we still hold fast to our religious beliefs."

"Why can I stop talking about tomorrow?" Replied Minerva. "Am I experiencing mixed feelings between happiness and scariness? Am I also becoming paranoid of tomorrow? Search yourself, Pachouco; I wish you could see what I saw. Tomorrow night, you will understand much clearer that hallucinations have no power over my judgment. Again, tomorrow night before the Prom, you will understand the difference between reality and illusion, my king."

Minerva's intuition of tomorrow left Pachouco confused. She knew what she saw, but she had trouble explaining herself to him. Pachouco recognized the prophetical gift that his sweetheart had, and this was the first occasion he ever doubted her uncertain prediction. Pachouco felt she was speaking senselessly in the parable concerning tomorrow. He attributed her behavior to nerves. Whenever he glanced at Minerva that night, he saw the presence of fear. Pachouco concluded Minerva was highly nervous. The excitement of being chosen as the queen. Her studying for the final exams caused restless nights. The speech she had to prepare became nerve-racking for her. Pachouco misread her, and she was in a more excellent shape than he was. He walked her home, and in front of her house, they were doing their goodnight talks. Suddenly, Minerva shouted, someone, called her name from above and commanded her to look up. Both did; they admired the constellation of the stars. They noticed that two of the stars were brighter than the rest of them. Automatically, the scenery took Pachouco for a loop because it was the most beautiful stars from above, he had ever seen. The two stars got so close to each other, like they were embracing while hanging from the sky. Surprisingly, with their own eyes, they saw the appearance of an angel who gently removed one of the twin stars and vanished away.

“This represented you, and I” entered Minerva. “Pachouco, I told you that it will not be tomorrow night for us.”

“Not again, my love” replied Pachouco. “We had to say “goodnight.” I need you to have a fantastic night of sleep. We must thank Mother Nature for its

beauty and nothing else, goodnight baby. Be sure you dream about me, Minerva.”

“I always,” replied Minerva; “I hoped you do a better job in the dream than earlier.” They laughed and kissed goodnight.

THE LAST BREAKFAST

In the morning, she cooked breakfast asked her parents to invite Pachouco and his mother. Kirk and Ema were shocked by Minerva's willingness to cook breakfast. They quickly called and invited them over. At the table, Minerva specified to everyone how much she loved them. A combination of fears and sadness attacked her spirit without any mercy. The expression on her face and how she expressed her feelings toward every one of them activated the tears from their eyes. Contagiously, everyone was crying joyfully except Minerva. Pachouco immediately perceived a notable change in Minerva, her beauty was irresistible, and he requested an excuse. He touched Minerva on her shoulder. They left the table, went to the study room, and locked the door. There passionately, he embraced her. Romantically was the way she took her time to kiss him. The romance among them had almost gotten out of hand. They had forgotten where they were. Before he left to go home, he tenderly glared at Minerva, saying, "tonight definitely will be our night."

She gave him the prettiest smile he ever

received from her. She uttered, "We are in a rush hour. There is no time left. "I love you, Pachouco; I love you, man, and pick me up on time. Enjoyable seconds are all we have remaining for us."

Pachouco answered, "Yes, my love, Minerva just counts on me. Walking by my side tonight, your right arm into my left arm is what I am yearning for; I will hold you so tight just like it will be my last time holding you. See you in a few, my beautiful Minerva."

"See you, my King, my strength, and my lover." Pachouco opened the door said bye to Kirk and Ema. As he was going up the street toward his house, Minerva cried with a loud voice: "Pachouco, you have forgotten something."

He turned around came where she stood. He kissed her goodbye. She said, "thank you, now you are free to go. Wait a minute, Pachouco, I have one more question; if I die tonight, tell me, what are you going to do? Will you try to resuscitate me?"

"Stop talking non-sense my chocolate," replied Pachouco. "A kiss of mine on your sweet lips will revive you if you do."

She handed him a poem told him to read it as soon as he arrived home. Pachouco took off from her presence with significant steps. The curiosity to read the poem preoccupied his intellect. He sat down at his bedside and read these words: On an Island of beauty, one mile from the pearl gates There, we are appointed to be together on a date. On the street paved with pure gold, my steps were ordered in an orderly fashion, setting the way we were told. “Twelve gates to the city” gloriously illuminated my path one life to live was the motto of a city free from wrath. I was waiting forever for you to come. Oh, you never did. Alone I must go, the one I love stood me up, yes indeed. My disappointment, my need meets together, to cast away along the way, down in the sea of forgiveness, all the way All alone I reached my destination; here I am at the gate Without a date, He welcomes me to the city, a saint of old. Peter was his name, gentle as he could be, showed me the way.

After reading the poem, Pachouco kneeled to pray. He petitioned The Creator of the Universe in his prayer on Minerva’s behalf. “Lord, what is going on with my fiancée?” Soon to be official, was the theme of his thunderous prayer.

The hour for the surprise and the Prom sneaked on them. A beautiful black and white limousine arrived at Pachouco’s doorsteps. He got in the limo; the next stop was a few yards down the road. Minerva stood with all her classmates, family, friends, and even the news media. They were all gathering in front of her house as a troop assembled for a parade. Minerva had no idea of the valid reason behind this festivity. She thought the rest of the graduates and everybody else came as a part of the school plan because Pachouco and Minerva happened to be nominated by acclamation King and Queen of the class. She thought they assembled at her house again to form a cortege to follow behind their limousine.

When Daniel the chauffer saw Minerva, he said to Pachouco, "she appeared to him as an Arc Angel." A bragging Pachouco responded to Daniel; "This is my baby and my angel. I can sympathize with Adam in the enjoyable book of life. If I may quote his word, Adam said when he saw Eve next to him." "This is now bone of my bones, and flesh of my flesh:" (Genesis 2:23) Go ahead, Pachouco, said Daniel, the chauffeur of the limousine. Pachouco replied, watch that I'm about to make the angel rejoice by proposing to her, offering her my hands in marriage. People stood on both sides of the road, Pachouco invited the community to come to witness the proposition.

Minerva's friends entertained her. She did not look back to see the limousine was moving because Pachouco had had someone to distract her. Placidly and silently, Daniel rolled down the limousine windows. He got out of the limo. Minerva heard a romantic voice announce, looked back my Haitian Queen, the love of my life. What did she see when she turned around? A handsome Pachouco kneeled in a white tuxedo in the middle of a busy street. He opened a small box which contained a beautiful and expensive diamond ring. In addition, a loud voice was saying "Will you marry me, my Queen, and my life? We are well capable responsible enough to do this and still, pursue our education. Please say Yes Minerva because "NO or PERHAPS" is not an option.

With great happiness, she answered, "No objection, yes, yes, yes."

She held her dress with her hands to avoid tripping. She jumped into Pachouco's arms. Both fell, rolled on the ground, hugging, kissing, and forgetting they wore white clothes.

According to the media, the standers, family, and friends were at the scene. All concluded that it was the most outstanding marriage proposal the world had ever witnessed.

With their elegant tuxedos and beautiful dresses, their friends helped Pachouco and Minerva off the floor. The boys picked Pachouco placed him on their shoulders. They carried him from her house to his and brought him back to the limo. The girls had done the same for Minerva because they were many.

Pachouco and Minerva suffer a kissing disorder. They were still osculating inside the limousine. But one of their classmates, Frantz, a good friend of Pachouco's, played soccer together on the same team. Frantz and Pachouco resembled each other they could pass for brothers. They arranged to pick each other tuxedos to play a prank on Minerva. Pachouco and Minerva went together, he got a black tuxedo, but if it were for Minerva, he would have chosen a white one. Minerva did not want him to wear a black tuxedo. She felt a little disappointed because he ignored her choice of color. Frantz had already dropped Pachouco's white tuxedo at his house, hung in his closet. Later that day, Pachouco took Frantz's black tuxedo to his house.

The girl Frantz promised to take to the Prom went with him to pick the white tuxedo. She honestly thought he was going to wear white. She did not know of the deal made between Pachouco and Frantz. The girl's name was Marie Mode. She was highly obsessed with Frantz. Marie Mode planned to match him with a long white dress. They were supposed to ride in a black and white limousine. Marie Mode went and pawned all her furniture to cover their Prom expenditures for both. So far, Marie Mode has paid for everything. As crazy as it may sound, Frantz did not have any money.

Five days before the dance, Frantz broke up with Marie Mode. She caught him in the movie with a young woman named Lyrevol. Frantz knew that Lyrevol was the one going to escort him to the festivity since day one. He canceled Marie Mode out. Heartbreaking and humiliated was the state of her feelings. Outrageous, she indeed became. She slashed the tires on his car, which she had purchased. She also busted his windshield, but Marie Mode loved Frantz too much to hurt him physically and mentally.

Goodness, it seemed so hard for men to understand, never endorsed the habit of playing with woman's emotions to avoid resting in a tomb with ants and worms. With her spying skills, Marie Mode grabbed a hold on Lyrevol's phone number. She called and told her not to accompany Frantz to the dance and not to wear the dress he gave her. Lyrevol made it plain to Marie Mode; regardless of what she said, she was going with Frantz to the Prom; he was her man. Marie Mode would have gone through the phone if she could slap the taste of Frantz from Lyrevol's mouth. Marie Mode explained to her,

repeatedly, that the dress Lyrevol was about to wear was the dress she purchased.

"Thank you very much for the contribution," was the response Lyrevol gave to Marie Mode.

Furiously, she told Lyrevol over her dead body, may the best women win, and Marie Mode hung up the telephone. She calls her back anew. When Lyrevol answered the phone, Marie Mode uttered, "Let me share a word of wisdom with you. If you wear the dress that I paid for to go to the Prom, somebody is skinny behind will go back home naked you'd better believe, and it will not be me. You know what I mean."

FREE AS TWO BIRDS

Pachouco and Minerva were as free as two birds, enjoying the moment. They locked up in each other's arms, exchanging kisses. They arrived at the center where the ceremony was. A substantial number of people stood by, waiting for them to get out of the limousine. She asked Daniel to tell the people they would be out in five minutes. Strangely, she holds his face so close to hers; "Listen to me, Pachouco: Be strong! I am not hallucinating; I'm as real as honest can be, I am about to die, and my time is up. I know you love me. I know you are crazy about me. Pachouco, God's love for me is more profound than you imagine. Today He will call me home. Remembered, I kept telling you tomorrow for me was a thing of the past. I will not see tomorrow."

"Minerva, my darling, you are not going anywhere. If God calls you home today, I must make the journey with you so we both can go. Therefore, it will not be a tomorrow for me without you, Minerva."

"No Pachouco, I must take the trip by myself. Alone I must go. Alone I must travel. You do not believe me? In your spirit Pachouco, you feel I am overtired, exhausted, and in a delusion state. Let me hush Pachouco; otherwise, you will advise me to see a psychiatrist or have a few nights' rest. Pachouco, most people do not believe that God shows to some the hour of their departure from earth to glory. Pachouco, my love, yes, he does. As we speak, I hear the gunshots; yes, indeed, I listen to them. Everyone living has a way to die. Too bad, my way is associated with gunshots wounds. No one can escape death, and no one can hide from death Pachouco, no, not one."

"Please do me a favor, Minerva; in case you see tomorrow, would you allow me to take you to see Dr. Nya Enalee in the morning."

"Yes, Pachouco, is that what you want to hear. In the meantime, kiss me with everything you have, because this is our last time."

The street proposition was well attended. The people left there went straight to the place to witness the getting off the limousine and the entrance of the charming couple to the party. There, their speech will be made. Marie Mode showed up. She heard all the commotion, asked a stander, what was going on? "He answered, the man in the white tuxedo and the woman in the long white dress in the limousine, he had just proposed to her in marriage. Lady, you missed the event. He kneeled in the middle of this busy street. He asked her to marry him. Girl, this was the nicest thing I ever saw, mentioned the bystander."

Marie Mode interrogated him; "Do you know what her name is? Is her name Lyrevol?"

"Something like that, I'm not sure," replied the bystander. Madness entered Marie Mode's heart. She said to him, "Yes, this is that low-class whore; I got something to cool off her behind."

Daniel opened the limousine door Pachouco stepped out. The crowd went wild, clapping their hands. Pachouco, with a kiss, helped Minerva out. He placed his left hand around her thigh and squeezed her body against him. He whispered in her ears, "Minerva, you are my passion, addiction, and habit. I am a blessed man to have you in my arms. Tonight, you are too beautiful for me to look upon."

Marie Mode mistakenly thought Minerva was Lyrevol and Pachouco was Frantz. Marie Mode pulled out a gun and shot Minerva three times in the back. She tried to hit Pachouco with the fourth shot, but the weapon jammed up. Then she realized she had shot Minerva, whom she loved and admired. Marie Mode automatically made sure the gun was ready to fire again. She begged Pachouco to forgive her, and Marie Mode killed herself.

Minerva laid down in his arms. She smiled and said to him; "It happens, in the same manner, I told you; it would. Pachouco, I love you so much."

Pachouco's speech forsook him. He was crying, screaming, and she said with an imperative voice, "Listen to me, Pachouco, promise me you will not be suicidal. Promise me you are going to finish school. Promise me; you will take care of your mother. Pledge to me someday; you will marry a nice girl and treat her the same respect you treated me.

Pachouco, I've got to go now; a band of angels has come to carry me home. I wish you could have seen the angelical being's delegation that God sent to meet me. Pachouco, I did not know I was that important until now. Pachouco, I thank you for not having sex both times when I wanted to. I see why now. What about the girl that shot me? Make sure she is, okay? Deliver her this message for me. I love her, and I forgive her from my heart, not my lips. She had mistaken me for somebody else. Exempt from my will, I die to save someone else. Could you imagine Pachouco, how God felt when He willingly gave his son to die for us? Pachouco, please forgive her. Tell my parents to have a private funeral and bury me in this dress. Drop one of your pictures inside my coffin, okay. I will pray to God for your speech to return to you. When you can talk, words to describe how much you love me will flow from your heart to your lips as the raindrops in time of a storm. If you could speak, you would have asked too many questions." "Why, God took me from you so soon? What are you going to do without me?" "Pachouco, bullets round tear up my flesh. I am swimming in an ocean of blood. Still, God's providential care allows me the resistance to address my farewell speech to the class."

Minerva's voice was weakening, she said to Pachouco:

"Cover me with your tuxedo. I'm getting frozen cold, a freezing type of cold. The angels are a few feet away from me."

All Pachouco's friends took off their tuxedos and laid them on top of her like a large blanket.

With a benign smile, Minerva said, "I have no doubt you people love me in my spirit. Everyone, come a little closer, said Minerva, come on girls, stop that crying; your Minerva is fine. Before I go, I want to leave you these words." In a trembling, a weak voice echoed these powerful Words:

"Death is really a new life to see.

No more headache and pain, just free

No one lives forever on the earth,

Nothing is the only thing we are worth.

Class, I'm on my way to heaven,

Yes, in heaven where everybody is even.

Indeed, I will be in a better place.

We will one day meet face to face.

There is a better place beyond the sky.

Do not rush it. Underneath that blue sky,

Study hard, enjoy life to the fullness,

one day, you'll get there with gladness.

Why do things go in the way they do?

Why do people die in the manner they do?

God purposely ordains what's done.

He's an answer for all unexplained gone.

Class, appreciate your life all the way.

Do not cry, and I am not dead; I am just away.

Farewell, farewell; I love you but cannot stay."

In Minerva's dying moment, she proved to her classmates that she was ready to make this eternal trip. After her address, she charged Pachouco to tell her parents to write on her tomb, "Forgiveness is greater than vengeance." "Goodbye, Pachouco, and thank you for loving me with true love. Too weak to talk, she pointed at her mouth to Pachouco. He understood the signal. He moved her head toward his mouth, he kissed her, and Minerva died."

Pachouco remained numb, and he was incapable of saying a word. He was doing his best to say a few things to Minerva, but he could not. The media recorded everything she requested. The ambulances carried all three of them to the hospital: Marie Mode died on the spot, Minerva, who died fifteen minutes after she was shot and Pachouco, who became numb, passed out after she died.

Most of Pachouco's friends left the scene at the end believing he was dead. Children, men, and women were crying bitterly. This was the saddest night in the history of love.It was amazing how a great celebration such as this instantly gave way to such unforgettable tragedies.

Pachouco's nightmare had begun. From the Island of Haiti to the utmost parts of the world, all knew about this sad day. Everyone who was not present had their version of what took place that night. One thing is for sure; people are people. They had something on the inside that triggered them to believe more in a lie than the truth. Well, this is a part of life. Therefore, Pachouco faced the real-life as the malicious rumors began. The latest version was that Pachouco was cheating on Minerva with Marie Mode. Then, Minerva shot Pachouco, Marie Mode, and herself."

Gossip, gossip, gossip is quite an incurable mouth disease; it can be contagious at times.

Pachouco was admitted into the hospital, where he stayed for one year. Barbara Ann, his sister, was well known in the political arena. She flew back home to be with Faye Esther, her mother, who was about to lose her mind. Kirk and Ema took the loss of their daughter very well from the outside appearance, but inward, there was no difference between them and Faye Esther. In the meantime, Pachouco was in a psychiatric coma, fighting for his sanity. If Pachouco had a choice to choose between life and death, he would rather have died than life.

All the family and friends hated the fact that Pachouco missed her funeral. Kirk, Ema, and Faye Esther held her body if they could enough to see if Pachouco would recover to attend the funeral. Finally, they buried her. They concluded it was a good thing because they did not believe he could have handled it. Minerva's parents visited Pachouco every single day.

ALMOST A YEAR

Two weeks away to make a year since the cold-blooded murder occurred, Pachouco came out of the coma. The hospital staff called him a miracle. His speech still failed him. He was able to communicate through writing. He showed the sign he needed a pen and a piece of paper, and he drafted a short poem:

"Here on weak arms, no time left. She breathed her last breath, there on my feeble arms, she'd left. Please don't give up, wake up,

It was my desired charm. Make it brief on weak arms,

Belong to the earth needless to harm

When life is playing tough,

While the condition is rough,

Oh God, quite a death,

On weak and unlucky arms

Tears came down from his eyes. He gave the poem to his mother to read to the rest of the people. Pachouco planned to kill himself because life without Minerva was meaningless to him. She appeared to Pachouco in a vision as beautiful as always. She shared those words with him again, death is an exciting life to see, but do not rush it, Pachouco. “Live your life to the fullest was my promise for you to keep. I did not fall in love with a coward. Pachouco rebuked the thought of killing yourself. Enjoy your life, honey. If you happened to kill yourself, you would not see me beyond the sky. There will be a gulf separating you and me because you took a life that was not belonging to you but God."

The doctor let Pachouco out of the hospital on the date, which marked the anniversary of the incident. He wrote on paper to carry him straight to the graveyard where they buried Minerva. Barbara Ann drove him to the cemetery and their mother, Faye Esther, and Ema. They were not aware that a few news reporters were following them. The reporters wanted to see if his speech had come back to obtain an interview. Impatiently, Pachouco jumped out of the car before Barbara Ann arrived at a complete stop. He ran to the tomb and stood at the foot of it alone. He was visualizing the night before Minerva's death. She was afraid of tomorrow. She knew her hours were numbered. He remembered the promises she had made for him to keep after death. Barbara Ann and Ema grabbed him by his arms. They wiped the tears from his eyes and felt sorry for him. They wondered whether he would survive without her. While leaving the gravesite, a voice out of nowhere sounded like Minerva's, echoing, "Goodbye, Pachouco, enjoy life, please do so."

Everybody presents heard it with their own two ears. Fear fell on them all except Pachouco. A couple of news reporters took off running toward their cars to escape from the graveyard because they were too afraid to stand there. Pachouco turned gently around with a gracious smile, saying:

"Goodbye, my love, just for you, I will, Minerva."

Barbara Ann passed out because fear and happiness mingled together, accompanied her brother's reaction. Pachouco speech came back on the spot. Pachouco and Ema worked with Barbara Ann until she returned to her senses. Faye Esther was silently praying, thanking God for the marvelous work He had performed in her son. She was thanking Him again for His tremendous power. Ema, Minerva's mother, praised God with great praise, singing a song written by Pachouco before her death, "Walking the King's Highway with My God." They sang that song joyously as it was the last song they would sing together, from the graveyard to their front door.

Pachouco drove the van because his sister Barbara Ann was not in any shape to drive them back. He was ready to tell everyone how he felt about them. Faye Esther stopped him, and she said: "Minerva did the same thing to us a few hours before she died; that was her farewell to us. We do not want to hear it, Pachouco. We already know you love us, and we love you, baby boy, go have you some rest now."

The incident at the gravesite brought headline news on Pachouco and Minerva. Eight years later,

Pachouco still had not let Minerva go. Once a month, he visited the graveyard to place flowers on her tomb.

The Memories of a True Love Never Died

MATCH MAKERS

Kirk and his wife Ema considered Pachouco as their son. They wanted to help him forget about the past ordeal that remained fresh in Pachouco's mind as if it was yesterday. They introduced Pachouco to a young woman named Leslie, and they recommended they go out together. Pachouco was not interested even though she was beautiful. She resembled Minerva a great deal. The only difference was that Leslie was a white girl. Pachouco, in a joking manner, said to Kirk and Ema that he thought that he was the only child they had now. However, Leslie looked too much like their daughter. All three of them started to laugh. They coached him to date Leslie just one time to see how comfortable he would be around her. He followed their advice, and he enjoyed Leslie a great deal. Ema saw Leslie as one that was blameless. She had the potential to make Pachouco a good wife.

Leslie knew that Pachouco was a successful man. He loved helping people. Under the teaching of Ema, the young white girl learned how to capture Pachouco's heart and erase at the same time the memories of Minerva from his heart, which was impossible for her to accomplish. Leslie purposed in her heart to end Pachouco's eight years of harassment by an uncontrollable nightmare that visited him at least twice a week. Leslie had promised Kirk and Ema that she would deliver a brand new Pachouco.

They entered quickly into a relationship. Pachouco and Leslie decided to be married someday. They appeared to be in love. This time Faye Esther disapproved of the relationship, not because Leslie was white, but she was afraid of another drama as any other mother that went through the same ordeal with her son would fear. Pachouco's mother did not let her feelings known regarding the situation. Again, Leslie, a white girl, had not influenced Faye Esther's uneasiness. Of course, Faye Esther knew that love is colorblind. The problem was that she became overprotective of him, forgetting Pachouco was a grown man. In such a situation, if another drama should strike him, the mother may not be able to survive it herself. The love of a mother for her baby child could be outrageous. Pachouco and Leslie enjoyed each other's company with reservation. He continually had his guard up, refusing to let his feelings be known. Leslie, knowledgeable of what she was dealing with, reassured him from time to time of his safety with her. Leslie was tired of mistaking her name for Minerva's when he talked to her. He apologized to Leslie often. She usually said to him, "she understood," but deep inside, she did not. He began to open more to Leslie. She had a roommate living with her, whom she claimed to be her baby brother. His name was Yvon. Since Yvon laid his eyes on Pachouco, he developed a great love and respect for Pachouco until it was unbelievable. Yvon had just finished high school but could not afford to go to a local college. Besides, he did not have a job, and Leslie had been taking care of him.

According to Leslie and her brother Yvon, their father was a preacher. She was about ready to take Pachouco to meet her father. Before they left the house, he asked Yvon if he was also going. Yvon answered Pachouco that his father and he did not get along too well. His father wanted him to be in church "twenty-four, seven." He did not like that.

Okay, replied Pachouco, he understood. On their way there, Leslie was brought up to Pachouco; Yvon desired to attend college to be an architect. She went on and on with the conversation ending it in this manner one day; "I will be blessed enough financially to send Yvon to college. God will make way for me to do so." With a heart pure as gold, Pachouco answered her that it was already arranged. Really, advanced Leslie, how can this be?

Leslie, you just finished involving the good Lord in the matter, right. This is how quickly God answers prayer. "Tell Yvon to go ahead and register. I will pay in full his tuition for the next four years."

Leslie desired for Yvon to live on campus. She needed room to get Pachouco where she wanted him, to fall entirely in love with her. She felt he was there, but not sure. Yvon decided not to abide on campus daily he came home. Meanwhile, as years went by, Yvon did very well in college. Both Pachouco and

Leslie were happy for him. Pachouco promised to marry Leslie right after Yvon's graduation. She was excited concerning that because it is only a year of waiting. Pachouco had three years ago pledged that if Yvon had done great in college, he would send him and his sister Leslie on a two-week vacation as a graduation gift. He had had a great love for Yvon, his future brother-in-law.

A couple of months before Yvon's graduation, Yvon's conscience was not at ease for the mischievous role he played behind Pachouco's back. Yvon decided to come clean with Pachouco concerning Leslie's behavior. He planned to meet with Pachouco alone for dinner. Yvon wanted to school Pachouco that the love Leslie seemed to have for him is a false advertisement. Choosing Leslie to be his spouse was the poorest choice he could ever make. Her ability to serve Pachouco as a wife would diminish Pachouco's character and reputation. Yvon's heart filled with regret for his previous behavior. He was willing to pour out his guts. Yvon's warning could have been for Pachouco to call off the engagement while time was in his favor. One thing Yvon soon found out, Pachouco was a unique person. It was hard to create in Pachouco a doubt in someone he loved. Pachouco always believed everyone was trustworthy until proven different.

Regardless of how Pachouco felt after receiving the truth was a secondary matter. He needed to face reality.

At the dinner, which took place in a nearby restaurant, sitting at the table peacefully, Pachouco was not in a hurry to hear what Yvon had to share. Sitting across from him, Yvon was scared and nervous, having no idea how to strike up the conversation. Finally, building some nerve, he said, "Pachouco, thanks a million for sending me to college. There is no way I could have done it without you paying for everything."

Pachouco answers, “Yvon, Man, this is my mission to help people like you who have the potential to understand the help. They engrave it in their heart for the rest of their lives. They will never forget they do not come this far by themselves. You see, Yvon, in this life, we are all users. We are all advantage takers. The worst scenario is when we forget those, like our parents, friends, teachers, and good Samaritans. We have used them; we have taken advantage of them to get where we are today. Yvon always chooses to be grateful over ungrateful considerate over inconsiderate, good over evil, and honest over dishonest. Never forget where you came from always remember where you are going. I saw in your eyes the day I met you, Yvon, you were hungry for an education. By the grace of God, I have possessed the bread. I shared a portion of it with you to lessen your hunger. I expected you to do the same for somebody else one day. You do this, and then Yvon, you can say, remember where you once came from” ended Pachouco.

More tears came out of Yvon's eyes remorse was taking a toll on him. “Shame, shame, shame, I'm so ashamed of myself, Pachouco. I must analyze with you: a few things about Leslie. She is not fit to be your wife.”

Pachouco cut him off saying, “Listen to me, young man, if you think I'm going to sit down at this table entertaining you, talking junk about your sister, my fiancée, you are as wrong as two left shoes. If she is not befitting me, what about letting me find out for myself, okay.”

Yvon replies, “she is no good!”

Pachouco furiously utters, “I do not care if she is or not, and I'm blessed with two eyes. When I see it for myself, then I will believe it. In the meantime, finish your dinner, Yvon. I do not want you to tell me what your sister Leslie is doing unless you show me with my own eyes. Yvon, this conversation is over.”

“Okay, Pachouco, I will show you. It is in my heart to help you. Pachouco, you are too good of a man for me to let you do the unavoidable.”

Pachouco left the restaurant, thinking how hypocritical his future brother-in-law was. He needed to keep an eye on Yvon because of his traitor spirit. Otherwise, Yvon would have Leslie, and he separated way before they married. The same night Leslie and Pachouco went out on a date. Yvon nervously expected Pachouco not to mention to her the outcome of the dinner they had had. The plan that Yvon had in mind could easily mess up. He hoped Pachouco maintained the unforgettable conversation quietly. He prayed for Pachouco to observe the basic twosome rule: "Whatever happened between he and Pachouco stayed between them."

The date occurred on a sizzling summer night in a friendly country club on a peninsula out in the ocean. Romantically, they are holding hands, admiring the constellation of the stars. The moon and its illumination got the best out of the night. It provided light to see during nowhere. The sound of the waves created melodies in their hearts, begging for romance. They reaffirmed their love. In addition, romantic indeed became the night. The vows once made were in danger of being broken. The flesh was getting messy, and they ended up in a bedroom alone. A queen-size bed, well known for its welcome address, was tempting. In that bed, teasing each other and their imagination overnight reached the high mark of creativity. That is what makes love all about the precious gift of God for those who tie the knot. It is also a blessing that can turn into a curse. Pachouco, because of his belief, always started something he was unable to finish. However, this time was the other way around. The minute Leslie brought to Pachouco's attention she was a virgin, he felt, if she managed to remain a virgin at her age, she could also wait on the night of their honeymoon. On this night, the plan to stay was on the verge of being thrown away. Is it true, in love, promises made to be broken? Love loves to keep its promises.

Intensely, Leslie and Pachouco were graciously reluctant to allow love to follow its course. Pachouco was a talented player in the team of no premarital sex. He was so weak that night that he was willing to change the team for the first time. A well-prepared Leslie in this aspect knew the ball was in her court, and time was on her side. She decided to play hard to catch. Pachouco was not dealing with a similar novice as Minerva. This time, he dealt with an experienced woman who believed in her intellect. She had created all the sexual moves. Therefore, Leslie had the power to cause Pachouco to flush his belief of no premarital sex in the commode. Leslie wanted to hold on to the wedding day, not because of principals, but insecurity. She was in a dire predicament; her intention was not to fall in love with Pachouco. From the beginning, somehow, she became deeply in love with him. In the beginning, Pachouco's financial estate was what reached her heart. At this point, she did not care about his money, but he himself. According to Leslie, Pachouco would be her husband, regardless of if she had to lie to him. She planned to override honesty as the key to a successful relationship.

In a romantic voice, she said to Pachouco, “Let us enjoy my birthday.” Pachouco, who is a poet from his heart, knelt between her legs, his hands on her chest, Saying:

“Today is your birthday, Leslie, I could not tell where I was, When God, just for me, created you on a scorching summer day of June it was. Lonely, yes, I was before He formed you."

"Suddenly, a deep sleep got the best out of me; When I woke up Leslie, I was one rib short; God created you just for me with the shortage. Count on me, baby, and I'll never cut you short. Quite a day that was "Help Mate" Happy Birthday."

She screamed with excitement; you are the most wonderful man walking on the island. "I am blessed to have you by my side. I am grateful to God for sending you, my way. The day I laid eyes on you, Pachouco, I perceived you were too good for me from the things I heard of you. Still, I had decided to embrace this venture with you. I coached myself, Leslie, remembered falling in love with Pachouco was out of the equation. My soul has a pure love for you. Pachouco, my dear, try to understand where I am coming from. Three years ago, I was not fit to be a girlfriend to you. A year ago, you had granted me the privilege to be your fiancée, such honor, and I was not fit to be. Before this week is out, Pachouco, I will be fitting for you all the way. There are a couple of chapters of my life I need to close, close forever. One chapter regards Yvon, and the other one concerns Kirk."

Inauspiciously, Pachouco had not a clue of her unclear revelation. He felt the remorse of her conscience, and he was willing to forgive her for whatever she had done wrong in her life. She took not the advantage of the situation to confess what she needed to confess. Pachouco loves true repentance. He admired those that overcame those shameful things they did in life.

When two people are ready to tie the knot, a voluntary background report is healthy. Anything in the past life, which can come back to haunt them, therefore disclose it before marriage. It does not matter how scary the situation may be or how long ago it occurred, and it is best to discuss it before the wedding. Who is free from a skeleton in his closet? No one, I have to say. Some skeletons are worse than others. If one person somewhere knows about someone's skeleton, too many people already know. For this cause, attack it first before consenting to get married. Keep in mind love, trust, and honesty cannot function well without each other.

Pachouco encouraged her by saying, "Your honesty tonight will add a new beat to my heart for you. It also gives me a better understanding of the word TRUST. Tonight, Leslie, we have built a new home in which the structure is made with true love, the foundation built on trust, and the roof with honesty. Who can destroy this well-put-together home? Besides God who ordained true love. We have made heroic efforts to reconstruct this home tonight. What has passed has been done already. We will welcome both the present and the future. The past has already evaporated as a vapor."

Leslie is so close to seeing her dream come true. The desire to be Pachouco's wife enslaves her faculties. She would like to bring him much closer to her; she refused to allow nature to take its course. How blind can she be? The man loves her crazy.

Pachouco is in a good mood for love. The time is perfect, but she is playing with his emotions. She recognizes his weakness. She teases him half of the night. She uses her body as a trap to manipulate him. Leslie has full knowledge of how he feels concerning sexual encounters before marriage. She entices him until she turns out to be his temptation. He is willing to yield to it, not knowing she is fooling him. In a desperate voice, he utters:

"Are we going to make love tonight?"

Leslie answers, “Come on, honey, let's do it.”

As he is ready to penetrate her, she pushes him away by declaring “I have a great necessity for it, but I promised myself years ago never to lose my virginity in casual sex. I wait for the honeymoon. I must do this for myself. I do not mean to reject you, Pachouco. Will you forgive me, love?”

“Leslie, calling Pachouco, you see, your wishes are my wishes. The promises that you keep for love are also mine to adopt. I tell you what, Leslie, I pledge to you this night, we will wait until we married. I promise to keep my values, as well as yours, from this day forward. Leslie, my darling, I enjoyed you tonight. You see, Leslie, I only have two relationships in my life, as you know. You are the second one, and I am proud of myself. I am also a virgin like you at my age. All I ever expected from the two of you was honesty and faithfulness. I cannot stand a liar. In both instances, I consider myself blessed. Both of you are honest, trustworthy, and full of integrity. I love you, Leslie, my wife-to-be."

The night already made room for the day, a deep silence overshadowed Leslie on their way home. She had a strange look upon her face, as she was before a crossroad having not a clue which way to go.

The hardest thing in individual life is to find himself in a situation where what must I do becomes confusing and unknown. In love, confession is good for the heart. Even though through confession, the heart could also experience a major breakdown. This is the first time in Leslie's life she is in love. She is afraid of her past life as well as a portion of her present one. She is not too deep to quit, but there is a price to pay. The heaviness of a ransom is usually associated with blackmail. She grabbed Pachouco's poetry book, took a long breath, and said, "you and I still need to talk."
I'm listening, says Pachouco.

She thinks for a minute while reading one of his poems.

The fear of sharing her secret with him fell on her. What did she read?

LEAVING

I'm not a lover anymore, nor a fool as before.

A victim of infatuation.

The heart knew pains with passion.

If you kept that promise,

Be faithful and honest,

My heart would not be in a mess.

Second and last creature

My heart was in love with,

Now messed up my future.

Now I get to say if.

Whenever I think of you,

How I hate the way I feel.

I hate to hate you,

To forgive you make me ill.

Pachouco inquired of her, what is going on, Leslie? “Talk to me.”

“Pachouco, not now; I will talk to you later, okay.”

He answers: “Leslie, it is always best to wait for the right moment to discuss specific issues. Leslie, the moment is here.”

“Pachouco, my love, you do not understand; the moment right now is not a favorable one.”

Amazingly, an opportunist like Leslie missed all the opportunities a night could offer to an individual to receive forgiveness for any wrongdoing. Even Pachouco could have been honest with Leslie concerning his sterile condition. After the death of Minerva, his doctor explained to him that the shocking death left him with a permanent condition, the incapability of producing offspring. Pachouco cried bitterly and begged his physician to keep the diagnosis a secret, especially from his mother, who is expecting a grandchild from him someday.

THE GRADUATION TRIP

The graduation trip with her brother Yvon approached fast, and it was a graduation gift from Pachouco to Yvon. Leslie never pushed the issue for Pachouco to come along with them since the genesis of the trip. She had found herself between two opinions. One mind told her to cancel the trip, regardless of how Yvon felt. The second mind advised her to have a good talk with her brother.

When the trip was initially planned, Leslie was not in love with her fiancé. She did not have any room in her heart to love anybody to keep it accurate. If the truth is told, she was ignorant of what love was a gold-digging ideal was her mentality. She was all about herself, admiring her beauty daily in the mirror. Now Leslie loved him too much. She struggled daily with that incontrollable disastrous feeling of betrayal. Insecurity and paranoia were her qualities. She did not trust any female, not even his mother. Without any knowledge of it, her brother Yvon raised her blood pressure whenever he spoke over five minutes to Pachouco alone. To break up the conversation, Leslie would invent a task that required the immediate attention of one of the two. Speaking of her love, what started as a game became extremely serious. According to Pachouco, to play with love is to play with matches and gasoline simultaneously. Leslie spread over Pachouco's heart like cancer. He was in a hurry to marry her. She hated the idea to leave him for two weeks straight, but before, she would have counted it as a blessing. Pachouco craved to ask her to cancel the trip but instantly reached his division of the unfairness of this decision toward Yvon. They were a couple of hours away to board the plane to the Spanish country next door to Haiti. Yvon was the only one excited, not knowing he had a surprise waiting for him from Leslie. The departure drew near, Leslie's excitement to teach her brother a lesson cheered her up. She had a great need to let Yvon see she was a changed woman. At the airport, Pachouco prayed with them advised them to have fun. He commanded Yvon to watch over his beauty queen, and then he said, "Bon Voyage."

Leslie quickly used the last statement made by Pachouco to her brother as an opening to discuss with Yvon her heartfelt love for Pachouco. Leslie explained to her brother some things could not be anymore because she was truly in love with Pachouco. Yvon knew since the beginning how his sister was playing games with Pachouco's feelings and that Yvon was an accomplice himself. Pachouco now had a special place in Yvon's heart. Yvon was so grateful for the things Pachouco did for him. From time to time, the flashback of his wrongdoing against Pachouco visited the faculties of his heart. The visitation often left Yvon overwhelmed with remorse for the bad treatments he had paid Pachouco in return. Guilty, Yvon was guilty. His conscience was built around his desire to protect Pachouco in any way he could from Leslie's sneaky and disappointing ways.

Yvon demanded his sister to let that good man go on his merry way. He said Pachouco needed to find someone else that loves him for himself, but not for his finances. Yvon and Leslie spent their vacation as two enemies sharing the same room in the same concentration camp. The tension between them spoiled their well-planned vacation; everything near them was sour. Leslie made it clear to Yvon he must leave the house to create room for her and Pachouco. Yvon agreed to it with a condition: "ONE LAST TIME." He will tell her when and where.

Leslie was mad at the condition imposed by Yvon. She answered him; “I will do anything you want me to do, to get rid of you. Yes, I agree; I warn you, Yvon, not to break the covenant one last time.” Those two spoke in code mainly if Pachouco listened to the conversation.

Three days before their vacation ended, Yvon and Leslie fought physically. Leslie lost her temper and slapped Yvon for adopting a bad idea to spill his guts out to Pachouco of the things she did. Leslie, ashamed of herself, of the trashy love she had had, wanted to start over after realizing Pachouco was the man for her. She tried hard to leave those thoughts, including Yvon, behind her. It became much harder to accomplish when her brother often reminded her of her yesterday’s pain.

The one last time, mentioned above, was also a part of the ransom. Leslie had to pay him to move out of the house and never share her secrets with Pachouco. Yvon's demand tied Leslie's hands. She had no other choice. Leslie instead complied with his demand to avoid shame, embarrassment, and loss of respect. So far, so good, the blackmail appeared to be irrevocable.

Being a novice, raised by his sister Leslie, Yvon had no moderation about himself. At an early age, thirteen years old, Leslie forced him to perform a man's duty. His sister declined the opportunity to enjoy his boyhood. Surely, "she created a monster." The worst sin was when she allowed the monster to wise up. Now he knew the right from the wrong. Yvon's gratitude for Pachouco was unseemly by Leslie.

For the last couple of years, a spirit of being grateful to Pachouco rested and abided in Yvon's heart. His willingness to protect Pachouco from Leslie's acting energy had no limitation. Yvon was determined to show him she was never what she pretended to be in his presence.

Now, Leslie, on her trip again, thinking about the conversation she had had with his mother a few years ago, blamed herself for not applying those words of advice when the time was perfect, and the ball was in her court. By now, all explanation would be gone, and the storm of the past would also cease to rage. A brand-new chapter could have opened because Leslie came to Pachouco's mother three years ago to ask for her blessing to date and someday marry him. Faye Esther answered Leslie; “You have obtained my blessing.” Leslie, an opportunist to the bone, wasted no time forming a question for his mother. Since Pachouco was her son, she knew him well, "what must I do to keep Pachouco and my relationships strong?" Faye Esther replied there were three ways she would answer her question. She advanced; if they followed them, they would not have any reason but to make it. Leslie leaps for joy inquired what those things were. Faye Esther replied, “Be honest, be honest, and be honest.” It sounds like a moral story, added his mother.

Faye Esther was not too fond of her future daughter-in-law. She perceived Leslie had an excellent capability to be a great wife to her son. From a woman's perspective, Faye Esther felt Leslie had dishonest ways that could create trouble for her son. Nevertheless, said his mother, Leslie, will overcome all sentimental dishonesties at the end of the day. She will embrace complete honesty. She will make the best wife a man could ever ask.

Every occasion in life brings its own momentum but remember, the lost momentum will never recapture.

The battle of the minds had begun. Being away from a sweetheart for two weeks straight can tell the story of how much one cares.

The two weeks apart disproved the concept "out of sight, out of mind." For Pachouco, Leslie was out of sight, but she was there in his brain. The fourteen days appeared too long. He entered a diet, not by choice. He missed her so much that his appetite went on strike against him. If his mother Faye Esther did not know any better, she would have believed his appetite went along with Yvon and Leslie. Since the day they had gone, Pachouco and his bed became the best of friends. Early he went to bed. He tried to rush the night to open a new day. During the day, he kept himself busy, a way to put pressure on the day to convert it into the night. He counted down from fourteen to one. His attitude convinced and confirmed to Faye Esther that Pachouco was seriously in love with Leslie.

Pachouco let his mother help him calculate when his suffering would be all over. According to Faye Esther's math, timewise, all he had left was twenty-nine hours, five minutes, and fifty-two seconds to see his beautiful Leslie.

He complained to Faye Esther of the longest two weeks of his life. He felt the day had taken a rest somewhere before it ended. Each night belonged to the turtles regarding how slow.

It was moving. Pachouco claimed the emptiness within changed his heartbeat to abnormal. The voice of Leslie was all he needed to hear about normalizing his heartbeat. His manner over her absence raised an exciting observation: Can he survive without her? What if something terrible happens which requires a breakup? He is a man that classifies honor before love.

Love is something else, and it can bring the best or the worst out of someone. Surprisingly, many people's greatest desire is to find out what love is? They are in the market for someone to show them. Leslie does not have to worry. Pachouco is showing daily how much he loves her.

SURPRISE

Pachouco arrived at the airport two hours before the plane landed. His patience, who knew where he misplaced it. He functioned as if the woman had been gone for a year. To be in love felt so good, so he said. Pachouco purchased another ring. He planned to kneel in the waiting room where the people picked up their luggage. The purpose was that he wanted to push the wedding up to four months earlier than the original plan, this time on Valentine's Day.

One thing about Pachouco, he knew how to draw a crowd because he had a unique style of doing things. He had friends that were news reporters. He invited them to be eyewitnesses. The plane landed. Numerous people gathered, waiting for their loved ones. Pachouco spotted Leslie, who tried to break through the crowd to find him. She missed him with a great miss. She got among the people. Pachouco shouted with a booming voice "May I have your attention please," followed by the blowing of a whistle. Everybody stood still; all eyes pointed at Pachouco. Then he kneeled loudly outburst please, "Leslie, my love, Leslie, my soul mate, would you marry me on Valentine's Day? Please, Leslie, say yes, say yes." The amazed crowd started to sing, Please Leslie, say yes, please Leslie say yes. As the crowd continued their chant, the shocked Leslie appeared unable to balance herself. She wanted to run and fall into his arms, but her legs refused to cooperate, too much excitement for her limbs. There was no glue on the floor, but her feet appeared to stick. She desired to open her mouth to say yes, but her tongue rebelliously raised against her speech. Leslie says yes, Leslie says yes, the chant continued, the crowd sung harmoniously like a mass choir singing the greatest love song for a promise-keeping couple.

Gloriously, the joy of loving, living, and enjoyment of happiness overshadowed the singers. The tears of many overpowered their eyes. Leslie shook like a leaf, she tried to gain a momentum of strength, and she did. She took off her shoes ran toward Pachouco, saying: “Yes, I say yes, yes, yes.” The crowd went wild, rejoicing, as if it was a countdown to the remaining second left from ten to zero, on a New Year's Eve, making ready for the New Year. They changed the tune, singing another song, "go, girl, girl, go get your man."

She flew into his arms. It was what the crazy crowd waited for and wanted to see. Pachouco and Leslie were a minute away from being arrested for public pornography. They tried to make up kissing in a day, what they had been missing for two weeks.

The experience in the waiting room at the airport placed a seal of relief in Leslie's heart. She was free from the doubt that Pachouco did not love her enough to marry her. Victoriously, she considered the moment as such.

Everybody was leaving the waiting room happy for them. People even asked them for an invitation to the wedding. Amid the happy crowd, there was "an unhappy camper." He considered Pachouco as a fool. Moreover, Leslie is a false pretender. Who was the unsatisfied customer? Mr. Yvon, Leslie's baby brother.

Yvon glared at Pachouco and Leslie, and he rolled his eyes. He added to himself their mothers should have named them after the two main biblical characters in the book of Hosea, Pachouco, as Hosea and Leslie Gomar. The bickering among the two brought a catastrophic disaster in their life. Yvon went outside the airport, wrote a note, and placed it on the windshield for Pachouco. “I congratulate you two on the outstanding performance you performed to win over each other. Pachouco, Leslie does not deserve your sincere love. I’ll catch a taxi home.”

The great proposition at the airport should have erased all the frictions between Yvon and Leslie. Instead, it made matters worse.

Pachouco and Leslie arrived at the house where Faye Esther had prepared a welcome home dinner for Yvon and Leslie. They assumed Yvon had gone home; surprisingly, he was in the living room watching television. Faye Esther announced Yvon's presence in the living room and how she enjoyed talking to him. He is a brilliant young man. Both Pachouco and Leslie had a concerned looked on their faces. They wondered what Yvon and Faye Esther were talking about? Leslie knew he was angry with her and Pachouco. Suspicious and nervous was the state, of Leslie. Being uncomfortable stole her beautiful smile from her lips, friendliness, and mostly appetite.

Pachouco decided to shop around for information from his mother. “Did Yvon tell you how the proposition went?”

“No, he did not. Since he came here, he had not mentioned anything concerning you two, no, not yet.”

Leslie, deep inside, did not buy it at first. She thought her brother had badmouthed her to Pachouco's mother. Quickly, Leslie marked with consideration Faye Esther was like her son; she would not entertain adverse reports without Leslie being present to defend herself.

The television news was on. Yvon, all excited, ran to the kitchen where they were. He announced, come on, guys, they are ready to show the script of the proposition. Amazingly, Pachouco's mother ran before all of them. Faye Esther saw how the crowd was into it, Pachouco kneeled, and Leslie flew in his arms. “Magnificently fantastic,” declared his mother with tears in her eyes. “Son, I'm so proud of you.

When you love a woman, you do not mind parading her for the entire world to see. The last thing I would hate you to do is not take safe care of Leslie, son. I want you to cherish her daily reaffirm Leslie of your great love for her from this day forward. Remember, love, is a daily prayer." Faye Esther held Leslie by her shoulder and, with a tender voice, said, "The same goes for you, honey. Love each other with perfect love. A love dressed up with integrity, honesty, and trustworthiness. Never fake love to marry a partner to please society; otherwise, misery will follow you everywhere. Unhappiness will mingle with grief, and it will dwell in the home. For this cause, so many homes have been destroyed, so many marriages ended up in divorce. Their love had not reached the standard requirement of a married couple's life."

Yvon was moved by the words of wisdom that came out of Faye Esther's mouth. He glanced at Pachouco and Leslie, and with watery eyes, he injected:-

"You two had better engrave these golden words in your hearts." They ate a delicious dinner, white rice cooked together with black beans, coconut juice, mushrooms, served with baked fish, plantain, salad, orange juice with milk.

They enjoyed telling jokes and talking about the trip for the rest of the evening.

Pachouco's mother told Leslie never to retake a trip and leave Pachouco behind; he drove me crazy. Leslie turned to Pachouco; "I thought you said you did not miss me much.'

"Girl, believe him if you want to, added his mother. If that man didn't know you were with your brother Yvon, he would have jumped in his car tried to cross the border illegally to find you. He concluded; you were well cared for. Leslie, the man, even cried."

Leslie leaned over his shoulder, singing, "Poor baby and my poor baby."

Yvon joined the conversation. Mother Faye Esther, check this out: Leslie was also crying, singing simultaneously. "I miss my baby. I wonder what my baby is doing. Yvon, Yvon, do you think Pachouco was with another woman? Mother Faye Esther declared Yvon; I told Leslie, shut up and let me sleep Pachouco is a good and faithful man. He is not like you."

Everybody was laughing senselessly, but Faye Esther pondered Yvon's joke.

The evening ended. Yvon and Leslie did not mention anything about their fight. They made the vacation sound enjoyable to Pachouco and Faye Esther, although it was a disaster.

Pachouco left to drop them off. His mother cleaned up the kitchen. While doing her tasks, Faye Esther was calling on God on Pachouco's behalf. It was made known to her by God it is a matter of time before a great deception will take her son by storm. "Please Lord, would you give him the strength to bear it? Nevertheless, not like before, when the incident happened, on their Prom night. Lord. You warned me already of his heartbreak which is coming soon. Lord, I'll try to tell him, but he fails to obey my voice. He has the spirit of knowing it all. For my sake, do not let him suffer long. Give him a quick recovery so he will move on with his life."

Faye Esther wrote the prayer, sealed it in an envelope, and addressed it to Pachouco, and she saved the prayer.

Leslie failed to ask her future mother-in-law if she needed any assistance cleaning up the kitchen. That showed, unbelievably, what type of daughter-in-law she would be.

A DANGEROUS JOKE

The last joke her brother shared with them before the ending of the evening's gathering rang a bell. His mother carefully examined the content of it. She wondered why her brother would indicate Leslie, "Pachouco is a good and faithful man, not like her." Was Yvon trying to give us a hint? Faye Esther found it challenging to cope with the statement. The more she thought about the two months before the wedding, many questions arose in her mind. The effect left her with a migraine headache. She reminded herself not to be so questionable of her son marrying his fiancée in a couple of months. She meditated too long on the subject matter. Increasingly, she became concerned about their engagement. She decided to have a confidential one-on-one talk with her future daughter-in-law. She refers to the date as mother and daughter day out. That night, she called Leslie on the phone and invited her for dinner in a nice restaurant. Faye Esther added, please, Leslie, let us keep it on the downlow. Leslie agreed to meet her for dinner. They set a date and time favorable for both. Happily, Leslie got off the phone. Speaking of Leslie, it was a privilege for her to go on a date with Faye Esther. Suddenly, Leslie felt heaviness in her heart. She accused her brother Yvon of talking.

And lying too much. Leslie recalled how her future mother-in-law was impressed with Yvon's conversation. Automatically, Leslie assumed Yvon had criticized her to Faye Esther. She knocked on Yvon's bedroom door. She begged him to come to the living room. He denied her invitation. Subsequently, he invited her to go to his room instead. She entered in went straight to the point.

"Yvon, did you tell Pachouco's mother of anything concerning us?"

"No, Leslie, I did not. I wanted to, but I changed my mind. It was not about anything negative." Leslie thanked him and tried going to her room. Yvon demanded she watches a movie with him. Leslie sat on the side of the bed, looking at the movie with Yvon. There she fell asleep until the following day. Once again, after the sleepover, a feeling of disappointment had dropped on her. Guilt was the condition of her heart for the way she treated her brother. Yvon knew how passionate Leslie could be. A side of her, not even Pachouco had known yet. Of course, Yvon lived with Leslie day and night. Therefore, her strengths and weakness had never been a challenge to him. In the past, Yvon deviated both in times of need and satisfaction.

Yvon was well acquainted with his sister, like the palm of his hands. He never trusted Leslie. If Yvon had the absolute power to impose or end their engagement in a clean and fairway, he would have done it a long time ago. Yvon caught himself again, wanting to protect Pachouco from the wrath of Leslie. This was because Pachouco invested a great amount of trust and belief in her to such a degree of confidence and belief placed on an individual when it's violated can be destructive. The violation could convert a warm heart to a cold one or kill it at once. A part of Yvon strongly believed Pachouco, in this endeavor with Leslie, will experience a great deception. Time will tell, Yvon thought.

Various controversies and secrecies surrounded Leslie and her brother Yvon's mysteries that were impossible to solve. Whatever happened to the old saying: "Blood is thicker than water." Pachouco occupied a larger portion of his future brother-in-law's heart than his sister among these three.

One night, Pachouco invited Yvon on a fishing trip for the morning. Pachouco picked him up early that morning, and Leslie was nowhere near the house. A great concern fell on Pachouco. He inquired of Yvon, where was Leslie?

Yvon replied, "I have no clue."

Pachouco intervened with another question. "Did she sleep here last night? Was she up early this morning?"
"Yes, she did responded Yvon; she slept in my room last night. She was fast asleep when you called me; she went to the store." Yvon meditated for a minute and said to Pachouco, do not be surprised if Leslie

might already be there waiting on us when we get there. She is just like a fox filled with tricks.

Pachouco did not like the idea of Yvon referring to his fiancée as a fox. Therefore, he reminded Yvon they were going to enjoy the morning fishing. They will not discuss Leslie's personality. First, her character would not tolerate her quickly visiting them without an invitation.

Yvon tried to educate Pachouco on Leslie. He said, "Man, she has you wrapped around her fingers." You do not know her better than I do."

Pachouco madly asked Yvon "Why she would do that?"

Yvon was ready to teach him why, but Pachouco stopped him by answering "I do not care. I do not need to be informed. Let us forget about this conversation."

"Be my guest, Pachouco, but the beam will be off your eyes one day, and you will see much clearer. I'm attempting to prevent long terms trouble for you before it is too late. In other words, before you say I do. Again, I will not be surprised if Leslie is not there waiting on us."

Furiously replied Pachouco, "You do not know what you are talking about. Yvon, one more word concerning Leslie and the trip will be canceled."

When they arrived, they removed the fishing gear from the car and looked straight at the riverbank and who stood up, leaned over, admiring the water: nobody but Leslie. Pachouco glanced at her and smiled. He turned back to Yvon and said, “Man, you were right. You do know your sister a little bit.”

Comically, Yvon said, “I'm not going to say a word because I would hate for you to cancel the trip.”

“Oh yeah,” said Pachouco, “Now you try to be funny.”

Retorting Yvon, “Did I hear somebody apologize by declaring Am I sorry?”

“Okay, you won, Yvon. I'm sorry with a capital S.”

Leslie joined the conversation; “What are you sorry about Pachouco?”

“My darling, this is between two anglers,” responded Pachouco.

In the same token, he asked her why was she there? Who told her he and her brother would be fishing today?

Yvon was dying to hear how his sister would respond to those questions. Without any hesitation, she demanded of him to come a little closer. He entered a few steps; she kissed him very passionately for a few minutes as he drew near. She made it known to him that was the reason she was here. She desired to taste his sweet tongue. Then, she said, “I'm leaving now.” Pachouco begged Leslie not to depart because her company meant a lot to him. She said, “Well, if she was going to be his wife, she might as well walk before him in obedience."

Wow, she was an expert in using the right words at the correct times. That was what drew Pachouco heavily to her.

Yvon shook his head to insinuate his sister was fooling him. She did injustice to those questions by not answering them. Moreover, Pachouco was too in love to recognize it. It's the truth; the best way to betray the one in love is with a kiss. She was there because she did not trust Yvon alone with Pachouco. He might reveal stuff he had no business revealing to Pachouco. If she can help it, Leslie intends to keep them apart until the wedding is over. She was sleeping when her fiancé invited Yvon to go fishing with him.

Since day one, her brother was still ignorant that the telephone in his room had always been tapped. She
screened all his phone calls. Even when he was in high school, she did not permit her brother to talk on the phone with girls who had the potential to be a girlfriend to him. She played the tape last night and heard the morning's plan, another mystery to Yvon. Leslie went fishing with the two men.

While fishing, Pachouco, and Leslie shared their point of view on their wedding. Leslie advised her fiancé to switch the tradition upside down. Usually, in preparing for a wedding, the bride chooses the flower girl, the maid of honor, and the bride maid.

Then, the groom picks the ring bearer, the best man, and the groom's men. Well, Leslie was always thinking ahead. She comes with this brilliant idea for Pachouco to choose the girls, and she would pick the men, except for the maid of honor and the best man. Even with that, she already had a plan put together. Why did Leslie desire to go this route? Of course, she had more male friends than woman friends.

Pachouco kicked the idea in the beginning based on the traditional fashion of doing things. However, another gentle kiss from her to him overpowered his argument, and he became agreeable with her proposal.

Proudly they shared with Yvon the decision made for their wedding. Pachouco will pick the girls and Leslie the boys. He knew what was next whenever Yvon shook his head while pitifully staring at him. Yvon asked whose idea was that?

“The two of us agreed to do so,” said Pachouco. Yvon shook his head again and said something like this Leslie was the only person I perceived who could invent this. Do not pay him any mind; Honey happily retaliated against Leslie to her fiancé.

INSECURITY

Suddenly, a friendly and quiet voice echoed, longtime not see, godfather? Pachouco, before he even turned around, he replied that it must be Michelle; he recognized her voice. She is his niece and goddaughter. She is the daughter of Rosa, Pachouco's sister. Along with Michele was Pachouco's other niece, Myrla Niecy.

A jealous Leslie was enraged to discover who the devil they were, waiting to be introduced by Pachouco as his fiancée. It seemed to her the introduction was taking too long. Remember, she was very insecure, very bossy, and manipulative. Those girls were there to fish. In the meantime, insecure thoughts were crossing her insecure spirit.

Leslie, in her intellect, questioned those young women's presence at the lake. She wondered if they were here to meet her brother Yvon and Pachouco on a double date. She lost her patience and was too short with her temper. She stood up with her arms folded, still waiting to be introduced.

Pachouco was so happy to see them both. He was interested in catching up on the times lost in their lives. He had not seen them since his previous fiancée was killed. It was not intentional that he disregarded her.

Yvon, on his part, kept asking himself where he had met the beautiful Michelle? She appeared remarkably familiar to him. Yvon was confident of the fact he had been in her presence before. His memories betrayed him for the time being. He believed Michelle, and he went to school together when he was twelve or fourteen years old. He watched her until her beauty created a unique attraction in his heart. He could not wait on Pachouco to present him to her. He was also afraid of his sister's reaction. At Yvon's age, Leslie refused to let him date somebody while living with her. What kind of mess was that?

Pachouco, by mistake, ignored his previous company. He got a little deeper in the conversation with Michelle and Myrla Niecy. Leslie, at this point, was on the verge of having a stroke. Though her blood was boiling over, she still maintained her calm. Her limited patience was only seconds away from being exposed.

There was a side of her Pachouco did not know. Yvon, on numerous occasions, had met the other side of Leslie. If Pachouco ever married her, he would need to put down his foot. Otherwise, she would spank his behind.

This was one of her brother's concerns for Pachouco. According to Yvon, she was far from being nice; however, for her fiancé, she was a charming saint, an angel from the sky. Yvon often insinuated

Leslie was one of the fallen angels. It is true, the name of the game was "Enjoy the moment." Yvon continuously believed he was the only one who could lead Pachouco to an exit door to escape from his sister's grips. Even though Pachouco escaping would be a hard pill to swallow, times would heal his wounds.

Leslie was a natural-born jealous hearted person. She never experienced falling in love before until the latter part of her engagement with Pachouco. What started as a game, playing love on her part, now became her genuine issue. She got aboard the relationship with a gold-digging mind. Previously, with a teasing spirit, Leslie tried to delude him. Her dream was to gain control of his heart and his wallet. Yes, she did accomplish her goal of falling in love, but he was not the only one in love. She also became contaminated with the love disease. She got beat at her own game.

Leslie paced the ground near the lake, making inappropriate gestures, trying to get Pachouco's attention. Nothing worked; Pachouco's heart was on the old days. Leslie relaxed concerning Michelle. She knew Pachouco was Michelle's godfather and uncle when she first called him by this title.

Myrla Niecy was more of a threat to her now. Regardless, she wanted him to introduce her to them. He left Leslie no choice but to do it herself. Leslie was not the only one with this feeling. Her brother Yvon also wanted Pachouco to allow them to meet him. Again, Yvon was keeping a close watch on his sister.

He realized her impatience with the whole situation. He reached over and told her in her ears to be nice; it was an oversight not noticed by Pachouco.

After expressing himself to her, Yvon's admiration of Michelle arrived at his sister's eyesight. She pulled him to the side and threatened him. In the form of advice, the message she gave to Yvon was to be careful, or he was about to be embarrassed if he did not stop looking at Michelle, as a man who had never seen a woman before in his life. Madness, Yvon was a grown man again, yet she gained control over both. Truly, Leslie is a piece of work. Yvon shared with her that Pachouco, her future husband, should have been her only concern. Besides, continued her brother, that girl is, yes indeed beautiful. There was not an enormous difference between the toughness of a snake and Leslie at this moment. The effects of loneliness just for a few minutes abide in her insecure heart. It seemed to her all the attention was drawn to Michelle and Myrla Niecy. She made a big deal out of nothing. She acted as two men she loved had violated her womanhood. Her pain and her agony nearly reached an end.

Finally, Pachouco told those girls: “Let me present you to my beautiful…”

Before he even said her name, Michelle busted out, pronouncing, hello Leslie, and she reached her right hand toward her brother and shook his hand at the same time, entering, hello Yvon, how is everything with you?

They found themselves in a circle filled with surprise. Michelle made Leslie's day by injecting; “You are a beautiful woman; you will make my godfather a lovely wife. I saw you two on the news; that was the most exciting moment in the history of love. I enjoyed seeing my godfather kneel with the diamond ring in his mouth, proposing to you. I was chanting just as loud with the crowd. I wished you could have seen yourself, Leslie running to go after your man. Leslie, you for real, outdid yourselves. There was one thing that puzzled me, whatever happened to the ring that was in his mouth?”

A comfortable Leslie, who was crazy about flattery, replied, “Child, when I fell in his arms, I kissed that mouth. I took my ring with my tongue.”

Michelle intervened to say, “Go, girl. Did you see it, Myrla Niecy,” asked Michelle?

“No, I did not, but all my friends talked about it.”

Pachouco started the introduction all over again. He said: Myrla Niecy, this is my beautiful Leslie. The word love did not have its true meaning until I met her. She is my sunshine when I'm cold; she is my water when I thirst. Yes, this is my lovely Leslie and Leslie, Myrla Niecy. This is Yvon, the cutest man alive, my partner, son, and future brother-in-law. Yvon is single.

Myrla Niecy declared to Pachouco, “The Good Lord has blessed you with a nice girl. Who stands for beauty, honesty, integrity, faithfulness, and trustworthiness? I can smell all these characteristics in Leslie, your wife-to-be." Leslie continued, Myrla Niecy, "You do not need me to tell you, Leslie, you have a good man. He will make you proud to be married. Pachouco will treat you like a queen. He introduced you to me with a long speech, and he meant every word which came out of his mouth. You may wonder how I know so much about Pachouco. He is the model of the family, and he is my uncle. I am his sister Barbara's daughter."

Leslie was worried for minutes; she thought Myrla Niecy was also in love with her husband to be. When she heard they were uncle and niece, the pain from her heart dissolved. Right, on the spot, Pachouco asked both Michelle and Myrla Niecy, would they desire to be two of the bride maids.

"Perfect, that would be if you two agree to do so. Please do it for us?" Leslie repeated.

They answered, "why not? Because you guys' wedding will make history. Do you have any idea how many people are waiting for February to come to witness the solemn ceremony," mentioned Michelle? "You two excite me more. I really appreciate your entrustment of Pachouco into my hands. I promise to treat him right. I do not promise his safety on the night of our honeymoon. You know what I mean, girls. This will be my first time too. I'm going to enjoy myself," added Leslie.

Yvon addressed Michelle inquiring of her, had she met him and Leslie before? She answered yes, it was a long time ago. “Do you not remember me?” Has she asked Michelle?

MEMORY

Somewhat, responded Yvon, "You reminded me of a girl I used to love in seventh grade. I was thirteen years old. I often prayed to God to allow me to rejoin with her again. Her last name was Casimir, just like Pachouco. She was a beautiful girl. She resembled you very much. If I am not mistaken, her name was also Michelle. I am still mad with my sister until this day. Whenever I think of the situation that had transpired that day between her and me. Anyway, you have not told me your last name."

She answered, "For the time being it is a secret, especially from you."

She left to go on the other side of the river. Yvon returned to Pachouco implored him with Michelle's last name.

He responded, Casimir, is she not pretty? "She is also my niece. Are you too much of a chicken to ask her out?"

Yvon replied she has always been a cute girl Pachouco, always.

Michelle called Pachouco, she said, "Par adventure, Yvon solicited my last name; please do not tell him.""Sorry, Michelle, you are a little too late. He did, and I already gave it to him, is there a problem?"

"This is a long story that was dead and needed not to revive. How long have you known Leslie?" Inquired Pachouco of Michelle?

"I was thirteen years old when I met her. She forgot who I was. The last time I saw her, I was fourteen years old."

"My goodness," said Pachouco; "You mean to tell me you still remembered her and her brother after all these years?"

"Michelle took a deep breath reentered godfather; when someone hurts one's feelings, the offender tends to forget. However, the victim will never forget when, where, and why. Even though sometimes, forgiveness reminds us it is not an option, but a full force requirement. Still, we often struggle with its compliance. Godfather, please be careful. I do not have to worry about you. God is constantly dealing with you in a particular way. God will never let you fall into a trap. In case He did, it would be in your best interest. Thank Leslie and you for allowing me to be one of the bride maid. Leslie might change her mind later."

"No," replied Pachouco, "Is a done deal."

"We will see," responded Michelle.

She knew that as soon as Leslie found out who she was, Leslie would "fight tooth and nails" to eliminate her from the wedding unless Leslie had changed for the better.

Michelle curiously was interested in knowing where Yvon abides. Nevertheless, she refused to pursue that question.

Yvon followed the trail leading to the other side of the lake, where Michelle was. He reopens the conversation. Apologetic, yes indeed, he is. He reenters how much he always loved her. Yvon shared with Michelle how he often daydreamed about her. He has prayed to God to allow him to reunite with her in one of the school years.

Shortly after the incident, declaring Yvon to Michelle, her parents moved away from the neighborhood without a trace.

Then, Yvon thought to himself; there is nothing harder than to hurt the lady you love with stupidity. The pains from the hurt terrorized her heart, coldly knocking her on the ground. When common sense comes to her rescue, she will run for her life until she vanishes away. To have not had a chance to say how sorry and how stink your behavior was.

Michelle rejected his apology. It had been too long. They needed to forget about it. Michelle failed to understand that night's disappearance had left him with a guilty conscience, which could affect him for the rest of his life. The urge to say he was sorry to Michelle impregnated him for a while. He finally gave birth to it. He stood in front of her, face to face. Yvon glanced at her shamefully repeated those powerful words, please.

Michelle, forgive Leslie and me for the hurt we inflicted on you.

Not, Michelle thought she was delivered from this unfair and confusing moment. Even though mischief happened twelve years ago, tears were flowing from her eyes. Michelle remembered the ordeal as if it were yesterday.

The only time an individual can believe he has overcome the bad rap of his life is when discussing or talking about it has not affected him. Then he can claim deliverance. As for Michelle, she always wanted to know the ending of the conversation that night. She decided to comment on Yvon's apology to her.

She responded in this manner, "Why apologize to your sister? If there need be an, I'm sorry for something; she would need to do it herself. Besides, tell me what kind of explanation she could offer to me while preparing herself to marry my godfather, my uncle. Yvon, you were a boy then. Now you are a man with this package of being a man demands you to perform the right thing for the sake of humanity. As an inexperienced girl, I did not know any better I was a child. Now that I am a woman, want it or not, the same formula goes for me."

OVERPROTECTIVE

Leslie, in the meantime, searched for her brother around the lake with a pair of binoculars. She tracked him down and saw him standing up on the bank of the river from the other side. The binoculars seemed to glue to her eyes, observing Michelle and Yvon. She sat next to Pachouco, who was steadily talking to her. She heard not a word he spoke. Her concentration was in jeopardy. Leslie was too busy spying on them. For what purpose, who knows? She looked for Myrla Niecy and saw her fishing by herself far from them. Leslie's senses began to work fast, Leslie recalled Michelle's presentation to Yvon by her fiancé. Michelle did not give Pachouco a chance to present Yvon's name to her. She was automatically familiar with his name. Now Leslie wonders where they have met.

Even though she acted insecure whenever she saw her brother having a lengthy conversation with Michelle, she still wanted him out of the house to make room for Pachouco. Yvon was the one who refused to leave because he had no place to go. While on vacation together they entered into an agreement that would require Yvon to move somewhere across-town. The same plea demanded Leslie perform one last time something before he would leave the house. Leslie agreed to it without an objection. She loved Pachouco she persistently desired to be his wife. She was determined to walk or to jump on anything that appeared to be in her way and that included her brother Yvon. She also recalled again how Yvon got lost in Michelle's beauty, how he was debating where he knew her from. Michelle's face was awfully familiar to Yvon. Michelle's physical attraction developed a mystery in Leslie's intellect. The more Leslie glanced at her; the more Michelle's visage became familiar. Leslie was unable to pinpoint where she first met Michelle. Leslie also recognized that she was extremely close to Pachouco and his family. According to what Leslie learned so far, Faye Esther, Pachouco's mother, was the one who sent Michelle to college. She also graduated the same month as Yvon. Leslie quickly perceived they were the same age. She did the best she could to put the puzzle together. However, the missing pieces made it impossible to solve. Leslie is not a quitter her willingness to go with what she must complete her spying task required a lot of mannerism. The creation of an excuse to go where Yvon and Michelle were temptingly becoming her last result.

Pachouco asked Leslie to let him use the binoculars to see what preoccupied her spirit. Because for the last twenty-five minutes she spent it neglecting him. An excuse to go deep into others business was just created. She quickly gave them to him. In the absence of any shame, Leslie kissed him, while he viewed Yvon and Michelle exchanging words of peace.

From Leslie's mouth came out these words "I will be right back. I'm going to check on them over there, especially Myrla Niecy who is fishing alone."

Leslie thought she was home free and that her manipulative plan had worked. "Not too fast," entered Pachouco, "Come back here and sit down with your nosy self. Let us enjoy the day next to each other, leave your brother alone. You are overprotective of him. Besides, both are single, and they are afraid to date."

"Do you want to know why I'm overprotective of him, Pachouco? I have cared for Yvon since he was thirteen years old. His mother mistreated him. I opened an escape door for him at my house with our father's approval because Yvon and I have the same father. I went through so much hell with his mother over him. Finally, a judge granted Yvon to me at his preference to live with me for a better living condition. Since then, he has not seen his people from his mother's side."

Pachouco asked Leslie, "Were you the mastermind behind Yvon's escape?"

"Honest as I could be, affirmatively."
Pachouco reminded Leslie how much trouble she could have had with the law.
Comically answered Leslie, "I did the same thing to you. I made your escape from all the girls in your

town. Now, look how peaceful you lay your head on my lap."

Leslie's beautiful smile left her face and invented room for a sneaky frown. Leslie was forced to cooperate against her will. A glance from Pachouco brought her smile back to her face.

She wasted no time entering an outrageous statement.

"All I know is my brother is a virgin. He also does not believe in premarital sex." "Over my dead body" "Would I permit a woman to fool him to get involved. I'm in love with you, Pachouco, because you have never pressured me in sexual encounters. Remember when we both were vulnerable, and we almost made love. Then we both realized premarital sex was against our religious beliefs. We did stop pursuing it. Pachouco, I just can't wait to explore your beautiful island. I will be the first and last captain to explore your virginity, my island of beauty. We will be married for life. I am convinced we were born for each other."

"On Valentine's Day, Lord have mercy upon my lovely Leslie," replied Pachouco.

The day went on, and as the hours of the day passed by, the night drew near. They began to pack their stuff. Yvon and Michelle wished each other farewell until the wedding rehearsal. Yvon attempted to get her phone number, but she refused to give it to him. She felt nothing had changed as far as his situation was concerned. All five fellowshipped a little bit, even though the mosquitoes declared war against them.

Leslie asked Michelle how long she and Yvon had known each other. Michelle caught herself beating around the bush. Michelle referred to Leslie as her future godmother and said she preferred her brother to answer the question. Laughing, Yvon asked his sister to tend to her business. Myrla Niecy boasted out and revealed they were high school sweethearts. No way contested Leslie; otherwise, she would have known Michelle before. Myrla Niecy intervened again with her eyes fixed on Yvon. Leslie had but did not remember, right, Yvon? On this note, Michelle broke camp by kissing Pachouco and Leslie. She shook Yvon's hand. Myrla Niecy did the same. Yvon let Myrla Niecy know he was delighted to meet her. In addition to Michelle, Yvon insinuated, he had everything under control. Michelle offered Yvon the prettiest smile she ever gave to a man. She was not cheap with it and wished him good luck. They were speaking in code.

Leslie, endowed with vision, imagined a heart-to-heart conversation with her brother. She was suspiciously thinking something was cooking between Michelle and him. Whatever it was, had a lot to do with her. A one-on-one chat between Yvon and Leslie might result in a battle of exchanging nasty words. The existence of mutual hard feelings for each other had overpowered the peaceful union they once had.

The evening reached its ending. Pachouco left to go home, thinking how enthusiastic his fiancee was about the wedding arrangements. Pachouco had a firm conviction to ignore anyone who attempted to bring disunion between him and Leslie. In other words, negativity and gossip against Leslie were not entertained by him. Whosoever proposed to do so; hurt feelings lay waiting for them. Pachouco hoped Michelle was not engaged in any degrading remarks with Yvon about his sister. Anyway, he doubted seriously that Michelle would tolerate Yvon to persuade her to talk trash about Leslie. Pachouco quickly concluded that his goddaughter was good at minding her own business. Before terminating the above conclusion, another thought invaded his intellect. Pachouco remembered one time Leslie had told him why Yvon stayed with her. He and his father, who happened to be Leslie's father, also could not get along. Pachouco realized the two stories did not flow well together. He decided to keep his mouth shut. Reliably, time will tell because he knew one of the stories was false. Yvon himself shared with Pachouco he and his father did not agree completely. As a preacher, Patrick wanted Yvon in church all the time. Pachouco does not enjoy digging in other men's matters. He learned from his mother to leave other people's affairs alone and tend to his problems. Well, said Pachouco, one thing is for sure, family stories always contain lies.

When he arrived at his house, he called to inform her he had made it home. Somehow, he assumed a problem with how Leslie picked up and answered the phone. Pachouco suspiciously insinuated she and Yvon had fought. He noticed that since they were back from the trip, they were not speaking to each other when by themselves. Even at the lake, Yvon and Leslie had spoken off and on. Privately, she wanted to deal with her brother. Willingly, she expected to keep everybody else in the dark about his and her issues. Pachouco, on his part, refused to interfere in a family affair and kept his silence. The feud among them had the potential to ruin their personalities, so he asked Leslie why she was upset. There was a silence on the phone as if it was a bad connection. She did not answer him. He said hello, hello, he informed her that he was coming back over. Then she quickly responded, “No, Yvon and I just finished fighting.”

Pachouco replied, “You want me to come over?”

Pachouco, she uttered, in a pleasant and gentle voice, “How long have I told you that what is going on between Yvon and I is a family affair. The last thing I would want to do is put you in that unfair position. Besides, I called my daddy to come and give him a good talking. I will talk to you later, honey. Do not worry, Pachouco, my love, your sweetheart is okay. I will call you tomorrow and be sure you dream about me tonight.” He replies, “Will do, baby, bye.”

NIGHTMARE

Since her accidental outing with Pachouco, Leslie, and Yvon, Michelle had experienced trouble sleeping at night. She began to despise those hours.

Their time together at the lake left her with a guilty heart and troubles some spirit. First, Yvon was her first boyfriend. Her intention to meet him again someday was unthinkable. When she departed from their house, she cursed both the night she and Yvon met and the day she and Leslie met. Michelle watched the script of her godfather's proposition to marry Leslie on the news. Michelle thought about her name, and a cold chill traveled her body. She never doubted that in her spirit, which was the same, Leslie. How in the world could she miss it? Leslie looked like Michelle's godmother Minerva, Pachouco's former sweetheart. The major difference between the two was her godmother was black with a beautiful light skin complexion. Leslie was white as well as Yvon.

Michelle did experience some sleepless nights. She deemed it too hard, struggling to figure out how to cope with the information she had on her godfather's wife-to-be. Pachouco and his former sweetheart taught Michelle at an early age the importance of being honest, trustworthy, and holding fast to her integrity. The hurt Michelle suffered that horrible night caused her not to go out with another young man. That night's experience killed her taste for men, depriving her of the right to trust a male. After all these years, she realized her feelings had remained stronger for Yvon. Even though not possible, was her final verdict, as far as her loving Yvon. Still, she might need to reconsider the possibilities. At this point, she worried more about her godfather. He closed all the entrance doors in both his heart and ears to avoid listening to the truth. Michelle knew Pachouco was a sincere, honest, trustworthy man.

He never bases his love for anyone because of what someone else thinks or perceives about that person. Bad or good, he prefers to see it for himself. He will die believing people do change from worst to good daily. He is confident she could not change a made-up mind.

Michelle also knew if Leslie came clean with him, he would forgive her for whatever she had done. He could cope with the worse habit that she had. The most brilliant move Leslie could make was to disclose all secrets to Pachouco before the wedding. He would have given Leslie a brand-new beginning and a brand-new slate. Honesty is what he lives for, and Michelle hated to let him go in a marriage blindfolded. She had no clue; the happy couple had already put everything on the table. Pachouco will not respect anybody's feelings, or anyone who tries to speak to him about

Leslie in a negative manner. He will take the same stand for Faye Esther, Yvon, Myrla Niecy, myself, or any other loved one. The man is pure gold.

Yvon and Michelle touched the situation a little bit. Shamefully, he explained to her he was against the idea of Pachouco marrying Leslie; she claims she loves him. Deep in his heart, Yvon realized she does love him but not enough to trust that good man in Leslie's hands. Yvon stands firm in his decision not to participate in the wedding or advise them. He blamed Leslie behind her back for losing Michelle, a complaint Michelle Casimir did not value.

Michelle did not tell Myrla Niecy what her horrific experience was with Yvon and Leslie. Michelle still experiences sleepless nights. She was determined to talk to her godfather without reservation. Difficult is her task because of whom it involves. She teamed up with her cousin Myrla Niecy. They came up with the bright idea of inviting Pachouco to dinner. They planned to swell up his head to get him to the restaurant. They told him they wanted to check on his readiness to husband's lifestyle. Myrla Niecy was excited about the game plan. She invited him. Pachouco agreed with the condition he would not entertain anything negative concerning Leslie. He is again a firm believer, and if there was anything negative in her life, God would show it to him in due season.

Myrla Niecy gave the latest report to Michelle of his affirmative answer. Nevertheless, his objection had defeated Michelle's purpose for the invite. She was expecting a miracle somehow, a miracle for him to leave the door of his heart cracked open to obtain knowledge of his surroundings. They met at the diner joyfully. The day of the wedding approached them rapidly. Pachouco, if he could, would place a rush order on the day to come first class expressly. He sat down with a smile all over his face.

Michelle asked him why he was smiling without interruption?

This time, he laughed instead of smiling, answered her by tapping his right hand gently on Michelle's shoulder and his left hand on Myrla Niecy's.

He spoke these words, “My two beautiful nieces; it does feel marvelous to be in love. Truly family, it is so sweet to fall in love with a woman that gives the same love back in return. What I love the most about Leslie are her honesty and her integrity. She reminds me so much of my first love Minerva who promised me she would be my guardian angel in everything I do. Minerva came to me in a dream and gave me the green light to date my beautiful Leslie.”

Michelle finally found the door cracked open she wasted no time to ask him, “Did my godmother also come to you in a vision to authorize you to marry Leslie? Or is this what Pachouco wants to do?”

Humm, was the sound made by him, he injected “She never had, Michelle.”

Michelle is now playing offense with her godfather. “You jumped the gun too soon. Leslie may resemble my godmother, and there is no argument. They are carbon copies of each other. In character, they are night and day. My godmother, compared to Leslie, was a perfect woman.”

Pachouco, unbelievably, was agreed with Michelle.

Myrla Niecy took the conversation over. “Uncle, I agree with you and Michelle. Minerva was a brilliant and honest woman. There was a true family bond between us. Minerva was secure, and I missed her a lot. She would have been my favorite aunt if she were alive right now.”

“She was a trustworthy person,” responded emotionally Pachouco. Michelle and Myrla Niecy understood his weakness. In the blink of an eye, they flipped the conversation around to avoid spoiling dinner. Michelle was expecting to mark the beginning of a family open door policy. The rain started to drop on the table, this time not from the sky but from Pachouco eyes. Michelle and Myrla Niecy had no other choice, but to talk about something that contained the power to cheer him up a little. They automatically concluded to lift Leslie up above measure. Then his smile and laughter quickly revived. Yes indeed, it worked. Myrla Niecy congratulated him for his taste in the choice of a woman. “I applauded Leslie’s beauty queen face. She looked younger for her age. She proved daily to be a young woman like us, beauty has nothing to do with age. She will make a beautiful bride."

Myrla Niecy was fun to be with no one can expect what would come out of her mouth next because she loved telling jokes. She said to her uncle:

"Please tell me, I know premarital sex is not in your vocabulary. In other words, you do not believe in having sex before marriage. There is nothing wrong with that. Please, uncle, do not ask me if I am a virgin. Too late, I'm sorry."

They laughed loudly and continued Myrla Niecy, uncle open your eyes widely, "Look at me. Have you or have you not gotten a piece from Leslie's stuff for real?"

Michelle screamed, godfather that girl Myrla is plain crazy. Pachouco and Michelle choked in their laughter.

"No Niecy, I have not. There were a few moments in our lives when we were almost engaged in sexual affairs because our flesh weakened. One of us always remembered the vows we made between us. No sex, until after the rings are placed in our fourth fingers on our left hand. Can you believe it, she is also a virgin?"

Michelle's attitude changed she screamed from the top of her lungs "Say what?" Pachouco adopted an attitude also by saying, "Leslie and I, we both are virgins. There are people right now who would think I am lying for saying I am a virgin. Who knows,

Michelle and you may not even believe Leslie is a virgin. You guys might have already stereotyped her."

"Calm down uncle, we believe you," said Myrla Niecy. Michelle answered, Myrla Niecy, "Speak for yourself."

The family open door policy, Michelle was hoping for had just been flushed down the commode. Michelle built some nerves at this moment she was willing to play her last card. She said, "Godfather, you and I need to talk."

"Is it about Leslie's behavior, concerning Yvon, or concerning you and me," replied Pachouco?

Michelle with tenacity, answered, "All the above."

Her godfather glared at her. In her judgment she pictured the green light, he would give her the go ahead. She learned in a hurry the true meaning of the old saying, "Looks can be deceiving."

"Baby girl," responded Pachouco, "I purposed in my heart not to listen to any garbage from anyone about Leslie's family, nor mine. I gave Leslie the green light to be honest with me about everything she did wrong in her past. She did just that. Case closed. I love you, baby girl, now let us finish our dinner."

Michelle was embarrassed, but she whispered to herself how stupid can he be? Myrla Niecy again changed the train of the conversation to a pleasant one. Winking her eyes at Michelle with a smile and exclaimed to Pachouco: “Go boy, defend your woman!”

He could not wait to talk to his mother concerning his enjoyment over Michelle and Myrla Niecy. Pachouco was always amazed to sit at a table with other members of his family in an outing for dinner or supper, always trying to catch old family stories. If Myrla Niecy happened to be around, the stories would be on target, one after the other.

Well, everything good must end. He picked up the tab, Michelle and Myrla Niecy contributed to the tip. They left the restaurant satisfied. He dropped them off, and the gossip started. Michelle shared for the first time with Myrla Niecy her unforgettable nightmare. A shocking Myrla Niecy was dumbfounded and aggravated with that tragic and sad story. She would have never believed something that serious could have taken place on the island in their lifetime. Myrla Niecy lost in a matter of seconds her natural sense of humor. Emotionally, there was nothing left to do but cry. She knew her uncle had to learn the hard way. His stubbornness teamed up with his eagerness, confederated against good sound advice contrary to the wedding. What was so hard for Michelle and Myrla Niecy to understand? In so many ways, he expressed himself clearly, asking everyone to be preoccupied with their own business. His philosophy was whatever one apprehended about

Leslie in the past, and it was now irrelevant because they were headed toward the future. Leslie had nothing to hide at her age; she was still a virgin. What more could he ask for? Michelle was anxious to comment. She preferred to choose the best route, which was to shut up. Otherwise, she would become an enemy of Pachouco.

HONESTY

It is amazingly easy for family members to invade and gain control over the privacy of a lovely couple. They will break up friendships through their judgmental criticism. This was the reason Pachouco begged Leslie to be honest with him. He promised the same in return. There was always room for forgiveness when the confession was made willingly in the absence of force.

Pachouco and his mother are conservationist. Therefore, they got joy when talking to each other, and there is no room for a dull moment. He is the type that many call "a mama's boy." He does not care what they call him. He feels a man should love his mother like crazy. If a man loves his mother, he will learn to love his wife and take loving care of her. This is Pachouco's philosophy. During the conversation, he brings to his mother's attention if he ever breaks up with Leslie, he will not date another woman from the Island anymore.

“An American girl from the south, or I will remain celibate.”

His mother, in a second, replies, “Hopefully, things will work out for you and Leslie.” Regardless of how Faye Esther felt concerning Leslie, she would still love her as a daughter-in-law. The problem is Faye

Esther's motherhood instinct has played a distinguished role in her thinking. She insinuated something was wrong with the type of relationships existing between Leslie and her brother Yvon. Pachouco explained to his mother that Yvon and his sister had just engaged in a fight again. He does not know the motive behind it. It seems like they argue every single day. He asked his mother for her opinion.

She asked him if he was serious about wanting her opinion on this subject?

"Come on, mother," said Pachouco. He was serious as a "heart attack that can kill." His mother reminds him how touchy he is. He tells her to go ahead.

She started by saying; first, Yvon and Leslie do not act like brother and sister. Time will prove it. Something must be wrong; they do not strike me as such. They fuss and fight like spouses, whose experiences, hardships, and aggravation resulted in falling out of love. Financial difficulties force them to live under the same roof. That is what they remind me of.

Pachouco, with itching ears, does not support this theory. Yvon is just a twenty-two-year-old man, a spoiled brat, who believes his sister owes him the world. Leslie was twenty years old, and her brother was thirteen years old when he moved in with her. There are two things about Yvon he is a brilliant boy, and he loves his sister. Pachouco says therefore he went out of his way to help Yvon.

Faye Esther is not only a classy woman, but she has a way with words. She said to Pachouco, "he did not go far enough out. He needed to go a little farther until Yvon had a full understanding of love, never love abuse." His mother pried too deep, so he wanted to change the conversation.

His mother began some people in life to set them up for deception in their daily living by failing to yield to the warnings present before their eyes. They think they know better than everybody else, an incurable disease to them. It could cause them brain damage and become brain dead eventually.

Now Pachouco, Let us finish our conversation on Yvon. The love that Yvon has for you is highly respected. He sees himself as a son who has a great father. The son loves his dad so much and is ready to protect him at any cost, continued Faye Esther. Pachouco, Yvon will never forget what you have done for him. I would not be surprised if the arguments and the fights between him and Leslie concerned you. They may not have loved you earlier, but now you are growing on them like cancer. Both love you with a different form of love. I told you long ago, Yvon and Leslie, not strike me as brother and sister. First, she treats him more as somebody she wants to get rid of, and she wonders how to make it happen. She has been around you long enough to understand the way you operate. To make Yvon move from the house will not be an easy task for her to accomplish because you will demand him to stay home. Your plans are always for the three of you. If she can make him leave on his own, you will respect his decision after he gives a reason for moving out. The feud between them is outrageous; it requires the participation of a third person. If necessary Pachouco, it might not be a bad idea to visit their father alone. He is a preacher. He will be glad to listen to any concerns a future son-in-law may have."

They had another mess again this evening, mentioned Pachouco to his mother. "I will follow your advice tomorrow evening. I will pay their father, Rev. Patrick, a visit by myself. He might be able to bring peace between those two; that should be my priority."

"Pachouco, have you chosen your best man yet? Leslie and I discussed it, and I will ask Yvon to be the best man."

"Fantastic," answered his mother. "Have you asked him yet? Time is getting away from you and Leslie, but as for me, I seriously doubt he will accept. He is totally against you marrying his sister, and he thinks you deserve better than that."

Pachouco replied, "Mother dear, I do not care what Yvon's motive is. I am not going to find out. I love Leslie, and I am marrying her. He has made three attempts already to talk to me. You know how I do." "Yeah," answered Faye Esther, "You cut him off quick, fast in a hurry."

"Yes, I did. I rejected what Yvon had to utter before he started. All three times, clear, I explained to him that I'm a Saint Thomas, and I want to see it with my own two eyes to believe it."

"What did he say, asked his mother?"

"Okay, you will see for yourself before it is too late," he said.

THE DINNER

In the morning, Faye Esther and Leslie plan a future mother and daughter-in-law confidential day out to dinner. Leslie came and picked her up, and they went on a shopping spree. They checked out the bride's maids' dresses. They were nosy enough to inspect the groom's men's tuxedos too. They have enjoyed each other thus far. Leslie, the bride-to-be, is over excited shopping with her future mother-in-law. Faye Esther does make her feel like she belongs to the family already. She walks, talks, and laughs with Leslie. Gloriously, in Leslie's mind, Faye Esther's outing with her is a sign of welcoming her to the family. Leslie ponders in her heart; Faye Esther would be as proud of her if she treated her son as a king for the rest of his life.

Faye Esther purposed in her heart that day to help and to show Leslie how to conquer Pachouco's heart completely. However, the mother's intuition kept telling Faye Esther there was something in her future daughter's past that needed to become known before it was too late.

After the shopping spree madness cooled off, Leslie and Faye Esther's stomachs sang a hungry song. They decided to enter a nice restaurant. They chose a quiet place. They sat down, ordered their food, gave God thanks, and began to eat. Faye Esther expressing herself to the bride, said, "Leslie, I thank you for loving my son and being willing to marry him. Every time I see you, Leslie, you remind me so much of Minerva. You guys look identical. The only difference is she was a black girl with a fair complexion, and you, Leslie, are white."

Leslie interrupted to say Minerva's parents, Kirk, and Ema, say the same thing concerning her and me. “Both call me daughter.”

Faye Esther picked the conversation right back up. “Leslie, when Pachouco lost her in death, his former fiancée, I thought I was going to bury him also. Alternatively, if he lived, he would turn out to be a vegetable. Minerva meant the world to him.” "He worshipped the ground she walked on." “She loved him that excessively. He feels the same about you right now. Even after her death, unbelievably, she visited the family often. She is his guardian angel. Before he dated you, she came and gave him the okay. She told him not to let her mother Ema down because she loved him. Then, he agreed to meet you. Leslie, my son loves you with all his heart. He is crazy about you. Do you love him, Leslie? Woman to woman, please tell me the truth. I want you to be happy,

Leslie, but I am afraid. I do not know what I am fearful of, and I’m paranoid because of what happened on their prom night. He has spent so much money preparing for the wedding. Everything is paid for, and if you decided to marry him tomorrow, he would have no problem agreeing with you. He told me not too long ago you would be the last girl he would date from this country. In case the relationship between you and him ends, he will either remain celibate or marry an American girl from the south. Leslie, I come to you as a mother, as a friend, so you can consider me as your biological mother right now. Please, trust me for a minute; feel free to talk to me. I want to help you marry Pachouco. You did not love him in the beginning. Today, Leslie, you are in love. The wedding is close, and I do not perceive you two getting married. For some reason, I feel the wedding will be called off."

"I have invested too much time in this spoke Leslie, and I want Pachouco to be my beloved husband. I want to show him he is my king, my life, and that he is the best thing ever to come my way. Please, Mother Faye Esther, help me be the wife he dreams to have."

"Leslie, Pachouco loves you. You need to know one thing about my son; he also believes in honor before love. Daughter, you two still can repair and come clean with anything that can cause your marriage to cancel. Have a meeting and call it a cleanup day; just be honest with each other. For example, any hidden secrets that have the potential to create trouble before or after the wedding. I would advise you to disclose them to him. The son I took my time to raise will forgive you and still marry you. That may sound like a fairy tale that a politician would use to make one confess to a crime just to apprehend him.

No, my daughter, the purpose of my compromising is amazingly simple. I found out he loves you with true love. I recognize his incapability to sustain another life of deception. The same man is also capable of looking beyond your faults and will pardon you. However, the confession must be made before marriage in a voluntary fashion. If you have done anything worth discussing, please bring it to him before he finds out from another source. Daughter, you love him; he means more to you than everything. However, I do have a problem with you. I'm not too fond of the quarrels surrounding you and your brother Yvon. One day this may cost you a husband and Yvon a wife."

"Mother Faye Esther, I appreciate your advice to the highest. I am almost clean. I will be complete by the time I say I do. I have a habit I must break; Mother Faye Esther, you have no clue what I'm talking about but believe me, you helped me a lot today. Thank you for talking to me as a mother."

"I love you so much. It is time for us to go, my daughter. We will do this more often."

On their way home, Leslie glanced at her future mother-in-law and said: "Mother, do you know Pachouco, and I have never had sex in our lifetime? People these days would not accept that Pachouco and I are still virgins."

"Is your serious daughter? On this note, would you accept my apology?" Continued Faye Esther, "I thought you were already raping my son."

A laughing Leslie answers his mother, "Oh, you better bank on it; it is coming, mother."

“What is coming?” Asked Faye Esther.

Leslie, this time laughs herself crazy to respond to the question. She said to his mother, "The rape part is coming, oh yes; I will rape him the night of our honeymoon. Mother Faye Esther, you will not be anywhere close to coming to his rescue. After this white girl is finished with him, Lord have mercy."

Both laughed so hard until tears came out of their eyes. Faye Esther appeared to be in a state of shock.

Leslie perceived it. She asked her future mother-in-law, “Are you shocked at the fact, Pachouco and I are still virgins?”

“Yes, again, I apologize to you for thinking you were loosed, Leslie. I knew Pachouco was a virgin before meeting you because Ema's daughter was very conservative. After he came to know you, he became more mature. Leslie, you are more aggressive than Minerva was,” continued Faye Esther. “Did you get a chance to meet her, Leslie?”

“Yes, I did numerous times. I ascertain we are the same age. I used to see Minerva with her father when they came on vacation.”

“Leslie, I love you, but Minerva was my heart,” stated Faye Esther. “When she passed away, our lives remained void for a long time. Kirt and Ema, because you resemble Minerva a lot, they found relief when they saw you. We did have a meeting, and we advised Pachouco to go out on a date with you. I remembered that night when he got home, and he compared your personalities. Since then, I knew he would fall in love with you. According to his comparison, no hard feeling Leslie, he found you had all things every day, except a few things he found Minerva more honest and more trustworthy than you. However, you are more compassionate and outgoing than her. I imagine by now," mentioned Faye Esther, "And you make him forget all the similitude. He wanted my blessing to marry you. I told him, Leslie, you were a nice girl who might bring him happiness someday and one who has the semblance of a great wife. I told him again; the best is all I must wish him. Today, Leslie, my daughter, the same wish goes for you. If Pachouco, my son, brings you misery mentally, do not be any man's fool. Turn him over to God in prayer. God does not intend for anyone to be miserable mentally or physically in a relationship. There is happiness, understanding, compassion, freedom, liberty, and communication wherever love abides. Where there is love, there is love."

Those words were the last statements Faye Esther shared with her future daughter-in-law. Leslie thanked her for the golden words.

While Leslie was dropping Faye Esther off at her house, Pachouco was on the porch, saying, "You guys did not invite me." His mother pulled out one of the dresses she purchased. She told her son, “Next time, if you are willing to wear a dress, you will be the first person to receive the news when we girls are going out. So, you can be ready and on time. Besides, today was mother/daughter day out, not mother, daughter, and son."

He answered his mother, saying, "I love you, mother" she responded, “I love you too, Son.”

Leslie was ready to leave, but Faye Esther advised her to wait a minute and invited her to come into the house. Pachouco stood by the passenger side of the car, opened the door for his mother to get out; she did, and he shut the door and walked toward the house. Leslie, in the meantime, was getting out of the car to accompany them. Faye Esther commanded her to remain sitting in the car because Pachouco has a duty to perform.

What mother, he replied? With her arms folded together, Faye Esther was watching him with a mother-dissatisfied look. Then, he remembered to open the car door for Leslie and to escort her into the house. Faye Esther thanked him with an attitude, adding, “I thought I raised a gentleman Pachouco. Don't let that be the first and the last time you give Leslie this benefit for being the lady of your life. Leslie continued his mother, whenever you and Pachouco are going somewhere in a car, remain sitting or standing until he opens the door; this is one of the duties of a real man for a real woman.” Leslie left feeling special because he did let her in the car.

Pachouco thanked his mother for spending a day with Leslie. She replied, "You are welcome. She is a nice girl, but she can get better. I had to apologize to her twice today for prejudging her. I learned from her; she is a virgin."

"Mother, your conversation was deep, too deep for a man. Oh, no, son, it was nothing, but girls talk. Wow! Mother, you did apologize to her. Were your thoughts changed toward her for the best after hearing her confession?"

"Son, give ear to my words, these gray hairs on my headstand for life experiences. After hearing her confession, I respected it to the highest. The girl is under pressure, and she is not convinced she owns your heart. Do not get me wrong, she loves you. She is willing to try anything at any cost, bad or good. Just to have you on her wedding day by her side, to say I do. For some reason or another, she has trouble believing she has you in the palm of her hands. She does not intend to lose you because you're the first man or the first person she ever loved. Son, you're a good man; you are good enough to make the coldest person on earth fall in love with you. You are a dangerous man to any woman who never experienced love before. You are easygoing, and you are not very demanding. All you expect from someone is for them to be honest and trustworthy.
Pachouco, let us insinuate you have a beautiful wife, and you never had the opportunity to see her under pressure financially or with great want. You do not

know her regarding integrity, strong personality, and low self-esteem concerns. Attentively, Pachouco is listening to his mother lecturing to him. Pachouco, my son, let me show you a mystery; many people nowadays find themselves revising wedding vows. Some even have the audacity to fabricate their own. They cannot digest the traditional one, which excludes divorce entirely from a marriage. When worse comes Pachouco, instead of fighting together as the traditional vows recommend, they prefer to leave behind their flesh and blood. They call it quits. When poverty strikes Pachouco, some of them could exercise anything that is not healthy for their integrity or self-esteem, cheating, lying, and even selling their bodies. They refute the idea that together they are going to make it. Instead, they embrace the concept," "Money talks," "No money and no honey. Pachouco, when severe sickness reaches their doorsteps, if it carries a long-term package, they start to mistreat each other by ignoring the fact that God can heal. Instead of praying for healing, some of them wait for the sick one to die and collect life insurance."

"Pachouco, my son, the idea of freedom limits their patience as far as death is concerned. Then they hire fancy lawyers to undermine what God has ordained. The victims in these scenarios, Pachouco, are usually the children. The victors of these scenarios are usually the lawyers. The big-time losers, yes indeed, are the divorcees. Pachouco, on Valentine's Day, when you and Leslie tie the knot, observe the traditional vows. Meanwhile, examine her ways to see if they are in harmony with yours before you say, I do, then it's a done deal."

"Thank you, mother, for your words of wisdom. I'm so blessed to have you as a mother. You will make Leslie the most fabulous mother-in-law in the world."

"Have you applied for the marriage license yet?"

"No mother, not yet. All the excitement made us forget. You see why I love you, Mother; you keep me in check. Let me call Leslie to see if she has found her birth certificate yet."

"Son, promise me you will be strong no matter what happens in the next few days. I tell you regarding Leslie, and I do not see you two getting married. I do not know why. I love her, but I do not think she is the one for you. Not now, maybe ten years from now, she will be ready."

"I doubt it now seriously one more time, mother darling, injected Pachouco. You are usually right in your intuition. You have felt the same way on the day of graduation. You did mention something terrible was ready to happen. You did not see Minerva and me graduating together, but this time, my beautiful mother, "you will be as wrong as two left shoes."

"Time will tell, honey, and meanwhile, Pachouco, my son, promise me, whatever it is, whatever takes place, promise me again Pachouco, you will be strong. My future daughter is on a trip. I love that girl. She told me she planned to rape you if it is the last thing she does. She wants to be the one who steals your virginity and your heart."

"Right, answered Pachouco, I will take hers too."

"You children are crazy," said his mother. "Who is the maid of honor? You and Leslie keep on changing, on me."

"Carolle supposed to be," replied Pachouco. "Things changed though she will be on a business trip for the government. We decided to ask Michelle. Leslie is supposed to call to ask her if she can fill in for Carolle. If not, she will ask Meneika, Melissa, or Vanessa."

"The wedding is a few days away, and you guys need to get your act together. Thanks, Mother dear."

While departing in the presence of his mother, he made his own song from the top of his head. He started singing: It is so wonderful to be in love. Love has found me a second time. "Leslie, Leslie, Leslie, you are the woman of my dreams, my wife to be." "Flesh of my flesh, bone of my bone," "God has created you just for me, for me alone. Leslie, Leslie, Leslie, you will always be my soul mate. I will never hurt your tender feelings. In case I do by mistake, Leslie, please, please, my sweet cakes, take it for love. If you are upset with me, I promise to make the reconciliation worthwhile when I kiss your gentle lips. Honesty, integrity, and trustworthiness are what you stand for, and I will never stop "kissing the ground you walk on. I will wake you up with a kiss on your tender lips each morning. Leslie, Leslie, Leslie, if loving you is a crime, I am guilty as charged. Imagine with me the beautiful life we are going to have, Yvon, you, and I on an Island built on trust, integrity, and mutual respect. Oh Lord, it is so wonderful to be in love with the woman I love. Leslie, you are, yes, indeed my dream maker. Your lips taste like pure candy. The sweetness of your tender lips daily starts my day as an activation for my morning prayer, like an alarm clock to wake me up. Leslie, why are you so beautiful? In the morning, you are my sunrise sitting high in the middle of the ocean. In the evening, you are my sunset, making ready for a goodnight of making love."

He ended up the song not knowing his mother recorded every single word of the song. She became more afraid for her.

Soon after listening to the lyrics. The song he had sung a minute ago finally rang in Faye Esther's heart that her son was not only in love with Leslie, but he was also plain crazy about her.

A PRAYING WOMAN

He went to take his shower, and his mother entered his bedroom. She is a praying woman. She kneeled on the floor; her head bowed down on his pillow. Faye Esther recited a word of prayer: "My God, how great thou art," "I come before your presence humbly as a mother, as a steward over your son Pachouco. Lord is excited about Leslie, his wife-to-be, and his future brother-in-law Yvon. Lord, for some reason, you have not shown me a wedding. All you allow me to see is a forswearing of their vows, a disaster in the making. Lord, Leslie loves him more than she ever loved anyone else. Her past life had her bound until today. She acts like a slave planning an escape, which came to be unsuccessful. Oh Lord, deliver Leslie of whatever it is that could end the dream of marrying the man of her life, our son Pachouco. Their minds are made up, leaving no room for anyone to counsel them. Leslie stated the other day to me, Lord, she has a habit to break, an order to execute, and a promise to keep, then she will be clean. Whatever she meant, give her the ability to come clean with Pachouco before someone else will on her behalf without her consent. Lord, I need the assurance of certainty there will be a wedding between them. The only answer I received from the petition I addressed to you was negative. You told me that was in his best interest. Please, Lord, have mercy upon them. Do not allow either one of them to victimize beyond repair. Lord, I love you, and I thank you for the doing of your will, Amen." Up off her knees, she went into her room, closed her door, and meditated on the song he sang earlier.

Faye Esther waited after he left to talk to Yvon to consider being his best man. She called Leslie demanded she come over for a second. She had something she wanted her to hear. Leslie loved stuff like this. She enjoyed being in the presence of her future mother-in-law, so she agreed. One hour later, she was at the house with Faye Esther, listening to the song he made off the top of his head. Tears were rolling like a river from Leslie's eyes. She completely examined the words from the song. She realized how sweet again her husband be, was. In her presence or behind her back, he was the same lover boy that cared deeply and powerfully for her.

This type of love she has never experienced before. Imperatively she expressed herself; imperatively, she carried herself in the past. Her strong passion for Pachouco required her to be submissive toward him. She wanted to eat his heart out by converting him from "a sugar daddy" to a husband. There were other sides of Leslie, Pachouco never dreamed of, besides being beautiful, charming, and intelligent. Yvon could author a book on her. It would have been the best seller without a line dedicated to Pachouco. Yvon took his time to know her. Leslie enjoyed the song. His mother uttered; do you have any idea why I let you listen to the music?

Leslie stated to his mother that it was beautiful. "I have one problem with its mother; why does he want to include Yvon in everything we plan to do? Yvon is leaving my house sooner than Pachouco imagines. Oh well, this is another story, declared Leslie."

"Yvon is your baby brother. Pachouco love him as a son. I believe Yvon loves Pachouco as a father," declared Faye Esther.

"I understand he hates the fact that I'm marrying Pachouco. He feels I'm not good enough, and my self-esteem is too low for Pachouco. I made a deal with Yvon, which is one of my requests. After it is done and over with, I only want to see him occasionally. Otherwise, he will stay far away from our lives if need be. Then he will understand that I changed; I meant business. Sorry mother Faye Esther, I did not intend to bore you with my brother Yvon and my problems."

"Not at all, pronounced his mother. I told Pachouco, you and Yvon acted more like boyfriend and girlfriend, husband, and wife on the verge of breaking up."

"That was funny, repeated Leslie." "I let you listen to the song he composed for you because I want you to cherish it. If you feel like causing him grief one day, pay attention to these words and have mercy on him. Leslie, I might be on the verge of being paranoid. But I cannot shake the vise that you will hurt my son very badly a few days before the wedding officially occurs."

"Mother Faye Esther, do not worry about that for the time being, but on the night of our honeymoon, yes, take it from me, I'm going to put a hurting on him, mother. I waited too long for it, my goodness!"

"Shut your mouth girl, declared his mother with a happy laugh. On a serious note, do not move him too far away from here because I don't particularly appreciate flying or taking a long ride."

"What makes you say that Mother?"

"He was talking to me last night. He envisioned facing a great deception where he would be so confused and not know how to respond to it. Whatever it involved, you and him. I told him, Leslie, the wedding is approaching faster than you two realize. Cold feet can start to make his presence known in your lives. He went, sat at the table, and

drafted this poem. He instructed me in case you stopped by to let you read it. The poem dropped in his thinking is titled.
A New Life is born.

A NEW LIFE IS BORN Those days are gone.

A new life is born. The past is evil

The main event of the devil,

Let us turn everything into an ash

Then, all could be thrown in the trash.

So let us start our life anew

Making our dreams come true.

Let us get away from our people

Moreover, live our lives in the temple.

Where love will be a priority

Understanding without authority,

Our hearts are breaking

Let us take off on behalf of the King.

Lovely, we do know what we want

In addition, I swear that is all that counts.

Nobody can live our lives for us

If so, we would still be acting like a horse.

Let's again take off from the woods

Where we will meet either bad or good.

At least, both belong to us

A new life is reborn.

Leslie was always excited about Pachouco's poetry because it often re-assured

her of the grand amour, he possessed for her.

Leslie left Pachouco's house went straight to Kirt and Ema, who was well known for the tremendous marital lifestyle. They were high school sweethearts. Kirk was Ema's first boyfriend, and she was his first girlfriend. They claimed never to have an affair with each other. Kirt and Ema were well respected in the community because of this fact. For years, Kirt and Ema often hosted a workshop at the area's churches. Kirt was a great lecturer. He was a technician on how to remain faithful to your partner from the beginning to the end. Again, the way Kirk and Ema stood in their community as role models were superb.

The part of his presentation that impressed everybody was the story of how he met his wife when they were in the sixth grade. Kirk was often bragging about the fact that Ema was the first girl he ever kissed. She was also the first lady he made love with, he had been married for fifty-five years, and still, Ema was the only female he knew. Kirk always received a standing ovation for his faithfulness. He was Pachouco's role model. Pachouco desired to live a love life patterned after Kirk.

Leslie went in, and she asked Kirk to be Pachouco's best man at the wedding. They got overly excited over that. In the meantime, everybody she asked to fill in for Carolle turned her down. She seized the opportunity to tell Ema to be the maid of honor. The three of them started to dance, but it was not a custom for husband and wife to be best man and maid of integrity. Leslie charged them not to say anything to Pachouco. Leslie wanted the idea to be a surprise to her husband to be. Leslie knew Pachouco's desire for Yvon to be his best man would be rejected because Yvon had told her how he felt.

Sure enough, Pachouco had a talk with Yvon concerning his desire to have him as his best man. Without any shame or hesitation, negatively, Yvon answered, "I prefer again not to be near the church where the wedding ceremony will be performed. I still, believe Pachouco, and you don't have any business marrying Leslie."

Badly, Yvon hurt Pachouco's feelings; here is a young man he embraced as a son, he took safe care of Yvon and sent him to college. Now Yvon had the audacity to deny Pachouco his presence at the wedding.

Pachouco shared the news with Leslie about her brother's refusal to participate in the wedding. Surprisingly, she acted concerned about Yvon's behavior. She uttered to Pachouco, no problem. "Why not ask Kirt to be your best man, and I will ask my aunt, I mean Ema, to be my maid of honor."

He picked her up, turned her around, and said, "Honey, that was a superb idea. They will enjoy it, I remembered him campaigning for the best man's position a long time ago. When we first met, we were not even serious. Kirk mentioned to me that could he be the best man and his wife, the maid of honor at our wedding? I thought Leslie was kidding, I completely forgot. I cannot wait to run that by my mother. We know this is a done deal. We can rely on that. They will not turn us down, as Michelle and the others did. Wow, my love, you get me excited increasingly about marrying you, Leslie. I'm the first man on the Island who suffers from an addiction to marry a woman named Leslie."

Keep in mind Michelle was patiently waiting for Leslie to call her about being her maid of honor, and Leslie never did. Deceitfully, Leslie led Pachouco to believe Michelle had also turned her down.

"We do need to apply for the marriage license, if not, mother will be highly upset with both of us, Leslie."

"I'm glad you mentioned it, Pachouco. Please, help me look for my birth certificate."
Leslie stood on a chair pulled down a box from the top of her closet filled with papers. It was in here somewhere. Suddenly, the telephone rang. Leslie answered it from the kitchen. The caterer for the wedding reception was on the line. Leslie spoke to him longer than she expected. The first envelope he opened had plenty of check stubs from Kirk's firm. Fifteen hundred dollars ($1,500) on each stub set up as a monthly payment. She was off the phone came into the room where Pachouco was. He gave her the birth certificate and the envelope which contained the check stubs. He questioned Leslie concerning the payments. She replied "My mother left me 800 acres

of land. Kirk purchased them from me to build a new development on a thirty-year plan. He pays me a monthly mortgage. This conversation is confidential; I don't believe Ema had been informed of the deal.'

THE HEAT

The heat between Yvon and Leslie grew worse. Pachouco decided to talk with his future father-in-law, who lived almost four hours away. He was a great gospel preacher. The last time Pachouco visited him, he gave Pachouco an open invitation to stop by anytime. Pachouco debated seeing if it was best to go there that day or the following day. Anyone could tell from his breathing he sounded incredibly stressed. He prayed to God to help him in his decision-making process.

There was a strange thing that occurred. A man was by the side of the road begging. Pachouco gave him a couple of dollars. The beggar thanked Pachouco and recited, "Go pay the preacher a visit." Strangely, the beggar disappeared.

Pachouco, confused about the mystery at hand, through obedience headed to see Pastor Patrick. He arrived in no time, knocked on the door, and said, "The preacher's relationship with his children stink." Patrick opened the door and declared to Pachouco, "What wind blew you this way?" It must be a bad one. It is not often a city boy travels this far alone.

Pachouco, with a benign smile, replied in a joking manner to Pastor Patrick, "The wind that blew me to you is your children's behavior, they fight all the time."

“My children,” inserted Pastor Patrick. “God has been good to me, better than I ever deserve. He richly blessed me for some reason but never secured me with a child in my own. What children are you talking about, my son?”

Pachouco, in a state of shock, asked to the preacher, “You are not Leslie's and Yvon's father?”

“No, son, I'm not.” Leslie used to be a member of my church. “I counseled her mother many days before she went to glory. She was the only child her mother gave birth to. The other name you mentioned earlier might be a cousin. Let me borrow your ears for a few minutes, Pachouco. In my dream last night, I was charged to tell you the truth because you would not listen to anybody else. You hate gossip. Right now, Pachouco, your spirit is telling you to get up and go home. Young man, there is the door. Whenever the dumbfound angel, which is Satan himself, tells you to leave, do not forget Pachouco, the door is right behind you. In the meantime, let me educate you on facts. Leslie's father is Kirt.”

With that introduction, Pachouco wanted to go home. He was afraid he might hurt the preacher's feelings.

“Rev. Patrick repeated himself over; Kirk is indeed Leslie's father. Kirk and Leslie, both know it.”

The word liar was on the tip of Pachouco's tongue. The tasty desire to call Pastor Patrick a liar and leave was a fire burning his mouth. That dumdum spirit was working inside him big time.

"I know, declared Pastor Patrick, you have an ardent desire to call me a liar right at this minute. Anyway, the noble Kirt has been paying Leslie fifteen hundred dollars ($1,500)

monthly for her to hide her identity as his daughter. Otherwise, she would go public."

Patrick finally got Pachouco's attention when he brought up those payments because Pachouco recently found the stubs.

Pastor Patrick said to Pachouco, "Did you meet Kirk and Ema's only daughter together? That, that crazy woman killed."

"Unfortunately, yes, sir" entered Pachouco.

Patrick continued "She and Leslie, yes, could indeed pass for twins. This strong resemblance was not by accident, young man. Leslie's mother was a white woman. Her name was Emanuella. She was the half-sister of Ema. Can you digest the truth, my son? Asked Pastor Patrick."

Pachouco nodded his head to signal yes, but he refused to agree with him deep inside.

"Emanuella and Ema had the same mother but different fathers. Emanuella, Leslie's mother, used to stay with Kirk and Ema under the same roof. She became Kirk's lover and got pregnant with him while living with Ema. Kirk moved Emanuella to another town away from her until she died to keep Ema from knowing that risky business. In fact, the two sisters got pregnant around the same time. Their children were born two days apart. Ema, until today, does not know that girl Leslie is her niece and stepdaughter. Why are you crying, young man? I knew you were coming to see me. Last night, in a dream, I saw Ema's daughter. She died on her prom night. I always wondered about the boy that was with her that night. Did he ever recuperate in the hospital, or did he die there? As I said earlier, she came to visit me last night in my dream to warn me of your visitation today. She asked me to be honest with you concerning her sister Leslie and her parents. She added in the dream she is indeed your guardian angel."

A speechless Pachouco could not believe again what his ears had heard. He wiped the tears from his eyes stood up to head toward the door.

Pastor Patrick asked him, "If the wedding was still on?" Pachouco shook his head to mean, "I do not know, I do not know."

While shaking Rev. Patrick's hand as a good-bye gesture, he burst out in tears mingled with these words: "I was the one engaged to marry Kirk and Ema's daughter Minerva. She was killed in my hopeless arms. Now I wish I were dead along with her. She was the only honest girl I ever knew." He left thanking Rev. Patrick for his honesty.

Pachouco had too much truth in his hands and had no knowledge of how to handle it, how to dispense of it, nor to disclose it.

The biggest mistake one makes in love sometimes is to go after the truth. No question about that, but the fact also has excellent potential to make one suffer. What is the truth? When knowing it and unable to do anything about it, what sense does it make? When an honest person discovers the truth that was covered a long time and is afraid to say anything, the truth is still hidden, and the honest becomes dishonest. Do not go after the truth unless you are ready and willing to protect its freedom. It is incredible how one second can change a life for the best or worst. Here poor Pachouco was in trouble, and his mind had converted to a valley of confusion. On his way back, his sense of direction had betrayed him. He stopped at a crossroad and calculated which side to turn. The evening was far from being over. He desired it to get out of his sight as quickly as possible. The day was a revelation for him, but he despised it passionately. If he had suspected this unintentional discovery of the nagging truth, he would have stayed far away from Rev. Patrick.

Pachouco arrived home and declared he must tell someone else besides Yvon and Leslie, the guilty pair. It was challenging for him. The two people he would have trusted confided in, concerning this matter of importance, they were the matter themselves. Moreover, regarding Kirk and Ema, whom he trusted, one was the accomplice, and the other was the victim. Pachouco was not ready to involve his mother in such a messy situation, which might cost her some sleepless nights. The pains that he bore from the disturbing news required a remedy. Someone who cared enough to loan him their ears, willing to pay attention and advise him how to handle this sensitive nightmare. When he could not find anyone suitable to be his confidant, Pachouco drove to the cemetery where Minerva was buried. Love and sorrow met Pachouco there. He went to her tomb, bowed down with care. He prepared to spill his guts. He uttered these words "My love forever, my guardian angel, please prays to God on my behalf so that he can make all my troubles quickly end. Darling, what must I do after learning that Leslie is your sister? How can I face your father, my role model, my inspiration, after the way he treated your mother and her sister? How can I meet him when he knew Leslie was your sister and arranged for me to date her? I am in love with her, ready to marry her in a few days. Your father and mother are our best man and maid of honor. Tell me again, how can I face your mother when I know something she should have known a long time ago? Am I a part of this incredible betrayal? If I choose for my tongue to cleave to the roof of my mouth as a dumb man, never speaking on this matter anymore. Would I violate the code of ethics, to be honest, if I keep my silence? Speak to me, my guardian angel. How can I face the fact of being betrothed to Leslie, who is a liar, a false pretender, and a blackmailer? The vain thing that charmed me the most with her was that she reminded me and everybody else of you. She and I have been sharing all the good moments, but she failed to tell me the truth about her identity. Should I blame her and call off the wedding? Alternatively, should I look beyond her fault while knowing the real picture? I wish I were dead along with you. Why have you left me behind, Minerva? To suffer hypocrisy from Leslie, who is filled with deceit, yes, as your sister and first cousin Minerva, Leslie has the right to look like you. However, speaking of character, or personality Minerva my first love, your sister or your first cousin Leslie, is far from being "worthy of unbuckling or shining your shoes." Let me go, my forever love Minerva. I'm stressed out."

The day was over, and the night was drawing near. Pachouco stopped talking to the dead. He left the graveyard the same way he came, with many questions and no answers. He made it home. Leslie was at his house waiting on him. She was in his bedroom, sitting on a chair, crying. He realized she was not acting like herself, but he was too upset himself to question her regarding what the matter was. She called his name. She apologized for using his room as a place of retreating. She had been there nine hours straight. According to his mother, she did not eat or drink. Faye Esther was having trouble calming her down. She did not speak to Faye Esther in detail. She told her there was something she had been keeping secret all her life. However, Leslie had seen the need to share it with Pachouco before marrying him. She refused to tell it to his mother first.

The tears from Leslie's eyes symbolized the fear of cancellation of the wedding by Pachouco after revealing her secret to him. Pachouco might not be able to handle the tearful confession of Leslie. In addition, desperately, she was afraid of Faye Esther's reaction toward her, when, later, knowing Leslie's lifetime secret, which involved a family member. Faye Esther appreciated Leslie's desire to be truthful to the man she loved might cause him to get rid of her. He may treat Leslie as a soldier who violated the code of ethics and received a "dishonorable discharge." When he came in, his mother was taking her shower. She had had a long day with Leslie, who wrestled too hard to be consoled. Leslie's intention to change her lifestyle had just begun. In Leslie's situation, her future mother-in-law believed it was never too late to do the right thing. In Leslie's case especially, Faye Esther's belief had flipped. In other words, she felt it was a little too late for Leslie.

The period between Leslie's tearful confession and the wedding is a few days apart. She wished that Leslie had followed that advice earlier she had received from her. His mother was speculating. She did not have a clue what Leslie's secrecy was.

Leslie stood in front of Pachouco, called his name, and again apologized for being in his room. She saw a Pachouco she had never seen since they had known each other. Leslie quickly understood he was strongly angry with an unfamiliar rage. He demanded of her to get out of both his face and his home. Pachouco's reaction proved that there are two spirits in every man, a good and a bad. Whichever spirit he feeds the most is the one that controls him. Leslie started crying aloud, and she had never experienced anything of this magnitude from Pachouco. He steadily yelled at her to get out of his life. “You low down the traitor.” His mother getting out of the shower, frightened by the commotion, ran into his room naked. She told Leslie, do not go anywhere. She demanded of Pachouco to apologize to Leslie, and he did. Faye Esther reminded him, saying, “Never, you hear me, boy, never talk to her in this manner again in this house. As long your name is Pachouco, your father's name is Fernand Andre, and your mother's name is Faye Esther, you will not talk like that. Do you hear me, boy?”

“Yes, mother, I heard you. I apologize to you and Leslie.”

“Son, for future reference, Pachouco, Leslie has as much right in this house as you. As long she is your fiancé or your wife.

Leslie, in her catastrophic moment, was in a state of shock. It was the first time she had seen his mother upset. She was well acquainted with Faye Esther's sweetness and humility. Surprisingly to Leslie, his mother was on her side, the way she promised to be with fairness.

Pachouco's intention was not to see Leslie until a few days to give him time to study the matter. She was the last person he wanted to lay eyes on right now.

In love, a second is enough time to destroy any relationships that experience hardship in communication. Not too many things can function or get along well, where communication is lacking.

Faye Esther explained to her son that the girl had been here since he left this morning. All she did was cry because she had a burden desire to come clean with him in a particular issue of hers. “She pressed her way here to meet with you. She was already afraid of the outcome of the meeting. Look what kind of welcome she received from you.” She did not bite her tongue in expressing her concern about how he gave Leslie a bad deal. He had not told her the reason he flared up. His mother continued that Pachouco's behavior was an injustice toward Leslie. Anyway, what provoked this reaction? What had she done so badly to deny her an explanation? It would be a shame to dismiss her from his sight, over hearsay.

Leslie in his room listened to his mother lecture him on her behalf. Leslie was too jolted to stop crying. She shook like leaves on a tree, which was on the verge of being blown away by a stormy wind. She was unable to control herself. She uttered a roar, which reached his attention.

Pachouco apologized to his mother again with a benign smile that could mean that he had one of the most excellent mothers in the world. He went back to his room, where Leslie was. He kneeled at her feet and reassured her how sorry he was. Then he said, "however, Leslie, I have a motive behind my action that needs to be discussed soon." She waited this long to talk to him. Yes, she became more afraid than ever. She had no other choice but to play the card on the table. Whatever would happen would happen. Leslie had plenty of things she would like to reveal to him. Leslie preferred to disclose one situation at a time. How he handled the first secret would determine if he was competent enough to hear the next one and so forth. She was carefully doing her homework. Leslie could be a little too late. Pachouco focused on her, and he automatically discovered she had been lamenting for a few hours; her eyes swirled up, her makeup departed from her face, and she was unidentifiable. Pachouco's heartfelt love fit well with his compassion. He pulled out his handkerchief and attempted to dry her tears. Exhausted, yes, she was. Her appearance tormented him. He moved her head from the pillow and placed it gently on his chest. In a minute, he kissed her forehead at least ten times. He praised her for being the queen of his heart, the blood that ran in his veins. The woman that caused his heart to beat. He finally received a beautiful smile from Leslie, and she prompted him to query.

"What have I done to you to originate your conduct that surprisingly seized me earlier? I am in the state of being benighted, lingering for you to escort me to the marvelous light. Please, Pachouco, tell me, what have I done?"

"Please permit me to enunciate Pachouco, to listen to your voice since your mother notified me. You have an outstanding obligation to partake in secret with me. When you terminate, I will expose to you the reason for my previous posture toward you and your mother."

Leslie kneeled and demanded Pachouco to do the same. She embraced him tightly whispered a prayer. She petitioned the "Supreme Being" to equip her husband with a greater understanding. Understanding, he never had before to discern good judgment. Pachouco was exceedingly impressed by the manner she initiated the petition. On the other hand, he was filled with anxiety. Pachouco perceived nothing could be worse than what he apprehended already from Reverend Patrick.

Leslie started her plea by uttering, "Pachouco, if you wish to split with me subsequently when I finish, you are welcome to follow your heart. Do not ever forget that I love you regardless of the outcome of this painful confession."

Leslie was bluffing. She knew over her dead body; she would permit him to leave in peace.

"Pachouco, do you recollect, I apprised you that my father was a preacher, and I rode you up there to introduce you to him. I lied to you, honey. Pastor Patrick was my former Pastor. Kirk is my biological father, and Ema is my aunt and stepmother, but she has no clue. Kirk knew since day one I was his daughter.

Pachouco interrupted her to interrogate when was the last time you spoke with Pastor Patrick? Leslie, please be truthful?

She answered, "The day you and I visited him."

"Are you sure," added Pachouco?

"Yes, I have not been communicating with Pastor since. Therefore, the last time you blabbed to me Leslie about calling your father concerning Yvon's nasty behavior, you were fabricating that also."

"No" answered Leslie, and "I did talk to Kirk that night with her head down, crying and retorting."

Suddenly, he articulated, "Save by the bell."

Replied Leslie, "You are not interested in listening to my shameful story. I'm not even halfway through, and you offer me deaf ears already. That is not fair to me. Are you ready to walk away? Or to call it a quit? Involuntarily, I am forfeiting my right to address you. Please, Pachouco, grant me a second chance. We've invested too much in our alliance to bring it to an end. Right now, confidently, for the sake of love, Pachouco, do not lose interest in me. I promise never to lie to you anymore. You see Pachouco, I am doing my best to come clean with you. On my first try, you are not showing me any respect. You block me out. I am an imperfect being, and so are you, Pachouco. I was stationed here all day long, waiting patiently for your arrival. I earned the burning desire to discharge the remorse of my wrongdoing off my chest for the welfare of our relationship."

Pachouco pretended to sleep because Leslie did not allow him the opportunity to enter a statement. "He agreed to disagree." She pressured herself too hard. He hoped for a favorable chance to speak because he had full knowledge of the issue. Nevertheless, a non-stop talking Leslie limited his elaboration on the subject. Leslie had a nasty temper, the side Yvon her brother, often referred to. Pachouco was not acquainted with that temper of Leslie's. How wrong was Pachouco to think she was only a lover and not a fighter?

During Leslie's observation, she miss-read him, madness entered her heart, and she grabbed him by his collar tried to strangle him for failing to heed her. Pachouco, in all his effort, was unable to remove Leslie's hands from around his neck. She told him how much she loved him while choking him. Pachouco did something that he had sworn not to do. He did not have a choice; he slapped her to bring her back to her senses so he could breathe. Leslie held her face and told him she was sorry.

She was used to the abusive lifestyle, but Pachouco was not. He kneeled at Leslie's feet begged her pardon. Pachouco felt that he was less than a man to slap a woman. He cried and cried again as she pulled him over gently to her. She said, "Why are you crying, Pachouco?" He answered, “I did not mean to slap you, but I could not breathe. You were choking me.”

Leslie gazed at him; “You must have had a bad dream Pachouco, my love. You did not hit me. Besides, you are not that type of a man to slap a woman. Your imagination is running wild.”

Pachouco said, "Are you serious? Are you fooling me, Leslie?"

She replied, “You know I'm crazy about you, right. I will do anything for you, but if you ever let the devil fool you to slap me, Pachouco, when Faye Esther counts her sons, she would be one short because you will be six feet under.”

Be-puzzled was the innermost part of Pachouco's body experience. Confusingly, he became incompetent to tell the difference between dream and reality. Leslie did an excellent job playing with his intelligence. She stared at him for a moment and feared the fall back on her.

Leslie implied, “let me pick up the story, where you made me lose my train of thought. Ema is my aunt, and you may marvel how that could be. Oh, my goodness, Pachouco, it is a shameful story.”

“Why don't you quit, for the time being,” stated Pachouco? “Breathing heavily, she exclaimed, oh no, I must fulfill this today! I need to be honest. Honesty is a virtue, and the wife of my cupcake Pachouco must be a "virtuous woman."

Pachouco pronounced, “Can I finish the story for you?”

“Are you kidding me,” uttered Leslie? “You could not distinguish where to begin.”

“Well, pay your undivided attention to me for a minute, entered Pachouco, your mother was white, her name was Emanuella. She was the sister of Ema. Your mother experienced some hardship and was forced to move in with Kirk and Ema. Your mother Emanuella and Kirt were having an affair. Both Ema and your mother got pregnant by Kirk. To avoid a family scandal, he moved your mother to another State. Until this day, Ema does not have any idea why the sister she loved disappeared from her house without a trace, without a goodbye. Ema had your sister Minerva on a Tuesday, June 7, and Leslie, you were born on Thursday, June 9, two days later.”

Pachouco bowed his head down, and tears traveled from his eyes.

Leslie benumbed at this hour, stared at him as she was in severe pain.

He continued the story, “Your mother after being sick a while passed away, you planned to go public with your identity after reaching a reasonable age. Kirk knew that you could destroy his marriage, their fame as the most faithful couple on the Island.

You and he understood the seriousness of the issue, and you two entered a private and shameful contract, where he paid you $1,500 monthly for his wife's lifetime. Meanwhile, Ema was still praying to see her sister one day on the Island. She heard she had a niece somewhere, and she would give anything to see her, anything to obtain a report of the sister she loved. You bring joy into her heart whenever she sees you. Leslie, because you and Minerva were identically favored. Is that sad? Leslie, Ema is with her niece every day and is unaware of such a fact. Through Ema's benefactor spirit, she considers you a daughter; therefore, she played the role of a matchmaker, so you and I could be together. Involuntary, I found myself proposing to two sisters."

Pachouco lifted his head and said, "Where would we go from here, Leslie?"

"I have no clue," responded Leslie, "But how long have you known this Pachouco?"

"I learned about it this evening, and I was agitated at you for lying to me, Leslie. We could have gone our separate ways, but you were about to disclose it anyway."

She injected, "What must I do now, Pachouco?" He answered her, "Within two weeks, we will get married. You have a week to study the situation and to arrive at a solution that would be best for everyone, especially us. All I know is you must come clean with your Aunt Ema before we go through with the wedding."

Surprisingly, Pachouco, in solving their problems, had left a big "stone unturned." He fails to question Yvon's kinship to Leslie. Anyway, Leslie was shocked by the manner Pachouco answered her. She did not expect an injunction that was based on the wedding. Worried she became because she did not know how to break the news to her aunt. Pachouco looked at the clock, and he advised Leslie to go home. It was getting extremely late. Leslie went home, got in her bed, and closed her eyes to fall asleep. Her sleep was on strike against her eyes, and she was wide-awake. She paced the floor all night long, imagining the mess she had created, resulting from her loving money too much. She blackmailed her father, cognized with greed, sold her identity and roots for a lousy fifteen hundred dollars a month. Leslie failed to comprehend her aunt, who showed her more love than money could ever buy and complied with her father's doggish spirit.

Leslie learned in a hurry, to transform from a crook to an honest person came with a price. Especially if those hurt and framed by the thief were still around. It's even more challenging when family members are victimized as prey in the fraud.

TEMPER

Was it a possibility for an individual like Leslie to change overnight? Her brother Yvon would answer no way to the question.

Last night, she took her time to make a fool out of Pachouco. He was not dreaming. She was choking him for real. She would have choked him to death if he did not defend himself.

Pachouco's biggest mistake was ignoring Yvon, who was trying to school Pachouco on Leslie's lifestyle and bad temper. Many nights, Yvon had to sleep with one eye opened, the other one closed, keeping a watch on his sister. Yvon could have had her prosecuted for man abuse. However, to avoid the upbringing shame on his manhood, he kept his mouth shut; in the meantime, she steadily whipped him. Since Pachouco joined the picture and was befittingly in love with him, she was forced to walk on a thin line.

Nevertheless, she had not been too confident of her mood swings behavior, which might cost her a good man. Pachouco, deep in his heart, thought he had been blessed with an angel. Last night he realized not. The tide of her furious temper would have almost carried him out of this world. When Leslie cannot have her way, instantly, tears would start dropping from her eyes, her hands gear up in choking or slapping whomever, her feet are ready to kick, jump, and her teeth prepare to bite somebody. According to Yvon, if Pachouco married Leslie, he would suffer many days and nights unless she changed. Otherwise, Pachouco has some whippings in store for him. Yvon was not talking about Leslie's uncontrollable temper, he knew it. He made up his mind to protect Pachouco regardless of the cost.

Yvon himself was heartless until he met Pachouco. He taught Yvon there was a better way besides using others for his gain. Yvon planned to move away from home at Leslie's request, based on Pachouco and her need to be alone. Yvon and Leslie decided to enter a plea bargain to make that register. After executing the order, he will move across town and not visit unless she sends for him.

Yvon shared his moving plan with Michelle. She advised him to call a friend of hers who had some vacant apartments for rent, approximately four blocks from where Michelle lived. The apartment complex belongs to Michelle, but she did not disclose it. A week later, he called concerning the apartment and spoke to Michelle. She gave him an appointment to view the home, and he said to himself that sweet voice sounded familiar.

He asked Michelle for her phone number at the lake, and she denied his request. She gave him the phone number to call the property manager, and that was her real telephone number. He wrote the number down. He understood nothing. Surprisingly to him, when he arrived at the place, Michelle was the host. She showed him a couple of apartments, told him what was, and he loved them. In his visitation, he flipped the conversation twice to him and her. Twice she reminded him she never mixed pleasure with business. She bid him farewell and told him she would see him in a few days at the wedding.

"I don't think so. Can I call you instead," uttered Yvon?

She replied, "No, that is not healthy for your living condition."

Yvon and Leslie were conversing that night. Michelle's name came up. Leslie was questioning him again about her. He said to Leslie, "Michelle was the girl I used to date when I was thirteen. She used to live across the street from us. She was the little girl that came to visit us and saw you and I in . . . ."

Leslie did not give Yvon a chance to complete his sentence. She took the conversation over, whooping, Michelle was that little heifer. "Did she have a recollection of me?" Spontaneously, Leslie was ready to fight him.

Yvon responded, "Calmed down Leslie that girl . . ."

"That girl what?" said Leslie in an uncivilized manner. She ran with the conversation. "As long you and her keep your mouths shut. You people do not carry any garbage to Pachouco's ears, so, I have no problem. However, I tell you what, Mr. Yvon, I swear on my mother's grave, if you two team up against me, I will make your lives a living hell until the devil himself has compassion on your two's soul. I will have no mercy on you people. Pay attention Yvon, I will turn your two into the worse enemies of Pachouco. Your biggest problem, Yvon is, you keep on confusing a threat with a promise, no Yvon dear. What I'm telling you here. I'm sorry if you take it as a threat, no honey, I repeat, it is a promise. You see, I tested Pachouco many times. My conclusion is his love for me is blind. I am going to marry him. I will move him to the middle of nowhere. I will keep his mother, Faye Esther, and the rest of the gang, including you, Yvon, away from my house and our lives. I am going to spend all his money by myself. I will stop him from keeping in touch with his mother, period." Leslie laughed and entered, "I fooled you, Yvon, and I will never do that. I'm in love with Pachouco, yes, I'm."

Yvon believed every single word proceeded out her mouth earlier. From experience, he knew that Leslie never spoke to hear herself talking. He glanced at her a couple of times; she appeared strange to him. He ran toward her and asked, "Are you okay, Leslie?"

"No, Yvon, I'm not. Tomorrow night is supposed to be when we separate for good after eleven years if I am not mistaken. I wonder what you think of me. If you had another place to go for the past five years, Yvon, you would have gone. It never occurred to me that I was maltreating you until a few days ago. I went out with Pachouco's mother. She reached deep inside me and pulled out the better person living inside me. I abused you so much, I saw you as a toy. I deprived you of having friends. I ran Michelle off because you were my baby, my sex supplier, and my pleasure. I stole you from your mother. She trusted you with me. She asked me for a favor to watch you overnight. You woke up in the middle of the night, asking me to take you to the bathroom. You had to pi. I was a grown woman; however, I was amazed at how big your penis was for your age. I put you in the bed with me. I showed you how to use it. I made love to you all night long. I promised to kill you and your mother if you told anyone. You happened to satisfy me that night. We found ourselves in bed every time you spent the night at my house. We both loved it. Then, I started to raise you for your mother; she could not afford to take care of you anymore. She went to the courthouse signed you over to me as your legal guardian. Then, she passed away. I lied to Pachouco about everything concerning you. Yvon, you and I had sex every day until now. When I was seventeen, Yvon, I was diagnosed as a nymphomaniac. I slept with every one of the boys in my class, the cute ones. After graduation from college, I met you. When you turned fourteen, you made me hire you for sex, no more free toy. The night Michelle came over, she saw us naked having sex; I set her up. I was the one who invited her over so she could see it for herself. I knew she was moving the next day. I gave her something to remember for the rest of her life, for calling me a penny and a nickel whore. She got mad because I ran her home for you to do your homework for school. On her way home, she turned around and said that I was the cheapest whore on the Island. She is blessed because I almost slapped the word out of her mouth. Later, that night, she did so apologize to me. It was too late then; my mind was already made up to teach her a lesson. After all these years, Michelle is back home, and I am ready to marry her uncle. She could say anything; Pachouco would not allow her to. Pachouco, deep down in his heart, thinks I am a virgin. Tomorrow, you and I will call it quits, and this will be our last time making love. I will let you choose the position you requested in the plea bargain. I will execute the orders. You asked me to be your whore and your private dancer for the last time. You got it. Yvon, Pachouco is my passport to gain my dignity back. I love him with all my heart. Yvon, forgive me, and thank you for listening to me."

Yvon answered Leslie; "We cannot change the past. However, we can be sure the mistake we made in the past will not repeat themselves in the future. I do not think you are ready to marry Pachouco. I know you love him, but I am sure you will break his heart if you marry him now. Any man would prefer his heart to be violated by a girlfriend instead of a wife. Leslie, Pachouco has been so good to me. He may disagree; as you know, he is the only male figure I ever had in my life. I do consider him as a father. In the beginning, you and I were taking our moments to use him. Somewhere, somehow, his love grew in us with solid roots. When he came to see you, he always brought us something. Whenever he was leaving the house each night, he kissed you goodnight, and he usually knocked on my bedroom door to say, goodnight son. I never expressed how good he made me feel. Right after he entered goodbye, often we did not give him a chance to start his car. We were already in bed having making love. Of course, having intercourse is an addiction to you and a habit to me. You need to explain to him the nature of your sickness, being a nymphomaniac. He might not be able to deal with the fact you must have sex every day. He sent me to college, and he found me a job.

Tomorrow, my contract with you will reach its expiration date. I invested and wasted my entire youth on you. The only remorse I have, right at this minute, is Pachouco. I asked myself on many occasions, what can I render to him for all his goodness toward me?"

Leslie answered, "well, honor the wedding with your presence that will brighten his day. Yvon, you hurt him when you turned down the invitation to be his best man.

Yvon picked up the conversation again, "You are perfectly right, Leslie, but there is a problem, I do not visualize a wedding between you two."

"The devil is a liar," Leslie fired back; "I am sick of Faye Esther, his sisters Barbara Ann, Rosa, and you, commenting it will not be a marriage ceremony. I assume you and his mother have been talking behind our backs. I got news for you four jealous hearts. If I must be the preacher and the wedding participants, Pachouco and I will tie the knot. It seems to me; I'm obligated to accomplish this task with or without you guys. Run and tell that to Mother Faye Esther, Barbara, Rose, or Rosa, whatever her name is."

"Tell me this much, Leslie. How do you plan to fool Pachouco with that virginity mess?"

"Easy," answered Leslie, "All I need is some fake blood. His experience in love affairs is so poor, yes, he will be fooled.

"Leslie, you're something else," injected Yvon.

"You got that right little brother, but if he has any suspicion that you and I have been lovers since you were a child, I would be a dead woman. Wow! I have to get rid of Michelle; otherwise, she will cause trouble for me with Pachouco."

"Leslie, don't you go there with that girl," cried Yvon. "Is your frame of mind off track? The truth will reveal itself in due season."

Truth, not before I marry Pachouco, mentioned Leslie.

Yvon curiously demanded of her, what difference does it make?

Leslie smiled and elaborated, Pachouco hates divorce. "It does not matter what he learned concerning me after the wedding, bad or good, he will not get a divorce; either way, he will stand by my side, he is old fashion. Thus far, I have everything under control."

"So, you think, we'll see," expressed Yvon, under his breath.

That night, it was a miracle; Yvon and Leslie conversed that long without a physical fight. He was expecting to hit the bed. It had been a long day. Oh no, said Leslie, "You did not fulfill your sexual duties for the night." He went and did whatever he had to perform.

Yvon despised Leslie more and more. When he heard how she set Michelle up for the first time to watch him sleeping with her, he hated her even more for the tricky, nasty plan for Pachouco's life. The contempt of her behavior toward her father was disgraceful enough to open the gate of hell, which is where Leslie deserved to be abiding thereof perpetually. She knew Kirk was her father from day one. She extorted him with a monthly ransom. As a token of the extortion, Leslie required her father to make passionate love to her. When he refused, she threatened him to go public with her identity, including a false charge of rape. To protect his marriage, name, and reputation, he did it. "How sick can Leslie be?"

SAFE KEEPING

Yvon and Michelle had a burning desire to protect Pachouco's goodness.

Yvon taped the conversation he had with Leslie earlier. Yvon woke up happier than ever since deliverance was on the way. He moved over half of his belonging transferred them to his new apartment. Then, he called Pachouco on the phone rehearsing.

"Guess what, man, can you stop by the house tonight at 10:00 pm for a surprise pre-wedding gift for Leslie. No matter what, do not ring the doorbell because the door will be already unlocked. Walk straight to her bedroom and look on the wall, then I will open the champagne. One more thing, Pachouco, there will be a bag at the entrance door, do not open it. Put it in your car, unseal it when you arrive at home, and you will understand how much I love you as a father figure."

Pachouco happily answers, "That sounds like a winner, and I will see you at 10:00 tonight. Have a good day, son."

"Good day Pachouco," replied Yvon.

Later, that night, naively, Pachouco did as Yvon instructed him. However, Pachouco heard music playing, the music he had never heard play in this house before. He proceeded toward the bedroom, and a bright light was on. What did he see? Leslie and Yvon, both naked, were having sex. Pachouco desponded. His knees got so weak. Instantly, he became as feeble as an older man and fell on the floor. He was in a state of shock. A tremulous spirit trespassed his being, and with quivering lips, he entered, "You invited me here, Yvon, just to see this?"

Leslie furiously and madly said, "Oh, you set me up, Yvon?"

"Yes, I did. Was it not the same thing you did to Michelle? You made me have sex with you invited her to the house so she could catch us in bed. It was the same thing you did to Kirk by blackmailing him. You knew he was your father; you forced him to sleep with you, and he did against his will. When I was eleven years old, she started to sleep with me, Pachouco. Pachouco, she is a nymphomaniac. She must have sex almost every day.

Pachouco, you are a good man. I consider you as my dad. I met with you twice to tell you what was going on, and you shut me up. I love you too much to let her trick you into marrying her Pachouco. I wanted you to see for yourself who Leslie really is. She has a bad temper. She beats on me all the time."

Leslie punched Yvon in his mouth to shut him up. She kneeled before Pachouco and declared, "Please, give me a second chance. You see, when I first met you, Pachouco, I was on a mission to show you good moments. I was getting paid to go out with you because I look like my sister Minerva. My job was to stop you from living in the past because she was dead. I was there for the money, and I got beat up in my own game. I fell deeply in love with you. My dear, give me a second chance to redeem myself to show you how much I care. Pachouco, when I first met you, I was lost, I did not know who I was, but you did help me find my identity. Please tell me you forgive me, and you still love me."

Pachouco, with an anguished heart, opened his tearful eyes, looked at her, and added: "Leslie, inside of me right now, there is a war going on between hating and loving you. However, my love for you is too strong to hate you but too weak to forgive you at this point. Leslie, why are you so deceitful, so devilish, and so lecherous?"

Leslie was still nude. Pachouco gained enough strength to look at the floor. He picked her to dress up off the floor; with a sense of humor, he said, "I examined the dress; there was no blood from the virgin. How can this be Leslie? Leslie, you petitioned the wrong person for a second chance; God is the only person dealing with this type of provisional care. Yes, he is indeed a God of a second chance but not me. You are heartless; here's your dress. Cover your naked body. You've defiled it long enough."

Pachouco asked Yvon, "Do you have any money in your pocket?"

With bleeding lips, Yvon answered: “I have a nickel.”

Pachouco recommended that he gives it to Leslie.

Yvon handed the nickel to her. Pachouco nodded his head to tell her to take it, and she did.

Leslie asked Pachouco what she was going to do with this nickel.

He answered her; it’s yours to keep. Yvon paid you for the sex.

“Now, Leslie, you beat the record of being the cheapest whore in the world. To conclude this mockery, Pachouco added, go back to bed, Leslie, and finish what you have started. Leslie, our engagement is over, the marriage is off.”

“Don’t tell me, you’ve called off the wedding Pachouco. Please, I’m begging you, give me a second chance.”

Pachouco responded in this manner, “Gomer, sorry I mean Leslie, I love to read the story of Hosea in the Bible. He was a good man. As for me, I’m too far away from being a Hosea. He was the only man who would have purchased you back. See you around, “Gomer the harlot.”

Yvon forgot the condition of his mouth and laughed at the statement made by Pachouco. Here comes the Leslie that Pachouco never met before. The other day, he glanced at her now that he had met the real deal. She pulled out a nine-millimeter handgun, telling both not to move. Pachouco intended to call her bluff. Yvon begged Pachouco to do whatever she said. Otherwise, she was going to smoke him. She was seriously yelling at Yvon and Pachouco. She was totally a different person. Pachouco tried to take a step, and she added, I swear one more step, just like I mentioned before, your mother Faye Esther will soon be minus a son.

Yvon said to Pachouco, take it easy again; she was serious. "Hearkened to my voice Pachouco, you never came close to this woman right here, but I have numerous times pleaded Yvon, if we are not careful, she will kill both of us and think nothing of it."

She apologized repeatedly. Pachouco demanded the gun. She replied, "If I give it to you, will you still marry me?"

Pachouco, with his strong conviction, still let her understand she blew it a few minutes ago. She asked Pachouco to take off his clothes, he did. She pushed him on the bed. Leslie gave Yvon a set of handcuffs. He handcuffed Pachouco on the bedpost. She tied Yvon on a chair in the kitchen area. She inserted a lemon inside his mouth tied it down. However, she had a silencer on the gun, and Pachouco heard a tiny noise of a gunshot. Automatically, he did what he should have done since the beginning, calling on the name of his God. Pachouco, nude on the bed, lay on his back. He had a great concern for Yvon's safety which activated his curiosity. He interrogated

Leslie, "I heard you fire a gunshot. You did not hurt that boy, did you?"

"He's used to it, answered Leslie. Be a good boy Pachouco. I will be right back. Do not try anything funny nor participate in a mutiny. Remember, Pachouco, swimming in your own blood could be messy. It will only take me a minute to be ready. She kissed him."

He lay down, wondering what she was up to. He began to sing in his heart the wishing songs: "I wished I had paid attention to Yvon. I wished I had listened to Michelle and Myrla Niecy. I expected I had endorsed my mother's advice. If I were opening my heart to receive factual knowledge from them about Leslie, my heart, my soul, and my body would not be in this mess."

Suddenly, Pachouco heard music playing, and the sound was coming closer and closer. The voice of Leslie echoed all over the house everyone; please stand to receive the bride. She played the song "Here comes the bride; she is going after her man."
Pachouco, amazingly, surprisingly was in a dumfound stage. He saw the beautiful Leslie on a white wedding dress trimmed in black. She was so beautiful in her outward appearance but nasty and dirty on the inside. She was appearing as an angel seemly perfect. However, wisdom proved differently to him. "Beyond the mask of seeming perfect was a fallen angel." The crazy Leslie, before she went back in the other room to get her dress, removed

Pachouco's engagement ring from his finger. He questioned that move, and she answered, be patient. "You will see." Leslie was about to perform the marriage ceremony herself. "She told him to repeat after me: I take these beautiful Leslie, from this day forward to be my wedded wife, and death is the only thing that can ever separate us."

Pachouco refused to say her vows, and Leslie was angrier now than before. She told him, "Either you say it or on the count of five, I'll kill you." Leslie started to count, and Yvon tried to tell Pachouco to repeat the vows, but he could not talk. Pachouco finally said it, and Leslie uttered the same vows to him. She helped him place her ring on her finger and forced him to say, with this ring, I marry you in the name of God." She had done the same with his ring, and she said joyfully, "Now we are spouses. Kiss me, Pachouco."

Pachouco said, "Leslie, you are a sick woman. You need help. Do you hear me? You need help?"

"Yes, honey, I do reply to Leslie; I am going to get some right now."

She raped Pachouco six times that night. Pachouco could not escape from this terror. If he were "The legendary Hercules," he would have the ability to break those handcuffs from his hands and the chains off his feet. Leslie subdued him and enjoyed herself.

Leslie made a believer out of Pachouco and his mother, Faye Esther. Under any circumstances, they should never accuse her of not keeping her pledge of raping Pachouco. Whatever she did to him, she had previously given him the scoop; it would take place one way or another.

Pachouco, who did not believe in premarital sex, cried bitterly during it. He felt worse than a woman did. His religious beliefs were sabotaged, his right had been violated, and his virginity had been stolen forever. Where would Pachouco go from here in case she released him? Would he go to the competent authority turn her in? If the second question was Pachouco's choice, would he go down in record as the first grown man ever to be the victim of a rape? It could be the first case that would bring laughter to the face of the most cynical judge in the world.

Yvon and Pachouco, if they escaped from this ordeal as men, would need to approach what to do next with care because the pride of their maturity was at stake. Just the image of the headline of a newspaper article on their story alone could force one to laugh in a scornful manner.

Pachouco asked Leslie to turn them loose.

"Sure," replied Leslie, "Will you prosecute me for what I did to you? I do not worry about Yvon, and he will never report me to the police. Anyway, after I let Yvon loose, he will unlock you okay. I want you to watch me kill myself, and I also want you to do the eulogy."

Pachouco, all nervous, tried to reason with Leslie saying, "I promise that I will not go to the law. You can count on me. Do not hurt yourself over foolishness. You have too much to offer, Leslie. Yvon and I understand what caused you to behave this way. However, you do need professional counseling, both secular and biblical. I'm willing to pay for both treatments."

"Man," tenderly uttered Leslie, "You're trying to fool me, the minute I let you go, you will forget me. I am a disappointment to Yvon and you. If you really meant what you said earlier, kiss me passionately as a token before your God, you will not have me put in jail."

She moved her mouth closer; he initiated the kiss, and as a result, she raped him one more time. Angrily, Pachouco begged Leslie to kill him and be through with it instead of humiliating him like this.

"Pull the trigger," said Pachouco. "My misery will be over after I die. What have we done to you which require you to use such methods of inflicting pain on us? Why are you so torturous to Yvon and me?"

Leslie rejoined the conversation; "Pachouco, if you want me to pull the trigger, that can be arranged. I have nothing left to lose, but I love you too much to kill you. One has to die between the three of us; relax, Pachouco, it will be me. You will have the opportunity to be the eyewitness to the death of two sisters. One died in your arms, and the other will die on top of you."

"Please, Leslie, don't you do that to me? Physically mentally, I am too weak to bear another tragedy. I am begging you, Leslie. If you need to destroy somebody tonight, let me be the victim, so you and Yvon can live."

"Would you still marry me, Pachouco? Without you, I have no reason to live. You are the first man I've ever loved. Do not let the gun in my hand entice you to lie to me. Honesty Pachouco was what you preached to me daily, and I failed to let the sermon take roots in my heart so I could be a "doer of the word." Integrity Pachouco was the daily prayer you taught me, but I failed to memorize it and use it in my daily walk. Trustworthy was the living word you gave me to survive in this life, but I ignored its content by choosing the negative side of the word. I do not blame you, Pachouco, for considering me as a low-class harlot. Inside of me, there is a much better person living. Please, Pachouco, I am thirsty for the truth. Just consider for a minute the way I treated my aunt, my father, even Yvon, and you; Pachouco agreed with me. I deserve to die. I messed up with you people, and I messed up with God. When I die Pachouco, I am not sure where I will spend eternity. Pachouco, my love, my soul is too good to go to hell, not good enough to make it in heaven. Am I beyond receiving forgiveness from God, Pachouco? Being a nymphomaniac Pachouco is a serious sickness. My body craves sex twenty-four hours a day. Be honest with me. Do you love me no more? Is it truly over between us?"

"Leslie, listen to me, baby. You know where we stand right now. I do love you, Leslie, more than you could ever imagine. Leslie, do you think love has something to do with what is going on between us right now? Look how long you've had me bound. Is it what you call tough love? "Bound or free," I'm still in love with you, but this time it's agape love, the love required by God for every man to owe to another. Sincerely, God expects all men to pay this debt. Leslie, time is still on our side. Untie Yvon and me, and we will be sure you obtain the proper treatment."

"Do you want me to be your wife, Pachouco? Honesty from you means a lot to me. Even if the word honesty slapped me on my face, I would not know what hit me. I am a dishonest woman filled with deceit. I was worst before I met you, but you retrained my thoughts. You introduced me to a new lifestyle. Please, look beyond my faults and reassure me of the solidarity of our future."

As honest as he could be with a tearful confession, He says, Leslie: IT'S OVER BETWEEN US Tonight is our last night. If you had seen the light, it would be our first one, too bad, I had to run.

You did understand what was killing me.

I never had an affair; I was faithful and fair.

Gambled our future to run an adventure, never was your intention to pay the sanction.

You are the one I trusted when I had a choice.

Even though you stood by, I have to say goodbye. Cheat, you already cheated, needless to kiss my feet. Let me go, I am not pissed; just add me to your list.

A terrified Leslie carefully paid attention to the words of the poem that Pachouco recited from the top of his head.

When Pachouco left his house, he promised his mother that he would be right back. He told her he was going over to Yvon and Leslie's house for a wedding surprise. Faye Esther happened to wake up exceedingly early that morning. She realized the cover from Pachouco's bed still stayed the same way since last night. She automatically perceived something was wrong with Pachouco. First, his mother knew he would have called to inform her of the delay. In other words, what took him long to come home? Second, she knew he would not defile his fiancée's house by abiding there all night long. She knew her son that well. She called Leslie earlier when the trouble had just begun. She did not answer the phone. His mother called again; Leslie completely ignored the phone.

Who can beat a mother intuition? Now Faye Esther was convinced something was wrong. Pachouco, on the other hand, advised Leslie to ring his mother back before she involved the police. Leslie agreed to do it under one condition; Pachouco must talk very nicely to his mother. Tell her they are playing cards. Otherwise, she is going to blow her head off. She called his mother back and said, “Are you looking for your baby? You know Mother Faye Esther; he’d better be here with me if he is not at your house. We are playing card.”

“Is that nice, Leslie? Who is winning,” asked Faye Esther?

“I am! Mother, I beat Pachouco all night long.”

“May I speak to him for a minute?”

“Yes, Mother, you may.”

Pachouco picked up the phone began to apologize: “Mother, I’m sorry for not informing you I will be home late.

“Where is Yvon, Mother asked?”

“He is in the other room,” answered Pachouco.

“Tell Yvon, I would like to speak to him now.”

“Yvon, Yvon yelled Leslie, Mother Faye Esther wants to speak to you. Tell Mother Faye Esther, Yvon is sleeping.”

Pachouco delivered the message, and she hung up the phone.

Again, who can beat a mother's intuition, especially when she knows her child? Faye Esther smelled trouble. She chatted with Ema concerning the situation. Both Ema and Faye Esther were aware something was not right. They concluded that Pachouco would have never pulled something, such as spending the night at Leslie's house. The absence of a phone call to his mother raised a "Red flag." Ema decided to ride over there.

Remember, when Yvon invited Pachouco over, he left the door open for Pachouco. When Pachouco went in to avoid making noise, he did not close the door behind him. Leslie herself thought the door was locked. Leslie entered the room where Yvon was, adding "I've come to tell you goodbye. I will see you on the other side. I do not want anyone to cry at my funeral. My great desire and last request are for Pachouco to offer the eulogy. My heart's desire is for you to marry Michelle. She is a wonderful girl. Michelle will make you a good wife, of that, I am convinced."

Bitterly crying, Yvon could not respond because his mouth was still tied up. Pachouco heard the conversation; he did not know what to say to change her mind. He called Leslie by name and said:

"Give me the gun," please. Sweat and tears mingled together dropped from his eyes like heavy rain.

She put the gun in her left ear, about to pull the trigger.

Hold on, screamed Pachouco, "I'll do whatever you want to make you change your mind. I'll marry you, Leslie. Hand me the gun, I promise."

“No, Pachouco, I'm not good enough for you. Wait on that American woman you've dreamed of having. If you marry me, Pachouco, I would be your worst nightmare. You deserve someone better than me.”

“I have to die. Besides, you wanted me to come clean with my Aunt Ema, and I hate to be the one to destroy their untroubled home. I deserve to die because of how I treated her and my dad, now you and Yvon. How can I face her to share the story? Pachouco, my aunt, has always shown me, love. Tell her I'm sorry. The way I treated her stinks.”

She put the gun on her left ear again, saying, "Farewell Pachouco, farewell Yvon."

RESCUER

Unexpectedly, a female's voice was echoing in the room. “You are the only niece, the only family member I have left. I lost Minerva, your sister, with gunshot wounds. I cannot afford to lose another one-off the same way. Hand me the gun, Leslie. Leslie, I've known you were my niece and daughter for a while. I love you with all my heart. You are my consolation. You are my paint remover. You see, Leslie, when my daughter got killed in the arms of Pachouco with a couple of bullets in the back of her head, she did not have a chance to dance at her prom nor receive her diploma. An engagement diamond ring from Pachouco, thank God was the highlight of her last day with us. I remember that afternoon just like yesterday. No one understood what I went through. I was on the verge of losing my mind. I became well acquainted with some sleepless night, addicted, yes, I was, to sleeping pills. I even tried some strong drinks to ease my pain, but they did not work. Here I was, a Godly woman. I was supposed to depend on the words of God. I sat down in the middle of a church service, imagining how I was going home, picking up a gun, and blowing my head off my body. I heard a fast-talking voice deep inside me, coaching me on how to do this without an ache. Believe me, Leslie, my daughter, who trained me to destroy myself was a great and deceitful trainer. His instructions appeared to me as the best-fascinated one I had ever received. Right in the church, he took control of my faculties. After rehearsal, he smiled at me and gave me the green light.

Right in the church, he showed me how to load the gun. He assured me all my sufferings; soon, all my trouble would be over. He agreed with me all the way. Life for me without my daughter Minerva was not worth living. He commanded me to leave the service because it was expedient to do this on time. Leslie, my daughter, I heard another voice which sounded like a well-mannered gentleman, who said to me, "Did I ever lie to you? Did I ever forsake you? Your daughter is not dead; in fact, she will never die. She is on an angelical mission. I promise to fill the void of your heart." That gentle voice required me to look to the opposite side of the church. Who did I see? A beautiful white girl named Leslie looked identical to my daughter Minerva. As shocked as I could be, I thought you were an angel. I went and spoke with you and invited you to my house. Since then, my distress and grief all took an eternal hike from me. You helped me overcome my fear of living. I am aware of the fifteen-hundred-dollar extorted deal between you and your dad. However, today you have the power to do the right thing in your hands. Doing right, Leslie has a beginning, and you can start now by giving me the gun." Leslie was filled with shame uttered, "I must kill myself, auntie. Thank you for loving me."

Leslie was about to meet somebody she and Pachouco had never met before. They had known the spiritual side of Ema as the sweetest and meekest person. Both, Pachouco and Leslie were too young to remember the worldly and the tough side of Ema. If Faye Esther had been at the scene, she would tell Leslie, Girl, to mess with your Aunt Ema is to mess with an "atomic bomb?"

Leslie continued talking junk, and she was determined to end her life. Her readiness to pull the trigger became more tempting now than ever. Plenty of junk was what came out of her mouth carelessly.

Unexpectedly, Ema, with a loud and scary voice, yelled at Leslie, "Shut your mouth. Hand me that gun before I kick your skinny butt."

Surprisingly in awe at the last statement made by her aunt, Leslie froze like a thanksgiving turkey that had been in the freezer for five months, waiting for "Thanksgiving Day." Unrealizable, she handed Ema the gun.

They shared their love for each other. Where is Pachouco, asked Ema?

Leslie handed her keys to those handcuffs. Leslie pointed toward the bedroom. A shameful Pachouco lay down on his back. He wanted to cover himself, but his hands and feet were useless. Pachouco was very weak because Leslie raped him without mercy six times back-to-back; what a way for a man to lose his virginity. He heard Ema was coming into the room to set him free. Embarrassment fell big-time on Pachouco.

The sound of a weak voice saying, "I'm naked;" had reached Ema's ears quickly answered, "Boy, do not make me spank your behind. I cleaned this for many days. The only difference is before it was a tiny organ, now it is a little bigger, I hope."

When she saw Pachouco on the bed, she thought her eyes had fooled her. She asked Leslie, "what in the world did you do to Faye Esther's Boy? Ema removed the cuffs and untied his feet, but he was too weak to stand up. Let me call an ambulance. You needed medical attention, expressed Ema."

Wait a minute, said Pachouco, Mother Ema, "There are two decisions I beg you not to make. Do not involve the ambulance or my mother. Just allow me a couple of hours to sleep. If you call the ambulance, the police will be involved. We don't want her to go to jail. Please, Mother Ema, let Yvon loose. He is in the other room."

She glanced at Leslie and asked her, "Do I need a key to unlock him too?"

No, answered Leslie, "You will need a knife."

When Ema proceeded to the other room, she found another nude body. She untied his mouth, and he spat the lemon out. She cut the rope and set him free. Gracious, is there anybody else, Leslie? "No, that is it, Auntie." Ema told Leslie, "I did not attend nursing school because I could not stand looking at grown folk's naked behinds. A minute ago, I thought I filmed a pornographic movie.

Ema prayed to God to give her the wisdom to provide Leslie with some personal counseling and teach her how to control her nymphomania. This disease ran in the family, but Leslie had the worst case.

Leslie poured out her heart to Ema without any reservation. It was the greatest moment of Leslie's life telling the truth had become a part of her.

In the meantime, Pachouco awoke from his sleep. He went to the kitchen and talked to his mother on the phone. Pachouco was playing it cool in their presence. He longed to be home in his bed. The completeness of Pachouco grief, aches, and torment had the remotest of being over in a few years. Sometimes, time is the best remedy to mingle back together with a broken heart.

Pachouco's healing was delayed for a couple of reasons. Firstly, Leslie's love has had the upper hand on Pachouco's love. Second, Pachouco was a member of the upper-class society, the hanging out places of the conservative and pride. Honor before love was his motto. His pride was severely injured to the point of death. Not too many people could comprehend how unpleasant and pernicious, this statement is, "I told you so." With a surety, he ascertained the minute he faced his mother, he would hear those words, "I told you so," which she did say. Pachouco was not in any shape to receive any smart comments. He longed for words of wisdom such as "Life goes on." There are some good fish left in the sea. "Somehow, you are going to make it."

They sat down, in a roundtable discussion, in the kitchen. Ema's motherliness techniques had Pachouco, Leslie, and Yvon temporarily forget their shameful ordeal. They were joyfully laughing and relaxing as a big happy family.

Pachouco reassured Ema, as he was the chairperson of the three, how much they loved her. They were impressed with how she handled the situation; it had the capability of being disastrous. Pachouco developed a burning desire to ask Ema a question on principals. He did not know how to pose the question. He was afraid of hurting both Leslie and Ema's feelings. If Pachouco could have read Leslie's mind, he would have realized she wanted to inquire about the same principle issue about her aunt.

Finally, Leslie shamefully bowed down her head. She said, Mother Ema, "Why are you still with my father? How do you find room in your heart to forgive him after engaging in an affair with your sister? He had her pregnant with me while she was living under your roof. He hid me from you. He shipped my mother off to a new city to hide her pregnancy. When she died, my father had complete knowledge, but he kept you in the dark. He did come to the funeral. I am seeking understanding; please, tell us, how did you do it? We all around this table Aunt

Ema acknowledge that he is a good man. We know you two love each other, but how did you find a place in your heart to forgive somebody like my father?"

"Well Leslie, I'm glad you asked. I did not vanish away from my husband for a few reasons. The greatest syllogism was the beginning of the traditional wedding vows. What took place between you three could have been far worse if you and Pachouco were married. What Kirk has done to me, even to you, contained the same sickening effect. Stupidly I would have reacted if I had left and divorced him. Never forget children; old age does tend to force one to digest things they disagree with. Age was not in my favor when I found out how your father defiled himself. Besides the vows, I was too old and feeble to start over. Kirk and I worked too hard; let me rephrase this: I worked too hard. He did not care to divide our blessings with two lawyers. When older people like Kirk and I, or any other couple, seek a divorce, the hiring of lawyers always comes out victorious, and the divorcers gain the unprofitable, which is nothing. Defaulters the divorcees become. In the case where children are involved, deprivation always makes itself known in their lives. Divorce, divorce, and divorce is nothing but a leach, killer bees, and children's haters. Leslie, how did I find out you were my niece? Kirk perceived I was worried about my sister Emanuella. After Minerva went home with the Lord, my wanting to see Emanuella grew worse. He had told me earlier he learned from a friend of old that Emanuella had passed away from yellow fever. He educated me of your existence. According to his imaginary friend, you lived in the northern part of the Island. I hired a private investigator familiar with the northern region to find you. The task was unsuccessful because you were in the eastward of the country. On the day after the burial of Minerva, I had decided to invest every single dime I earned to find you. My statement frightened him, so he moved you nearby, eight miles away."

"I saw you in church the day I planned to end my life. I could not cope with the emptiness of being deprived of my sister, my daughter, and my niece. I introduced myself to you; similarly, I invited you to my house. I asked you right then if your mother was still alive. Negatively, you answered. Then I launched you the invitation to be your mother. Right on the spot, you agreed to be my daughter. Kirk manipulatively knew the minute I glanced at you, and I could see the family resemblance. To be honest with you, at first, I did not believe Leslie was a natural person. I thought she was an angel sent from heaven, in the likeness of Minerva. I was so alarmed to approach her."

Attentively, they all listened to Ema's dissertation as the best they had ever heard in their lifetime.

"I wondered about your identity in the back of my intellect, Leslie. A mixture of the family's ways overshadowed you, and it spiked my curiosity.

Sometimes, Leslie, you reminded me of Kirk, Minerva, and Emanuella, even myself, in your actions. Not the one like you put on Yvon and Pachouco. That one was your own "specialty."

"I spoke to a doctor friend of mine, soliciting her help for a paternity test. You took sick one day, and she drew some blood out of you. A week later, your father went for his annual check-up. She drew his blood also. She did the test, bingo, it was ninety-nine-point ninety-nine percent (99.99 %) that Kirk was indeed Leslie's father."

Ema expressed herself to them in an exciting manner. They applauded her to the highest. "Money is a defense," continued Ema, money also has the gift of tongues when you have everything at your fingertips. Thank God for money. To put the icing on the cake, I did a lineage test, guess what? This little girl right here is indeed my niece. Let me stop right here; It was not my intention to bore you like this.

They shouted at once, please, Mother Ema, finished the story.

Pachouco jumped in, Mother Ema, what did Papa Kirk do when you injected the information in his ears?

"Are you ready for this," asked Ema? "Yes, in unison," they answered.

"Kirk and I were making love." Yvon was tickled to death at that statement. Very lively, Yvon boasted out that's gross, “Mother Ema, you and Kirk are too old for that.”

Pachouco and Leslie laughed hard.

Ema answered, “Yvon, baby because we are old folks does not mean we are dead. Kirk and I are still familiar with the way, and we are still burning wood.”

Ema had everybody rolling on the floor with laughter. She continued, “While we enjoyed ourselves, I whispered in his ears. I had something to tell you. I knew Emanuella, my sister, was your lover. Leslie is your daughter from her. Stop all the foolishness I had the paternity test done. In the morning, you are going to call Derrick, our lawyer, to draw the papers”

Kirk screamed, “Please do not divorce me.”

“No, I will not, honey.”

“What papers are you talking about, Ema?”

“We are going to will everything we own to Leslie. Do you have a problem with that, Kirk?”

“Oh no,” answered Kirk.

“Can you handle it, Kirk?”

“Oh yes, Ema, those papers will be drawn in the morning.”

“I thought so,” said Ema, “A man that sleeps with two sisters, should have been able to handle anything, Kirk, even death. I looked toward heaven that night, children, and I said, “Emanuella, my twin sister, the ball is in our court.”

THE WILL

Leslie, your father, and I have decided to leave things the way you thought they were. Leslie in a couple of months, I will go on record and make you my daughter officially."

It is not necessary Aunty, I'm too old now to be adopted," added Leslie.

"My daughter said Ema, one is never too old to enjoy reaping the blessing of a true love."

Mother Ema uttered Pachouco, "Minerva in my ears repeated the same statement at least a million times."

The moral of the story beyond this quote is this, said Ema, "When Minerva was eight years old, she drafted a poem in the middle of the night about a dog name CJ. Subsequently after the vision, she called it Funny Dream. But she did not have any idea her father and I were going to get her a dog. Amazingly, she showed us the poem. Unknowingly, she was uncertain of where we were planning to take her. Benighted, she was on the issue of getting her a dog. We arrived at the animal shelter, she picked her a dog that nobody wanted except death."

"What so impressive about this poem? The dog she picked; his name was CJ. Minerva chose him and then asked for his name later. She drafted a story for CJ. Leslie, I want you to pay attention to this story carefully. One day, my family and I decided to visit The Humane Society. We wanted to adopt a young puppy. While we were touring the dog pound, all the dogs were barking except for one large dog. Later I learned his name was CJ. He sat quietly, looking as though he was lonely and forsaken, waiting for his dying day that was soon to come. Very quickly, my attention was drawn to him. In my mind, I immediately wondered why he looked so sad. Was it because he was sick or just unable to bark? I felt that he needed a friend, I asked my father, what do you think of this dog?"

He said, "The dog was too big and too old."

"Still there was something inside of me that kept telling me, there was something special about this dog. My curiosity drew me to one of the employees who took care of the animal; he told me "CJ" was old. He had been at the pound for the past three years. No one wanted to adopt him because again, he was too old. We will have no other choice but to put him to eternal rest soon. I am beginning to understand how CJ must have felt. Instinctively, CJ had to have lost hope. CJ looked at me with eyes full of sadness to say, "Baby girl, you are my last hope." Compassionately, I glared at my father. Moreover, these words proceeded from my mouth. Could you imagine being old confounded in a nursing home for so long and forgotten by family and friends, still hoping day by day for somebody to come and see you and no one showed? Quickly, the realization of no one cares rules the heart. Then, leave you with the desire to rush death so your trouble will be over. My dad replied, when you are old and feeble, friends and relatives tend to erase you from their lives. Sometimes, it will take a stranger to make your last day comfortable or enjoyable. Minerva said, daddy, you are right, allow me to carry CJ home with us, and his last days would be cheerful ones, I promise. Let us add him as the newest member of our family. We will show CJ what family is all about, concluded Kirk. Minerva went to the dog and uttered, your sadness is over CJ, I'm taking you home with me. Amazingly, the dog answered by barking to say to me, "thank you for taking me home with you." CJ has been barking ever since. A week later, I took him to the veterinarian. He asked me, how in the world I adopted an old dog? Most people would not do that. I replied that CJ might be old, but he brought the family joy. Every day, my mind reflects on older people who deserve a second chance in life. They never get it because no one has the time for them. Thank God for allowing CJ a second chance."

"Once again, Leslie," said, Ema, "One is never too old to enjoy reaping the blessing of true love. You are not too old to be my baby girl Leslie."

"We love Pachouco, and we were expecting you and him to get married." Moreover, Ema entered with a most serious tone of voice, "Pachouco, and

Leslie, this is my recommendation, all three of you need to seek counseling. The wedding has no other choice but to die out. Each one of you needs to go your separate ways. Thank you, Pachouco and Yvon, for looking beyond Leslie's faults and forgiving her."

"Pachouco, does Faye Esther need to take you to the hospital," asked Ema?

"I'm fine, Mother Ema."

"What about you, Yvon?"

"No, I'm good to go, Mother Ema."

"It does not matter how dreadful things seem to be. Lord knows it could have been worse," continued Ema. "Remember, children, life goes on with us or without us. Before departing from this table, let us be sure we understand each other. Where do we go from here?"

Pachouco called off the wedding. He reminded his former fiancée that God is a God of second chances. Keep on trusting in Him.

Leslie left the table, and went turned herself into competent authority. Quite a surprise for Pachouco, Yvon, Ema, and the whole Island. No one had pressured her to take such action but her conscience. When it came up to Yvon in all these years, Leslie finally realized the seriousness of her crimes, molestation, and statutory rape against an eleven-year-old boy. She stole his childhood away from him. Leslie felt this is a crime one should not go unpunished for anywhere around the globe. Voluntary, she arrived at the Police Department, and she signed a warrant for her arrest on two accounts, rape, and statutory rape. Pachouco and Yvon refused to press charges against Leslie. They asked her what made her do a stupid thing like that? She replied to them, saying "They did not understand, now I know right from wrong. It is up to me to do right. I committed the crimes alone, and alone I must pay the sanction."

Even though Pachouco and Yvon did not want to push the issues, the Prosecutor still found her guilty. Thirty days in jail and thirty days probation with counseling including a total of two months was the payoff of her debt. Leslie finally tastes the sweetness of doing the right thing.

Leslie planned to move to another country where she could start over. She stayed with her aunt and father. She was waiting for her counseling and probation sessions to reach their terms and conditions. Leslie's shamefulness demanded of her to move as far away as possible from Pachouco and everyone else. She did have a residence in the United States of America, so she might go there and live.

Yvon moved to his apartment and tried to obtain a relationship with Michelle.

Leslie, before leaving town, conquered her worse fear. She did make a farewell phone call to Faye Esther. Leslie apologized for disappointing her, and she brought to Leslie's attention to keep her head held high. “Life has just begun for you. What is for you, Leslie is for you? Who knows what the future holds? One day, you and Pachouco will get married.”

“Mother Faye Esther, I let slide from my hands a good man. He deserves somebody better than me. I am the sorriest woman on the Island.”

“Leslie” added Faye Esther, “it is needless to go anywhere to start over unless you are ready to leave the past behind you.: Faye Esther concluded, “Young lady, do not carry any bags of trash or any unpleasant memories. To start over is to start brand new. The beautiful memories of yesterday,” said Faye Esther, “Need to travel with you, not the bad ones. The bad memories of yesterday can be so cruel to your mind if you allow them to. They can kidnap your self-esteem from a higher standard to a lower one. Leslie, be your exterminator, eliminate anything contrary to happiness, joy, and love.”

Aggressively, Leslie answered, “Mother Faye Esther, you promised to be with me as a mother" "through thick and thin." “You did just that. I will never forget you for your wisdom and your sense of humor.”

“Where have you headed, Leslie,” asked Faye Esther?

“Mother” uttered Leslie; “it is a secret. I promise that after I get situated, you and my parents will be the first three to be informed.”

Suddenly, Faye Esther burst out laughing aloud.

“What is so funny, enquired Leslie? What kind of joke crossed your mind, Mother?”

Faye Esther replied, “You do not want to know, girl.”

“Try me, Mother Faye.”

“Okay, Leslie, you begged for it.”

“Yes, I did. Mother, tell me.”

In a laughing manner again, Faye Esther said, “I saw the way you raped my son. If you were pregnant, would you grant me a pledge? Promise me, you will never hide these children from me, no matter the circumstance.”

“Children,” shouting Leslie! “Mother Faye Esther, are you out of your mind? Stop before you jinx me with your mighty mouth.”

“I'll tell you what, in due season, you will know if that has taken place. Nice talking to you, Mother, I have a flight to catch, I love you.”

“Leslie keeps in touch, and never forget that I love you. Also, congratulations for allowing Ema to adopt you and paying your debts to society. Girl, I am proud of you; Lord knows I do.”

Three months had elapsed, and Pachouco still could not cope with the torture he suffered. The scenery of his ordeal captivated his photogenic memory. Therefore, it affected his thinking his sleeping condition, and it even declared war on his appetite. He pledged to his mother if something terrible ever arose between Leslie and him, he would remain in perfect condition. So far, it was not working because his mother had taken him to the hospital for a sleeping disorder. On this occasion, Faye Esther decided to keep quiet during his visit to the hospital. From there, he was transferred to a mental institution for a period of six months. Having nightmares concerning extreme rape with violence, through fasting and prayer, he bounced back. He spent a lot of money because of this mess. Through it all, he kept a heart full of forgiveness for Leslie. He still loved Yvon like a son. He felt deep inside that God wanted him to live a single man's lifestyle. Faye Esther disagreed with him because she expected grandchildren from him. Even though Faye Esther knew already about the scientific fact of his sterility, her faith in God taught her different that Pachouco would be a joyful father regardless of the physician's report. It was quite a surprise; he thought his mother didn't know anything about his situation because she discussed it not with him nor anybody else but with God only.

Pachouco mastered his fear and claimed victory over the high treason of Leslie against him, which had devastated his ability to discern good judgment. Through the power of prayer, the nightmares and his sleeping disorder disappeared entirely from his life. Pachouco recovered nicely. He came to his senses he realized life would go on, with him or without him.

This was the conclusion of Pachouco's first two deceptions in life. Now everyone should understand why his heart turned toward Loretta. No one would comprehend Pachouco and Loretta if the stories of Minerva and Leslie were not told.

THE BLIND SIDE OF LOVE

Let us recapture the love story of Pachouco and Loretta. The relationships between his brother Serge Gerard, Loretta, and Pachouco seemed unconquerable. The two incidents combined left Pachouco with a restless spirit. It is fair enough to bring the story up to date. Pachouco's brother, Serge Gerard, seized the occasion of Pachouco's recovery. He introduced Pachouco to Loretta on the phone. However, there was a problem, she only spoke English, and Pachouco only spoke French and Creole. Loretta knew a few phrases in French, not enough to carry on a conversation but enough to get fresh a little. Pachouco was the same in English.

Serge Gerard, in the agreement, was willing to be their translator. When Pachouco received the pictures, he made a big deal out of them. "Why was that?" Loretta looked like his mother, Faye Esther. Both ladies took their times to be beautiful and impressive. Serge Gerard knew what he was doing when he matched Pachouco with Loretta. Since then, the idea of Pachouco joining the priesthood or living a celibate lifestyle disappeared like a vapor. Pachouco thought differently from the average guy, his experience with women was not vast but very narrow. When he met Minerva, no one on earth could have enticed him to believe she was not his "Eve," his unique creation, one of his ribs.

Nevertheless, God called her home. Then he found Leslie, and he felt that Leslie was the Supreme, being formed for him with his rib. He put all his faith in her, and she presented him with a "breach of trust." Now Pachouco is still in the quest for his "Eve" in his intellect; he thought every woman had an "Adam," every man an "Eve."

Pachouco, in his love letters to Loretta, referred to her as his heartbeat, Eve, at the time of his creation. Loretta became overly attached to Pachouco. He may not be able to communicate with her verbally, but he scored many points in her heart in writing. The poems he sent to her sometimes helped her sleep like a baby. It was not because they were boring but too interesting. Loretta used to share his writings with Serge Gerard. Lately, she refused to inform Serge Gerard when Pachouco wrote her.

Pachouco, in the meantime, sold a few more of his assets. He sent the money to Serge Gerard to deposit in a savings account, opened in his name for Pachouco, in a New York Bank. Pachouco intended to buy a house for him and Loretta to live in after getting married. They decided to tie the knot the day after he entered the states. Serge Gerard advised him to sell his possessions, and Pachouco followed his brother's counsel. Pachouco had given him twenty-three thousand dollars to deposit so far. One night on the phone, Pachouco made mentioned the above amount.

His oldest brother said, “Man, Pachouco, we have way more money than that.”

“What do you mean,” asked Pachouco?

Serge Gerard replied, “The bank just credited three thousand dollars in interest to the account. Pachouco, I’m the man. I’m an expert in money marketing. By the time you arrive in this country, you and Loretta will be rich. Do you see how quickly we made an extra three thousand dollars? I asked you to sell all your possessions a little bit at a time. You sent the money to me to place in the bank. You’re glad you did! I can hear it in your voice, baby brother.”

“Well, big brother, I could not do it without you,” said Pachouco. “I’m tired of living on this Island, and I can hardly wait to marry Loretta. The bottom line is, big brother, I need a family.”

“Little brother, come on; you do have a family. You have me, and you have Mother Faye Esther. What more do you want, Pachouco? I did not mention the rest of our brothers and sisters. Since day one, they have never treated you and I right. I am so glad little brother; you have decided to date an American girl.

Otherwise, you would tarry in Haiti for the rest of your life. I recognize the fact that life in Haiti had been fair to you. Way better than it ever was to me. Nevertheless, life in New York City will treat you even better, Pachouco. Little brother, never forget, I am your family. It is not because of what you possess. I choose Loretta for you, Pachouco, for distinct reasons. Some of them, you will never imagine. Loretta will never lead you on to use or to abuse you."

"Serge Gerard, can I say something? I recognize perfectly well you are my family. We are all busy people. You and I, Serge Gerard, but we make time for each other. Family should never be too busy to stop checking on each other. Big brother, consider how far we are from one another, but we communicate daily. I ascertain some siblings who live within walking distance or a few miles from each other who are not seeing nor talking to each other in six to twelve months. Their selfishness allows them to adopt an "I'm too busy" spirit.

Serge Gerard, some people take things for granted. I said earlier, "I needed a family for myself, what I mean by that big brother is, I want children of my own, but I'm afraid this is an impossible task. I imagine it sounds good to you when Danielle, Eric, and Jeffrey call you daddy."

"Pachouco, I hear you, man, but hang in there.

You and Loretta are still young. You two will take part in replenishing the earth. I can feel it, soon and very soon."

Pachouco detected a problem between Serge Gerard and Loretta. The other night, they were on the phone. Loretta did not say much. It seemed to

Pachouco that his brother's translation was longer than what Loretta said. His lack of English denied him the right to dig for the truth. She wanted not to be bothered. That was the message he read from Loretta's attitude that night. Pachouco decisively asked Serge Gerard, what was the matter with his fiancée? She let him and Pachouco carry most of the conversation. In joking moderation, he answered, Loretta, will be alright. Serge Gerard said something to her in English. Of course. She came back with a concise statement. Okay, said Serge Gerard. Pachouco anxiously waited for the answer. After a few seconds of intersection, Serge Gerard took a deep breath. Little brother, she said, "She missed you. She has moments like this when she visualized Pachouco touching her all over."

"Tell Loretta for me; I miss her every second, every minute. Tell her, nightly, I kiss her pictures. The motion of my lips brings life into her photos. In my bed, she indeed becomes real." Loretta laughed so hard at Pachouco like she understood what he said in French.

"Pachouco, she wants to know how was it when she became real in your bed next to you? Was she nude, Pachouco? What happened next?"

Wildly answered Pachouco, "My goodness, it is the best. We recreated the scene of Adam and Eve in the garden of Eden. I was in a trance in the garden next to my Eve, Loretta. When I looked at her, I realized how beautiful she was. Tenderly and sweetly, I said, she was created for me."

Loretta laughed aloud again.

Serge Gerard, after his translation, cried out: "It is too hot in here!"

Pachouco, in his conclusive mind, believed Loretta comprehended French much better than before. He asked his oldest brother, "are you sure Loretta isn't sneakily studying French?"

"She only knows what I taught her, which was not much," contested his oldest brother.

"Nevertheless, Serge Gerard, I'm almost sure, she knew what I was saying. Tell her what I'm assuming."

His oldest brother told her, and she turned it into a joke.

According to Serge Gerard, she added, "You two gentlemen better be careful when speaking French. You two brothers do not have any idea what this American girl understands. Please do not make me bust you."

Serge Gerard shared her comment with Pachouco. They laughed as laughing was going out of style.

Suddenly he asked Pachouco, "who does this statement remind you of?"

Pachouco uttered, "My mother, Mrs. Faye Esther. They are too much alike, big brother."

"They are two comical beings, little brother."

They hung up the telephone. Faye Esther was aware that they often compared her with Loretta. That night, Faye Esther articulated to Pachouco her true sentiment. She admonished her son not to approach this New York venture heedlessly. "The Serge Gerard that I once knew as a son was a perfect man. You could consider it done if he shook your hand in a deal. The words from his mouth were as good as gold. He left the Island a long time ago. Therefore, I'm not sure if Serge Gerard is the same man I helped raise. People change my son, some for the best, and some for the worse."

"Mother, I trust my brother Serge Gerard with my life. He is a good man, the kind you described earlier. He is the person I talk to all the time. Besides you, he is the only person on earth never to violate my trust. He is an honest man. Mother, the minute he heard of my tragedy, he stuck by my side."

"Pachouco, you have a point there, my son, but be careful. I'm glad he introduced you to Loretta. I'm too old to learn her language. If she wants to talk to me, she will have to learn French or Creole."

"Mother, what about me? I speak not a word of English well. Son, believe me, you will speak her language. A real woman has the power to pull within her man, capabilities he never perceived he had. A man, who is deeply in love with a woman, has no other choice but to be her slave," concluded Faye Esther.

"Wow! Mother, where did those words come from? I forgot Mother; you did not get this gray hair overnight. Love you Mother, goodnight."

The following day, Pachouco went and had Loretta's pictures enlarged. He desired to place each one of them in a frame. Serge Gerard had commanded Pachouco not to expose those pictures under any circumstances to Faye Esther. Pachouco, all night long, contemplated the images. He realized if he framed and displayed them in his bedroom, his mother could not tell the difference. Those pictures were not in color, but black and white.

Pachouco thought he was being clever. He found a few old pictures of his mother. Pachouco mingled them together with Loretta's photos. He showed both sets to Faye Esther. She was incompetent to select which ones were hers or not. She glared at Pachouco; after admiring them, she said "Boy, back in the day, your mother was the most beautiful girl who ever walked this Island. Even when I became a madam, I still had it going on."

Pachouco, without hesitation, repeated, "Back in the day, Mother, you are still beautiful today, the most elegant and the most beautiful lady in my world. The older you get, the more attractive you become. Your beauty will never expire. However, according to my brother, you have competition out there."

"Who might that be?" Asked Faye Esther?

"Gloriously, he answered, my beauty Queen, your future daughter-in-law Loretta."

"Well, my son, beauty runs in the family. Loretta will fit well not as a runner-up but as one among the beauty Queens. Pachouco, I took so many pictures in my younger days it did not make any sense. People used to steal them. In Mardi Gras season, I was the Queen for our local bank. Every year, my float won the first prize. Anyone who desired to take my picture was welcome to do so. That was the part I did not care for. Therefore, I'm ignorant of whom possesses my photographs today? If Loretta looks a lot like me physically, she will need to be careful, Pachouco. When I was Loretta's age, I was afraid of being raped. I was fearful of being mugged by jealous girls who were mean to me. They picked a fight with me often. Those jealous girls purposed in their hearts to slash my face with razor blades. They wanted to destroy my pretty face, to eliminate me as a beauty pageant contestant. I suffered a lot because of my beauty. Various insecure women had accused me of messing with their men. I was friendly, outgoing, and sympathetic. Through it all, I held fast to my integrity. I remained faithful to the end. Son, I thank the Good Lord for Eva, my mother. She taught me how to survive and keep my head above water. Among all the excitement, which crowded my life, your father, Fernand Andre, was the only man who knew me. I was a virgin when I married him."

Faye Esther entreated Pachouco for the pictures again. Nervously, he handed them to her.

Even though he knew her eyes sight from time to time. However, that day, her visibility was graciously restored. Pachouco was dumbfounded when his mother divided the pictures into two piles, and she gave him all her pictures to hold. She retained Loretta's photos. She took her time to admire and study Loretta's pictures. Faye Esther said, "Loretta is more beautiful than I anticipated. She reminds me so much of my mother and me. Pachouco, with tears in her eyes continued; she even dresses the way I used to dress. Stylishly, even her hair is fixed like mine. She is a reincarnation of my youth. I am now in agreement with you and Serge Gerard. She is a carbon copy of me and my late mother, Eva."

"Son, Loretta is a nice-looking woman, attractive. She needs to be careful. Let me tell you what your grandmother warned concerning a beautiful woman." She said to Faye Esther, "A beautiful woman is but one step away from being a scant whore or a prostitute." "If she uses her beauty as bait to manipulate and to exploit people, she will find herself in bed with anything who owns a few dollars, male or female who cares. She is also one step away from being a woman of character and integrity. The choice is hers."

"To conclude, Pachouco, your grandmother, used to ask me, what is a beautiful woman with a trashy personality? She is nothing, my daughter. She is just like a beautiful flower without any smell. She is just like salt that lost its favor. People would tell her anything, exaggerating to get her in their bed as a low-class hooker. My daughter, your grandmother, would say again, "do not let your beauty turn into your curse; turn to your disaster."

Amazingly, Pachouco could not digest the fact that Faye Esther identified Loretta's pictures. Without a second guess, she picked them the first time. Pachouco has a great desire to ask his mother if she had seen the photos before? Her reaction had blown his mind.

Pachouco felt terrible and that he should have told her of his possession of Loretta's photos. He was sorry; he followed his brother Serge Gerard's counsel. Weird as it may sound, Pachouco asked his mother for forgiveness for not sharing the receiving of the photographs with her. His intent was never to hide from her their existence but to surprise her someday. She accepted his apology.

Following the acceptance, a remarkable gesture from her head reached the corner of Pachouco's eyes. He quickly intervened with a benign smile Faye Esther in her tactfulness, pointed at her gray hair. Pachouco received the message loud and clear. His mother knows how to have ways with words. She articulated to him that "You and Serge Gerard would have to rise early in the morning for you two love rookies to fool me. Even with my eyes blindfolded, I would still discover your game plan. In addition, I was patiently taking my time to beat both of you in your games, on your field. You know why I do not dye my hair black," said Faye Esther. "I am afraid I might stain all my wisdom. Then Serge Gerard and you will have picnics in my backyard uninvited whenever you two get ready."

She made Pachouco's day with those statements. He laughed until he cried.

He said, "Mother, please, the gray hair stuff needs to go. Promise me after today, and you will get rid of it. Please give it a longtime rest."

Faye Esther said, "Pachouco, honey, why would I do that? Loretta, Natacha, and I need some sense to be around Serge Gerard and you. Otherwise, you would be unruly without our leadership. Now call your brother and give him the scoop. Pachouco, I cannot wait for Loretta to speak French. I can hardly wait to recognize Natacha. I need to educate them of you two brothers, the Casimir boys."

"Mother, the Good Lord knows what He is doing."

Pachouco and his mother could bring joy in any joyless place, laughter where sadness abides, peace where struggle resides, unity where division sojourns, and love where hatred is tolerated.

Pachouco, happily satisfied, came clean with his mother. Now had a free hand to frame Loretta's pictures and hung them on the wall where everybody could see. The power of the truth always prevails. The truth outshines the lie and introduces it to freedom.

Since the time of old and today, being truthful has been the best remedy for a condemned heart.

Pachouco did not waste any time to grab a sheet of paper, an English dictionary, and write Loretta. He expressed to her how the day went how warm the conversation was between his mother and him. He started the letter to Loretta in this manner:

"Loretta is her name to the one that makes my heartbeat, the woman of my dreams. My girl, my sweetheart, I wish you were at my house a few hours ago to listen to your future mother-in-law talking about your beauty. I did not know my grandmother Eva, but her mother said, you favor her greatly. Loretta, it is hard for me to express myself to you on the telephone. You may wonder why that is. I must speak through my oldest brother to say something to you. I depend on him to translate for you and me. I am doing well in my English class. I have problem hearing words that are unfamiliar to me. I am more comfortable with you now. I do not have to hide your pictures anymore from my mother. She took her time to contemplate them. She cannot wait for you and me to meet each other. Last night in a vision, I saw us getting married. I could not see the face of the preacher who performed our wedding. When he asked me to kiss the bride, I did. I found myself in trouble with the law. They incarcerated and prosecuted me. The judge found me guilty, guilty of loving you too much. Sweetie, words are not sufficient for me to describe my love for you, and I need to show you how much I do. Loretta, I am not an artist by trade. I cannot draw on the wall like Fernand Andre, my father. Nevertheless, I could draw my heart for you to know we belong together on the wall of your heart. Therefore, I would sign my name "Pachouco Casimir Forever." I wish I could take a few x rays of my heart for you to see; your name is already engraved in gold, "Private Property, No Trespassing" was what the writing read. Loretta, you are my butter pecan ice cream on a hot night. You are the fruit, the syrup, the minced nuts, and the whipped cream on my sundae. On a freezing night, you are my fire in a fireplace. Loretta, my love, you are my sunburst through rifted clouds. I often imagine your beautiful anatomy, which the Architect of the universe has formed. Your breasts any day and any night could serve me as a pillow. If I were a baby, they would serve as my bottle. Can I play with words for a minute? Loretta, I am your baby; nourish me with your natural milk. Then, I will have no other choice but to attach to your sweet smell. I cry when I miss you, acting up when I am hungry. Your charm brings the best out of me, and you become a habit, an addiction to me. Loretta, what more can I do to satisfy you? Please tell me, love. I am at your service. Whatever you need or desire, if it had anything to do with love, darling, trust me, I would have it. Please, enslave me, Loretta, with your passionate love and never set me free. Everything about you is attractive to me, your smile, touch, and kisses. When you visited me in my dreams, we had never experienced a dull moment. Every single performance was intoxicating. Loretta, we will marry soon. Our love will be stronger. Death will be the only thing that could put out our fire. Loretta, I love you. Enclosed are three hundred dollars for bus fare to go to school. Loretta, make sure you say "hello for me, to my big brother. Tell him I sold some more stuff, and the package will arrive at his house in fifteen days." Love you, Pachouco.

POWER OF PRAYER

Yvon proposed to Michelle in marriage. She told him the only way it could happen was he would have to obtain permission from Pachouco. Yvon, bold as a lion, met with him. He asked Pachouco would he permit him to marry Michelle. Without Pachouco's blessing, Yvon would not be able to marry Michelle. Pachouco asked Yvon to give him a couple of days to contact Michelle. He made a memorable trip to her house. He spoke to her very highly about Yvon. He understood what Yvon did to protect him, even though it was painful protection. Michelle told Pachouco, "whatever you say is what will happen." Graciously, he gave her his blessing. Pachouco called Yvon and gave him his love and respect, and he gave Yvon his blessing.

Yvon happily thanked him and said to Pachouco, “I need one more favor from you.”

“What might that be, Yvon?”

“I will be so grateful if you do me the honor of being my best man.”

A laughing Pachouco glared at Yvon and uttered, “What goes around comes around.” “My answer is, Humm! My answer is yes!” Yvon leaped for joy, shouting aloud, yes, he forgave me, yes, he forgave me. While running with happiness, he turned around and said: "Pachouco, my father, I love you. Thanks a million. You have filled my heart with gladness. You covered the void and the emptiness of my life with education. How can I repay you, Pachouco? This belief was far from your heart besides an eye for an eye, a tooth for a tooth. You have shown me peace instead of vengeance. You offered me back my dignity, and you crowned it with your niece and goddaughter Michelle."

Pachouco's answered, "Yvon, my best man, the only way you can repay me is to treat somebody else right along the way. Yvon, keep on allowing the loaves and the fish to multiply. Share the blessing, son."

A few years had gone by since Pachouco departed from the presence of Leslie. Since then, it was the first time Yvon talked sincerely. However, the effect of the deception had left Pachouco discouraged about living on the Island. Pachouco right now would like to live in his native country forever. He felt all the Island had to offer him was deception. However, his incident with Leslie paralyzed his way of thinking. Pachouco blamed the country for his heartbreak. He placed all the girls from the Island in the same category as Leslie. He mistakenly felt all of them were deceivers. But his first love was not. In love, irrational thinking is a high-ticket item. Therefore, it is always costly. Pachouco, by now, sold way over half of his assets. He risked everything to run an adventure in New York with his brother. His finances are now in a New York bank in his brother's name. Pachouco has a two-track mind, Loretta, and Serge Gerard. If he talked to someone for one second, they would be the highlight of the conversation. He trusted them with an unhealthy trust. They could do no wrong in his eyes.Loretta herself now disliked the idea of using his oldest brother as their translator. Before it was fine by her, she was not in love. She was there to please Serge Gerard. She moved by how Pachouco expressed his love for her in the letters. She was carried away by his nice looks. His pictures alone had significant effects on her. Being in love with him was the condition of her heart. Her intention currently was to eliminate the three-way phone calls. Serge Gerard had no idea how much Loretta cared for Pachouco. Her love for him was greater than what he perceived. If Serge Gerard knew its magnitude, he would have cooled it down. Nevertheless, Loretta kept him in the dark about her true feelings for Pachouco.

Surprisingly, he never knew how often Loretta wrote Pachouco. She developed a system unknown to him. Pachouco was writing her in English, and Loretta was doing the same in French for practice. Remember, she did not speak French, and he did not speak English. Both were using dictionaries to form their sentences. Loretta had introduced the plan to Pachouco. She commanded him not to inform his brother of the written correspondence. He agreed that she learned enough French to transmit the message loud and clear to him. Pachouco thought its purpose was to get rid of the language barriers. Loretta was thinking ahead, and her goal was to remove Serge Gerard from the picture. The letters took too long to reach "Point A to B." In that case, it was not possible to do away with Serge Gerard's translation service. Pachouco had been studying English for quite some time now. He had a lot of vocabulary, but his pronunciation was inadequate. Therefore, he had trouble speaking the language fluently. Since a game plan, Serge Gerard and Loretta deliberately refused to understand him.

Pachouco was puzzled by Loretta's French writing skills. She was very stylish with it. He had trouble believing she was just a learner. She wrote as if it was her native language. She complained before she had no one to teach her the language. Finally, he realized that Loretta might be gifted.

Pachouco called his brother and reported that his mother had recognized Loretta's pictures. He was honest enough to admit he was playing a prank on Faye Esther, and he got caught doing it. There was complete silence from Serge Gerard, who expected to hear the outcome. However, Pachouco changed the conversation. With a trembling and scary voice, Serge Gerard said to his baby brother: "hold on, tell me, what she said, man?"

"I should have shown her those pictures a long time ago. Serge Gerard's mother's impression of Loretta's photos was fabulously great. She even had a few words of wisdom for you to translate to my beauty Queen. Mother also complimented you and me."

"Pachouco, you mean to tell me Faye Esther complimented us. She did not talk junk about you and me."

"Serge Gerard, are you kidding me? You know for yourself, if Mother did not trash us, we would have to admit her into the hospital."

"Did she not say anything concerning her gray hair to prove our ignorance?"

"Yes, sir, she did partner. To put all jokes asides, Serge Gerard, mother, and I appreciate you. Indeed, you are a blessing to us."

"Pachouco, how long have I told you I'm here for you, baby brother? I love you, man. If I cannot help my flesh and blood, I would not hurt him either. Every day, I harass the lawyer supposed to take care of your residency in New York. You know what he told me this morning, Serge Gerard; you are crazy about this brother. I answered him with all my heart. Pachouco, I need you here with me. I invited the lawyer to your wedding, and he promised to be a witness."

Pachouco uttered, "A friend of mine mentioned a ten-year grace period for permanent residence. Does that mean I have five more years left before entering New York?" He replied to the allegation by saying, "Do not forget Pachouco, I'm the man. Next year this time, you will be in the arms of your wife, Loretta. Who knows, she might even carry your baby. This is how fast things are going to move. Pachouco, in the twinkling of an eye, you will be right here kissing her all over."

"Well, said Pachouco, "I want to see her badly. I am at the end of my rope, and where is my sunshine tonight?

"She has just arrived Pachouco. Loretta picks up the phone before your honey goes into heart failure."

She jumped on the phone with this greeting:

"(Bonsoir mon amour, Je pense beaucoup a toi aujourd'hui.)" which translated; Good evening my love, I think a lot about you today. He answered, "(Moi aussi,) me too."

Faye Esther marched into the room where Pachouco was. "Is that your brother Serge Gerard and Loretta on the phone?"

"Yes, Mother Dear: if you do not know mine, I will enjoy speaking to them tonight."

Pachouco made known to them his mother's request. It was a pleasure for both. Faye Esther asked Serge Gerard to give the best translation possible. She needed Loretta to comprehend every word that proceeded out of her mouth. He pledged to do so. Loretta, for a moment, was in a state of mental uncertainty. A spirit of suspicions overwhelmed the two New Yorkers. All three of them became extremely nervous when Faye Esther joined the chat. "Why did this nervousness preoccupy their intellects?" The worst-case was Loretta.

She dreaded involvement in a talk with Pachouco's mother. She heard from those boys how sharp Faye Esther was. She had spoken to his mother many times from the background. Never had Faye Esther asked for a direct conversation.

Serge Gerard seized the opportunity instantly from Faye Esther and began to chat. He intended to lead the discourse until Faye Esther lost her train of thoughts. It did not happen in this manner. She forced him to hush. "She would like to know why Loretta cared not to visit Pachouco. All she needs as an American is a valid passport and leave the rest to us."

"Mother Faye Esther, she is afraid of flying," injected Serge Gerard.

Faye Esther asked him, "Serge Gerard, is your name, Loretta? You're supposed to interpret for me. I have not heard you say a word to her; you answered me already. What kind of interpretation is this?"

Loretta was dying laughing in the background as she understood what had been said. He explained it to Loretta. She giggled for a minute. According to Serge Gerard, Loretta enunciated that "I was planning to visit the Island three years ago, but something came along to deprive me of the trip. To be honest, I will be uncomfortable flying over there now. Pachouco's lack of English and my lack of French might bring chaos.

It is the truth; I hate flying with a passion. Besides, I may not want to come back without Pachouco. Then, what would be next for me? Pachouco could apply for a tourist visa. I'm sure he will obtain one, but he chooses not to engage with that. His problem is he detests going back on his words. He mentioned the day he ever flew to another country, and he would not come back home to live on the Island again. This conviction of Pachouco rejects all attempts for a tourist visa. I have offered him a permanent residence.

If he agrees to visit me here, I will marry him and file his papers. Mother Faye Esther the Casimir boys are too much alike. They refute the principle of taking a helping hand from a woman. Their pride encourages them to believe such a concept is unmanly. He had instead waited on his brother Serge Gerard to file for him. No matter how long it takes, it will take less time with me. He bases his refusal of my offer on the ground I will never let it rest."

Serge Gerard finished translating for Loretta.

Faye Esther cracked a joke, Even my American daughter is aware of Pachouco, and you are full of it. Tell Loretta; I see where she is coming from, and I grasped every word. In the meantime, she and Natacha need to team up and pray for you two."

"Why is that" beseeched Serge Gerard to Faye Esther?

"How long have I narrated the Casimir boys are too demanding? You two are just like Fernand Andre, my husband. The only difference is that I converted him from a tiger to a lamb with prayer. Loretta and Natacha will need to do the same thing. Serge Gerard, I have not heard you translate a word to Loretta."

A giggling Serge Gerard added, "Mother, I will not give them your secret to using on my little brother and me. We must remain strong, not too gentle."

"On that note," Loretta also chuckled."

Pachouco called Faye Esther, she wished them a blessed night and put him on the phone. They declared (bonne nuit) goodnight.

Another round table discussion will soon start. Pachouco always acknowledges his mother's discerning spirit. The digestion of the result is often too hard for him to deal with, "Lord have mercy."

Pachouco is a great person and a sincere lover. Whenever he loves someone, he dedicates his life to her. He staggers not from here to there. Pachouco learns to make a woman feel like a woman. Someone honorable who deserves to feel special and should not ever experience a slap, a kick, or verbal abuse from a man. However, her man ought to cherish every ounce of her being. She is too fragile, too precious to be handled roughly. Tenderly, sentimentally, gently, and lovingly is the ideal style to touch a woman. Any other turbulent fashion is a crime against creation. A crime against the Designer of such an important being called "WOMAN." If she chooses to remain in an abusive love story, she would be a degrader of the name "WOMAN." Vice Versa, if a man slaps a woman once, he will slap her twice. So let the first slap or kick be goodbye forever. The same rules apply to verbal abuse.

Pachouco does not mind expressing his feelings to the one he loves. Why is that? A man like him often receives the worse end of the deal. He always has in return something contrary to what he dishes out.

To introduce effective treatment to a woman that is satisfied with receiving harsh treatment is to "create a monster." Eventually, she will consider the introducer as her fool, who is inexperienced in love. A real woman will know the difference. Everybody has a promised land to reach in love. Everybody has their exceptional captain to lead them there. However, many men and women missed the entrance of their promised land. They had fallen in love with the wrong captains who knew not the way to happiness, love, peace, and success but the way that led to abuse, misery, and traumatic stress disorder is what they are familiar with. Now they live in the wrong land with the wrong captains, resulting from bad choices.

The round table discussion had begun. Pachouco questioned his mother about the talk she had with Loretta. What was her perception of Loretta? Faye Esther opened her mouth, played with her tongue a little bit. “I believe she is somebody I would enjoy talking to, but Loretta left me with the impression she is the one that could be very deceiving."

"Mother, are you going to share that impression with me?"

"To me, Pachouco, Loretta is fluent in French. She is fooling somebody. She did not pause for Serge Gerard to translate my jokes; she started to giggle. That occurred more than twice. I hope I misread her. Why would she pretend she does not speak the language?"

"Mother Dear, I feel she is a natural-born gifted when it comes to French. If I showed you the letters she wrote me, you would be convinced even more. From the back of my spirit, I shared your view. It was a grave issue for me. I confronted Serge Gerard about it. He only taught her a few phrases. She repeated those words without an accent; she sounded French. Pachouco, you amaze me big time. The energy you burned to keep this love going all these years. You prove that the word love itself is truly an action word. You and she are faithfully communicating weekly. You do not develop any feelings for somebody else while tarrying for her. I want you to understand there is nothing wrong with that. It does not matter how long it will take. Wait on her if she deserves to be waited on. In long-distance relationships, letters are the backbone of it. When the writing begins to experience slackness, something is up. When the interest has been shifted to negligence, again, something is up."

Faye Esther, articulately, tried to reason with Pachouco, a task that could be complicating of nature. Remember every word that he speaks; he spoke it with conviction. In his belief, he wavers not. His mother perpetuated him as a mule because he was stubborn. She portrayed him also as the most compassionate man on the Island. A heart filled with mercy.

The round table was still in progress. Faye Esther advised her son to seek a visa to visit Loretta and Serge Gerard for a couple of weeks.

"That is forbidden, Mother Dear, I will not do it."

"Pachouco, what harm could that cause? You are well known in the country; all it will take for you is to apply for a tourist visa by presenting your passport and assets to the American Embassy."

"No, mother, I'm not going this route. I would rather wait on Serge Gerard. He said, "I only have one more year for them to send my green card. When I leave the country that I love, I will not come back. For yourself, Mother, you would know that if we wanted to visit New York, we could. Loretta has a great desire to give me a green card. I refuse to accept it from her because of a joking remark she made. She laughed hysterically, saying, I will give you the card. If you get me upset, I will ship you back to where you come from. Serge Gerard answered her that day, so he is an American citizen; he can give his brother a card."

"How do you know Pachouco, she declared this to your brother? Do not trust Serge Gerard's translation to the fullness. I understand you very well, son. Still, you need a visa to go check something out. You are ready to leave Haiti, of which I have no objection. Would I stop selling the rest of my assets if I were you? I would also stop sending money to Serge Gerard to place in the bank for you. Sixty thousand dollars is a lot of money. There is nothing wrong with Pachouco if you want a house in New York. I tell you what, if I had that type of cash in a foreign country, I would have to have access in that country.

You need to take a trip to New York for your own experience. If you decide to do so, son, please let it be a surprise to both Serge Gerard and Loretta."

"Mother, mother, mother, it sounds like you are losing confidence in Serge Gerard. I trust him with my life. I've learned to take heed in the things you say. I will give it some thought. Mother Dear, suppose I decide to appeal for two visas, guess who the other one will belong to?"

Pachouco, my son, it will not be for me. It would be best if you had a break from me. It would be best if you handled this alone. You do not need any extra baggage like me. Pray and see what the Master will is for your future."

Faye Esther completely disregarded the introductory statement added by Pachouco. It sounds like you are losing confidence in Serge Gerard; he was right. The three-way telephone call became a revelation for Faye Esther. She disliked the manner Serge Gerard handled the translation between her and Loretta. Faye Esther's sentiment remained unchangeable. Regardless of what Pachouco rehearsed in her ears. She strongly believes Loretta spoke French fluently. Faye Esther could be wrong, but times will tell the story. Why would Loretta put on a show? If Faye Esther were right, Loretta would have gotten rid of Serge Gerard long ago. She preferred to communicate with Pachouco by mail. When Loretta wrote him, she had the freedom to express herself in a fleshly fashion. Pachouco mentioned that Loretta is a shy person on the phone. A statement Serge Gerard has trouble believing.

THE OPPORTUNIST

Unbelievably, Serge Gerard is a hustler, and this is a piece of information that Pachouco will not digest. He sees his brother as a great provider, as God's gift. Serge Gerard is perfect in his view. Faye Esther mostly wondered often; does he consider how much Pachouco cares for him? what brings the closeness between the two? Pachouco, neglected by his other brothers and sisters, called him a "mamma's boy." His prom night ordeal, the cold-blooded assassination of Minerva in his arms, reached the international ears. Then, his so-called brothers and sisters living abroad took advantage of his trauma. They gave an interview to upgrade their social status from left to right. What they had meant to be profitable to them became a blessing to Pachouco. With her busy schedule, Serge Gerard and Barbara Ann have stuck by his side since the news hit the airtime. Who could tell they might have their own hidden agenda also?

One thing about the time is that it does not keep a secret too well. It does not lie either. Just give time enough times, and the truth will tell. As said earlier,

Pachouco is an extraordinary person with the heart of a lion. He is not a quitter. The urge to see the end of his starting point of an adventure has created in him a courageous spirit. He does not stagger forever when the going reaches his toughness. Pachouco, in his life, experienced plenty of devastating blows. The effect of them knocked him off his feet. Nevertheless, eventually, he bounced back.

A sickly and troubled child displays a mother's unconditional love. Of course, the baby of a family, no matter how old they are, could prove the unfairness of a mother toward the rest of her children. Pachouco and Faye Esther fell in the above examples. The pair has been through so many heartaches together, which is why she suffers from this incurable disease being too overprotective of her son.

Will Pachouco ever learn from his mistakes? Can Faye Esther answer the question? Can Serge Gerard, Loretta, and Barbara Ann take a shot at it? When dealing with Pachouco and his goodness, the "Supreme Being" is the only one familiar with the answer.

One night, a distressful Pachouco was talking to his brother. He asked Serge Gerard this question, "Am I set aside to be used by those I love?"

"I hate to think so, baby brother. Anyway, I got your back, Pachouco. From now on, I will be your mad dog, your bodyguard, watching over you. You deserve better in everything. Again, why do you think I matched you up with a classy woman like Loretta? She stands for the same thing we stand, honor, and integrity. She will be your wife before and behind you, a team player."

Somehow, Serge Gerard managed to bring a spontaneous smile to Pachouco's face that night.

For the life of her, his mother is unable to understand Serge Gerard and his family. He and Pachouco are close. He married Natacha, who is a Haitian American. They have three children, Eric, Danielle, and Jeffery. All three live with them. Two years ago, Serge Gerard and Natacha, his wife, was financially challenged. They were facing foreclosure in their home. Pachouco delivered them from their trouble.

Faye Esther tries to do the math to see what adds up or doesn't. She remembered Serge Gerard reaffirmed to her that Natacha had a hearing impediment. Therefore, she was not able to communicate on the telephone. Bizarre was the manner it appeared to Faye Esther. There was nothing wrong with her hands. She could have written a thank you note and dropped it in the mail to her brother-in-law. Serge Gerard should have put the kids on the phone to show their gratitude to their uncle. Unbelievable, the whole matter came to his mother. She brought these facts to her son's attention. However, Pachouco had an explanation for each one of them. Faye Esther, for sure, started to attain bad vibes as the situation unfolded. She guards her silence because his resentments have gotten the best out of her. On the other hand, she planted some seeds in his heart that will require his undivided attention.

"Have you talked to Ema lately, Pachouco?"

"Yes, Mother, two weeks ago I was over there. She was sad-looking. She had heard from Leslie six times around the Christmas season for the last nine years. She called her and Kirk to wish them a Merry Christmas and a Happy New Year. Mother, you know she is in New York. She left four months after I canceled the wedding. Why did you ask me that, mother?"

"They heard from Leslie yesterday Pachouco. You know Ema shared with me when she first called two babies who were crying in the background. Ema asked her whose babies, were they? I'm babysitting she answered and entered a goodbye.

Pachouco left the table with his head down and entered his bedroom. This is the first occasion in decades, a goodnight from Pachouco to his mother did not end their chat. His mother quickly realized she had made a mistake. She said, "Goodnight baby." She was deprived of any feedback. She decided to follow her intuition, which required her to leave him alone for the night. He was devastated by the news. Pachouco knew after the death of Minerva he was diagnosed sterile by his doctor. He was incapable of producing a child. He felt this was something that could drive Faye Esther crazy if she knew. Yet Pachouco yearned for the accuracy of the age of both children. He recollected his mother had dreamt about Leslie with twins the day after her raping spree. The toughness of the situation was no one could vow where she was in New York. Her address was unknown, and her phone number was unlisted.

Now the curious minds of Ema and Faye Esther automatically presumed the two babies were twins and they were Pachouco and Leslie's. However, at the phone call, Leslie worked as a babysitter at a nursery near her apartment.

Faye Esther would not mind investing a few dollars in finding out where Leslie lived. Upon learning the news, a spirit of being too confident had fallen on Faye Esther, and she declared, "They are my grandchildren!" The exclamatory remark she uttered to Ema, who also partook her view. Everyone seemed to forget that night Leslie had intercourse with Yvon and Pachouco. Let's put it in this fashion; she raped Pachouco consecutively six times.

Ema's reason to believe those twins are Pachouco's was because of his mother's dream. Could a dream serve as evidence to determine the paternity of the twins? If there is, for actual a set of twins.

Faye Esther and Ema experienced many sleepless nights behind this. They will not be satisfied until the mystery is solved. They think alike often; it is the power of having a few dollars. Without talking to each other, both decided to hire a private investigator. They are not dealing with a domestic issue but an international one. They encountered a problem. They needed someone to recommend a private investigator. Faye Esther and Ema were secretly working alone. Their attempt failed. Now they had no choice but to enlighten each other on their undercover operation. They formed an alliance that would not surprise Pachouco or Leslie. These children are well acquainted with Faye Esther and Ema's devices. The danger of it is they worked well together. They are a force to be reckoned with, and "Here comes trouble" is best to describe the pair.

Pachouco, in his thinking, concluded he was not going to worry. He would leave the worrying for Ema and his mother. He knew they would do anything in their power to unrest the truth. In his heart, he felt they had begun working already. Faye Esther and Ema went to dinner to map out their plans. One person crossed Faye Esther's spirit; it was Serge Gerard. Unbelievably, he was the same person that Ema was about to suggest. Both repeated at once, what about Serge Gerard? They gave each other a high five.

I will take care of that and leave it to me, " said Faye Esther. She called Serge Gerard for a recommendation of a private investigator. She warned him not to inform Pachouco about this subject.

A week later, Serge Gerard announced that he had found a good one. He charged five thousand dollars upfront. Two thousand more when he found

Leslie. Ema and Faye Esther went half on the money and sent it to Serge Gerard. One thing about him is that he is a sweet talker. Serge Gerard leaves everyone with the impression he has the world around his fingers. He can perform all things but fail. Serge Gerard used to mean well before he became financially challenged.

Dr. Valada could have saved Ema and Faye Esther some money and kept them from fooling around with Serge Gerard. She was a good friend of Leslie. The two met in New York eight years ago. For some reason, Leslie and Valada had never discussed their background or the people they knew on the Island. No one should ignore that we live in a strange world where anything is possible.

In the meantime, the telephone rang. Pachouco glanced at the clock. It was 1:30 AM. Who might that be, injected his mother this late?

A down and out Pachouco picked up the phone. Surprisingly, a sweet voice came through the line. Speaking slow motion, "can I speak to Pachouco? Please, this is Loretta?" If Faye Esther did not know any better, she would think God Himself was on the telephone with her son. The man acted as if he was going crazy.

Loretta added Pachouco calm down. “I called to say I love you. Do not tell Serge Gerard that I called, okay. I must say goodnight; I love you, Pachouco.”

He replied, “I love you too, Loretta. Do not go yet.”

She responded, “I do not understand what you said, write me and kiss me, bye.”

He threw her a kiss as she was next to him. Anew his sadness had left. He has something to talk to his mother about the whole week.

Many questions arose concerning the surprise phone call from his fiancée. Is it the truth she cannot understand his English?

On the phone, or she's just pretended not to? If so, what is her purpose? Was she a false pretender in the genesis of her love for him? She could have been, but not anymore. Her drama had become something which was designed to be. A foul spirit from her heart is on the move. This type of ghost can be uncontrollable.

Certainly, Pachouco is feeling her love. Lately, she has been doing things she has not done before. She writes him more often. She was accustomed to sending a one-page letter. Now, she is writing from three to five pages with limited French and the simplest English words to arrive at his comprehension, bi-weekly.

There is nothing two-faced about love. When one is in love or falling out of it, the result is the same. Both bring changes for the best or the worst. Either way, the test result is clear. One may choose to play ignorant, but the fact of life is: "Never played with love," and it should be a constant reminder to everyone.

Pachouco had no idea what to make out of her demand not to tell Serge Gerard about their correspondence. That night, Loretta acted like someone having an extramarital affair. Sneaky seemed to be the dangerous side of her phone call. This was last-minute resignation to hear a lover's voice at any cost. In a state such as this, carelessness becomes the factor of risky business. Anyway, Pachouco cherished the moment,

hoping to hear from her again in the same fashion. Evenly, Faye Esther was happy herself over Loretta's boldness. Calling Pachouco without his brother to interpret for them is a big step toward their confidence. He charged his mother not to mention it to Serge Gerard because they had to respect her wish. Why did Pachouco have to warn his mother? He should have known by now Faye Esther would force her own two cents in his business.

Wait a minute, she said. “Do you mean to tell me; your fiancée wants you to keep this on the down-low? All I'm going to say and be through with it. Pachouco wakes up.”

“Mother, please. Loretta asked me not to notify Serge Gerard since that may touch him severely. In other words, we try to avoid an animosity spirit among us. You know for yourself; how important he wants to be in our lives. Besides, I must obey her request."

"Do not make me laugh, son. Do you love Loretta? Do you heed her request? You can settle that by going to the American Embassy and applying for a visa. Son, your priority is to see about her. Surprise both with your visit. You are wasting too much time and money, Pachouco."

THE HOODWINKED DECEIVER

It has been six years now. Pachouco received not even a piece of paper from immigration.

His brother could not furnish the receipt of the registration fees nor the case number from the immigration office. He had not filed yet for Pachouco; if he did not, that would be another devastating blow for Pachouco. Serge Gerard could be very deceptive towards him.

The urge for him to see Loretta grew worse. Pachouco had his passport done, willing to follow his mother's advice. He went to the American Embassy and filed his documents. Fifteen days later, they approved Pachouco. They granted him a three-month visa. Money and who one knows is power. An enthusiast, Pachouco planned to surprise Serge Gerard and Loretta for Christmas. He broke the news to Faye Esther; she was excited for him. As a praying woman, she took the matter to God in prayer. Backward sometimes is the typical way most believers work. She should have invited God into the situation first. Then, I prayed before advising him to go after the visa.

He called the travel agent. They booked him a direct flight from Port-au-Prince to New York on December 22, at 11:05 am. He had a couple more months in front of him. This allowed him to get in contact with Dr. Valada. She was the same woman he came close to putting out of his house. He accused her of trying to discredit Serge Gerard to his mother.

One had better be careful how he treats an old friend in life. One never knows when or where he will need that old friend again.

Dr. Valada is an old friend of the family. She is also a beautiful woman. A vivacious spirit crowns her beauty. She had a bad crush on Pachouco. Nevertheless, she learned of the statement he had made. "He will not date nor marry another girl from the Island." The setting of his mentality was encircled by a firm conviction that was unchangeable. So, he thought the terrifying truth was his egotism still in the intensive care unit. He had forgiven Leslie. Seemly, he thought Leslie imputed her injurious behavior in all the rest of the girls. Dr. Valada was also familiar with his saying: "Remain celibate or marry an American girl from the south." Why the south, no one knows? Well, according to Serge Gerard, Loretta is from the south. Pachouco perceived he had found what he wanted. Pachouco killed her taste for him. Dr. Valada, until today, sees his belief as impertinent and hazardous toward the Haitian woman. It is not because of the choice of an American woman. However, the imputation of Leslie's nymphomaniac spirit was unfair to the womanhood of the Republic.

Dr. Valada agreed to pick him up secretly from Kennedy Airport at 6:00 pm. that Sunday. Pachouco could hardly wait to surprise Serge Gerard, especially Loretta. Valada does not know Loretta, but she can draft a book on Serge Gerard. The book would be the best seller, and Pachouco would have trouble believing the contempt of the novel. Nicely, Dr. Valada fixed her guest room. She had the intuition Pachouco may need a place to stay temporarily. Keep in mind her heart is far away from him. However, she remembers Faye Esther's goodness toward her when she was incapable of taking care of herself. She is living in New York now. Graciously, Faye Esther has a lot to do with it. She feels she owes his mother and her household. It has been a minute; Dr. Valada came to Haiti on vacation. Pachouco handed her eight thousand dollars for Serge Gerard on her way back to New York. She took upon herself to give him six thousand dollars instead. The verbal message that Pachouco entrusted her to transfer for him was, "Tell Serge Gerard he asked for six, and I sent him eight."

When receiving the money, he and Loretta said to Pachouco, "Thank you for everything."

"No problem," answered Pachouco. "You know, I'll do anything for my baby."

Dr. Valada banked the two thousand dollars. What was the purpose behind this unethical behavior of hers? Will the future bring to light an explanation? Yes, it will.

Life is full of surprises as well as opportunities. The power to make the best out of them all is an individual thing option.

Pachouco was through chatting with Dr. Valada on the phone, and the mail carrier stopped by and handed him three letters from Loretta. Wow! Nobody can tell him anything now. His mother held her gaze at his contentment. She injected, my goodness, son, I hope you will shout like this when God comes for you. He went and kissed his mother on the cheek. Pachouco took off his shirt as a sign of relaxation. He began to read the letters. By his side was his best friend, who happens to be an English dictionary. One of the letters started in this manner:

To the man I love.

December 22, four weeks away, "we will celebrate our eighth anniversary. I found myself expressing to Santa Claus as a five-year-old girl. I have a list of things I would like to receive. Pachouco, my love, you are on the top of the list. I quickly remembered that I petitioned for the same things every year. It never took place. My first request is to see you in New York. We will celebrate both our anniversary and Christmas on December 25. I wish we could tie the knot. A voice knocked me back to reality. It said, stop dreaming. You have at least two more years before you see Pachouco. I cannot wait that long. I want to be with him in my bed, caressing him tenderly. The voice replied to me, have patience, and remain faithful to Pachouco as he is to you. I need a favor from you, Pachouco. Promise me in two years, and we will make up for the lost time. I lasted this long, waiting for our physical contact. In the meantime, I find consolation in the readings of your sweet letters. To read them makes me feel I'm with you in the flesh. As crazy as it may sound, your letters, poems, voice, and photo facilitate me. I get a sweet orgasm. What more can a woman like me yearn for? Satisfied, yes, I am. Pachouco, you are a dangerous man. Look how far you are away from me; you still overpower me with your charm. Financially and sexually, you fulfill my needs. How can I forget you, my darling? You are always there for me. In my dream, your name is all I'm calling. I hooked on your love. I hate to let go. I never have enough. Every night all I have to do is think about you, and the nerves in my body act up for yours. From my toenails to the top of my head, here comes that gentle orgasm. I cry at times; slow down, take it easy. It shocks my body like high voltage electricity. I hate to see that feeling go away. But I wonder if my heart could sustain it if it lasts permanently. Boy, I pray daily for your "green card" to come. On December 22, I will call you myself without Serge Gerard to translate for us. This is our anniversary; we will enjoy it any way we can. Have patience with my French, and I will have patience with your English. Yes, we are going to communicate. I will not get off the phone until we are satisfied in the flesh. Kiss Mother Faye Esther for me. Love you, Cutie." Loretta will be overwhelmed and lost for words when Pachouco arrives at her doorstep. Her expression and her demeanor will tell a happy story.

Faye Esther usually teased Pachouco about the fact he could not keep water. He talked too much. In this category, his mother had misread him. Contrary, he is too private; he would not have experienced the back-to-back life deceptions if he was not. He is doing a respectable job so far. He is determined to surprise them. He purchased many gifts to tag along with him. He wanted to make their Christmas one remembered for the rest of their lives. He brought Loretta a diamond bracelet, some earrings, and a ring. Natacha, his sister-in-law, will also have some diamonds. Pachouco decided not to carry that much cash on him. Why is that? He has at least seventy-five thousand dollars in a New York City's Bank. The money is in Serge Gerard's name. If his mother had not discouraged him, he would have more cash than that in New York.

Good news from Serge Gerard, he called Ema and Faye Esther. He let them know the investigator had located Leslie and her children. They live in Boston, and that is not in his jurisdiction. He does not have an address yet. He will charge us another five thousand dollars to cover blood work from the hospital and their birthday. He will go after the name of those babies' father she gave to the hospital for an extra thousand.

Please wait a minute Serge Gerard, and my daughter is supposed to be in New York. Is he sure she is in Boston?

Serge Gerard is an expert thinker and a compulsive liar most of the time. He said to Ema, “let me borrow your imagination just for a second. Let's say you were Leslie, and you did not want to be bothered with your family. Then you know you have two children the family wants. Moreover, you ascertain they may come looking for you and pursue you until they find you. Would you tell them the State you are living in? Or would you give them a fake one just to throw them off and dispatch them on a "wild goose chase?" Leslie could be the one who promoted this New York thing herself to confuse everyone's interest.”

“That is interesting, declares Ema; where do we go from here?”

In the absence of all reluctance, she said to Faye Esther, “Let us go for it.” Faye Esther had always admired and respected Serge Gerard. However, she refused to overlook how he conducted the three-way phone call between him, Loretta, and her, which diminished her admiration and respect for him.

“When is the money supposed to be in your possession, asked? Faye Esther? In a friendly manner he responded, “My mother's as soon as possible, trust me.”

“We will send it to you tomorrow,” uttered Ema. Faye Esther replied, “Why can't we wait and give it to Pachouco to carry to him.”

"What do you mean, Mother Faye Esther," advanced Serge Gerard?

Common sense had slapped Faye Esther in her mouth, and then she remembered she was about to reveal Pachouco's secret trip. To answer Serge Gerard, she started to speak an unknown tongue. The first two words that came out of her mouth sounded like the language a three-month-old baby would speak. One can read between the lines and see Ema's face concerning Faye Esther's mistake. What the devil was she talking about?

She answered Serge Gerard saying, "I mean, Pachouco is going downtown next week; we will let him send it."

Prudently Serge Gerard injected, "Mother, we cannot do that. I thought you two didn't want Pachouco to have anything to do with this."

Faye Esther was bugging out big time, and she came up with another excuse; she said, "Son, your mother does not know what she is talking about today. We will send it to you tomorrow."

Serge Gerard wished them goodnight and left.

"Ema joked: Faye Esther, next time, how about you keep your mouth shut when you do not know what to say."

They laughed hysterically and ended the conversation. Ema looked at her, saying, "Girl, what was the matter with you? You almost messed up the boy's plan."

"You got that right. We would be rich too if I blabbed his secret out."

Ema replied, "How is that?"

Faye Esther said, "Well, this is the first time the world would see a man having a baby. You hear me, Ema, Pachouco would have a child."

Not too long ago, Faye Esther accused Pachouco of not being able to hold water because he blabbed too much. She turned around and did likewise. He is his mother's son. Pachouco's mother felt that she would stop him from taking the trip if she could. She has a fuzzy feeling, but she was the one who planted the seed in his spirit. She felt guilty for advising him to go. Regardless, this will be the most incredible move he ever made. He shied away from talking to her. He spoke to Dr. Valada again, and she will pick him up tomorrow.

Late that night, Serge Gerard and Loretta were on the phone with him. The conversation was not exciting as usual. Pachouco's intellect began to wander. He questioned the coldness of the atmosphere. His brother had agreed Loretta was sad. "She hated to see the presence of tomorrow. Another year without you seemed unfair to her. I begged her, on your behalf, to have patience. You will soon be here; two years are nothing but seven hundred and thirty days, or one hundred and four weeks, or twenty-four months." Serge Gerard, said Pachouco, those two years are less than sixteen hours. Baby Brother entered Serge Gerard; "I do not comprehend how you came up with this computation, but it is fine by me."

Tell Loretta to hang tight; her honey will see her soon.

His mother also deserved a lot of credit. She went and kneeled by his bed and lectured him. Her last-minute advice was very brief but powerful. An uncomfortable feeling had built a mansion around her heart. Grievous was the condition of her soul. These sentiments were not the effect that she would miss him too much. Loneliness, no doubt about it, will dwell in that mansion of hers. However, it was not the major issue of her worries at this point. She acted as a mother preparing her son for the test of a lifetime. She was doing her last minute interrogation with a voice filled with wisdom. Directly, she asked him, "Pachouco, do you have a plan B?"

"What do you mean, Mother Dear?"

He lay down on his back, his two hands under his head, crossed his legs together, and was looking toward the ceiling. His mother is still kneeling by the side of his bed. Her elbows rested on the mattress, her hands under her chin. She shared with him her beautiful smile that used to drive men crazy back in the day. For Pachouco, it had another meaning. Readiness had become her strength as the toughness of a rattlesnake. Pachouco also understood beyond the frightening smile; a woman called Faye Esther never neglected to bring him to the light. Proudly, he enjoyed having her as a mother.

His mother declared to him, “Plan A that you would visit Serge Gerard, especially Loretta, in New York City. Valada will meet you and take you to your brother's house. You expect everybody to be surprised by your presence. Plan B will be thirsty for your understanding. Let us insinuate for a minute. You arrived there, and your expectation is contrary to what you have been led to believe. For example, Loretta does not resemble your grandma or me. Your brother is different from what he showed you on the phone. Let us insinuate your brother again in a wary manner, spent all your money. What would be next for you?”

Responsively, Pachouco smiles.

“No! Do not smile, tell me what you would do,” insisted Faye Esther?

“Mother Dear, which is too deceptive, negative, unthinkable, and unbelievable to imagine. Besides, Mother, my airline ticket is a round trip. I know where home is. I'm sure of how to come back where I came from. However, my brother is far from being a deceiver.”

“She handed him his passport and his ticket, expressing this thought you are ready to take this venture.”

“Mother, you mean to tell me, you have confiscated my passport and ticket.”

She entered; You had better believe it. If you have flunked the test, you would not be able to recuperate the ashes.”

Faye Esther waited for him to go to sleep. She prayed and anointed him with fresh oil. Off her knees, she went to the living room. She called Dr. Valada concerning the possibility of a cell phone in his possession. Dr. Valada assured Faye Esther that was her thinking also. She even had an extra room for him just in case he needed it. Dr. Valáda thanked her for calling. Before his mother hung up the phone, she reentered hello. Dr. Valada replied, yes, mother; in a soft voice, she uttered, Doctor, take care of my son if his going gets rough. Consider it done, Mother.

POSSIBILITY

No one should ignore that we live in a strange world where anything is possible. Faye Esther stepped into her bedroom, crying, and praying for God to be with him. She and Ema carried him to the airport. He boarded the airplane in Port-au-Prince. He was so scared. It was his first time flying. Pachouco's patience got shorter; if there were anything he could do to make the airplane go faster, he would. He began to daydream. He visualized himself marrying Loretta. His brother Serge Gerard was his best man, and Dr. Valada was the maid of honor. He also saw a bitter argument between him and his brother over Loretta. He left his brother's house. In addition, he killed some time with a friend of Dr. Valada until she came for him. He had an uncompromising vision in the air. The jet had finally touched down. An excited Pachouco arrived in the Big Apple. He went straight to customs to check out. He went downstairs; who did he see? "Lord have mercy," it was the beautiful and charming Dr. Valada. She wore black jeans, a red blouse, and a black shoe mingled with red. She looked like an angel from the sky. "Pachouco boasted you are so fine you can make a preacher sin."

She answered, "You are not bad yourself. New York City here comes trouble. Boy, with your good-looking self-somebody, is going to snatch you up."

He put his luggage in the trunk of a black-trimmed in red Jaguar XJ6. In his mind, he entered that Dr. Valada was always a classy woman. She drove him to her house first because it was near the airport. The crush she had on him was still there but undercover. Pachouco toured her beautiful home. She invited him to come and spend a few days with her. It was friendly and basic, nothing more. He barely listened to her. He wanted to see Loretta. Dr. Valada gave him a new cell phone to use. On their way to Serge Gerard's house, she said to him, "this is New York; before going to a friend's house, you need to call first. Otherwise, they might not be home when you arrive there. Instead of you surprising them, they may flip on you. She dialed Serge Gerard's phone number, and Natacha answered the phone. This is Dr. Valada; I will be over in one hour. I have a surprise for you."

"Tell me what it is," Dr. Valada.

"No, it is a secret, Natacha. I will see you in a few."

"Pachouco could not believe his ears. He asked her who answered the phone?"

"Your sister-in-law, Natacha," replied Dr. Valada. "I thought she had a hearing problem," replied Pachouco.

"Who told you that garbage? There is only one thing wrong with Natacha."
"What is that?" Asked Pachouco?

"You might not be able to deal with the answer."

Pachouco uttered, "Try me, Dr. Valada."

She should have never married your sorry brother. "You will see for yourself. Your brother needs help. He is an abusive man."

Pachouco became speechless. His freedom of speech seemed to be in solitary confinement. Dr. Valada thought he was upset over the statement she had entered. She knew he was a family-oriented man. Therefore, it displeased him when others criticized a member of his family. However, she was mistaken. He tried to figure out why his brother led him to believe Natacha was deaf. What possessed Serge Gerard to lie to him? Dr. Valada decided to break the silence because she glared at him, and he was in deep concentration.

She asked him, "Are you okay? Are you not mad at me, are you? No, I'm fine. Is my brother a

jealous man?"

"Is he?" Repeated Dr. Valada, "Yes sir, until it's sickening. We are five minutes away. They lived four doors away from my Pastor."

"That is great, Dr. Valada."

"We've arrived Pachouco." She knocked at the door, Natacha said, who is it? "This is Valada and your brother-in-law Pachouco."

Natacha opened the door in a hurry and hugged him tightly.

She acted as if she was a good friend of his. Valada declared to Natacha, “Have you met him in the past?”

She replied, in the pictures with his cute self.

He said, “Where is my brother?”

He is in Atlantic City. He left this morning. He will be back in two days.

Dr. Valada suggested she call Serge Gerard and announce him the great surprise. However, she did not have the phone number where he was. Dr. Valada added, is it okay for Pachouco to stay here until Serge Gerard comes back. Sure, why not? He is home. On that note, Dr. Valada said goodnight. She told Pachouco to call if he needed her.

She called Faye Esther concerning Pachouco’s triumphant arrival at “The World University,” which is New York State. She was scooping his mother on how Natacha received him as a close friend instead of a sister-in-law. Serge Gerard was not home.

His mother, with unspeakable joy, thanked Dr. Valada. She also instructed her to keep her posted on his well-being.

Natacha showed Pachouco great hospitality. She was treating him like a king. Pachouco could not comprehend her first-class treatment toward him. The most confusing part to Pachouco, surprisingly, was her face. There was nothing showing. She acted as if his visitation was expected because it was long overdue. She gave him the phone to inform his mother he had reached his destination. He explained to Faye Esther that Natacha erased from his faculty the idea of being a stranger in their house. Unbelievable and agreeable was the description of the manner she welcomed him. Ideally, he considered everything thus far. His mother said to him, "she wished Natacha could speak on the phone." She wanted to address her gratitude. Uneasy he became. He preferred to get off the phone than to lie to his mother. He avoided telling her that Natacha does speak on the telephone. To meet Pachouco is to meet his mother. Both are deep thinkers. If Pachouco told Faye Esther that Serge Gerard lied about something this important, she might never speak to him again. Pachouco took a break from bragging about Natacha with his mother. He ended the report by saying goodnight to his mother. He did something that impressed Natacha. He asked her whether he could use the telephone again. She genteelly replied, of course, "anything for you."

He called his mother back and said to her, "Mother dear, guess what? You are, and you will always be, the first woman in my life. Words cannot express how much I love you, Mother. Hey, guess what again? I love you."

Teary, was the condition of Natacha's eyes? Instantly, she became prouder of him. She wished that every man who has a mother alive could have been a witness to such a grateful address.

"Natacha, why are you crying?" He asked.

She replied, "I had not seen that type of love in this house for a long time. I only read about love in love letters. By your presence here for the last forty-five minutes, I find myself living passion again. Love was appearing dead to me in every aspect. Nowadays, everyone's love seems to have waxed cold. The talk between you and your mother rekindled my love."

"I understand, my sister. That could be a touchy subject."

She made a petition to Pachouco to be excused for a minute.

Now, the desire to see Loretta had become undeniable. He twisted and turned on the couch.

Nevertheless, according to his patience, the end of his rope was what was left. As strange as it may look, the number he had for Loretta was the same as Natacha's. She gave it to him earlier to share with his mother as a backup. He decided to inquire about Loretta. He was dying to see her reaction when she came in and saw him sitting down.

Pachouco was impressed with Natacha's style in speaking French. Her grammar is top-notch. She expresses herself as a grammarian. Her voice sounds like Loretta's.

He was dissatisfied with their condition of living. He quickly understood his brother was not honest.

Finally, Natacha returned where he was. She was through taking her shower. She smelled good. Beautiful, yes Indeed, she was. Pachouco's impatience called for her attention.

Voluntarily, she announced that Pachouco, Loretta is also out of town. She spent Christmas with her parents. "When I was in my bedroom, I did try to reach her. My effort was unsuccessful her parents had changed their number. However, her sister was going to get in touch with her. You see, we are living in a busy state where everybody minds their own business. An old friend can live next to you for the last five years, but you never knew it. Their schedule may not be your schedule."

Pachouco inserted; "I miss my baby. Do you know I left Haiti with a brand-new romantic embracement, just for my baby?"

With a slight attitude, Natacha said to him, "Do you mind calling me Natacha instead of my sister?"

"No, I do not. Natacha, how long have you and Loretta known each other?"

"I have known her all my life. She is truly a dear friend of mine."

"Were you born Natacha in Haiti or New York?"

"I'm a Caribbean girl. It was a figure of speech when I said I had known her all my life. She told me a lot concerning you."

"Sister, I mean, please forgive me. Natacha, what did she tell you? By the way, Natacha, your telephone is ringing," said Pachouco.

"Oh, Darling, I'm sorry, oh Pachouco, you have good ears. I will be right back."

She played with her phone, and he thought she dialed her own number by mistake. He realized she was not. She talked loudly he believed she was chatting with Loretta. Natacha intended for him to hear the conversation. He was eavesdropping, and he enjoyed everything he listened to this far. He grabbed a sheet of paper and wrote those words. When Natacha picked up the phone, she said, "Girl, your man is here. Who do you think, Pachouco?"

"Loretta, I am not lying. He's been here a good four hours."

Natacha called herself speaking terribly slow so that he could understand every word. Apparently, he did. Pachouco was still trying to be nosy as the conversation continued. He is in the living room with his cute self. "Lord have mercy," The man looks good, Loretta. You do not want to talk to him now. You are on your way. Okay, Loretta, I know you have waited almost seven years for him. That does not mean you have to destroy him in one night. Girl, you are crazy. You do not want him to see your face for three nights straight. What do you plan to do? Loretta, come on, are you serious? You are serious, as a severe heart attack which kills. Excuse me, well, I will tell him. Nevertheless, Loretta, Pachouco may not go for that. Oh, Pachouco told you he would let you do whatever you desire when you first meet him. Anyway, Loretta, you will need to save some for the honeymoon. It will be 2:00 am when you arrive here. I need to take the light out from the room he is sleeping. Girl, why are you doing this? Oh, I see. You desire to know if he loves you because you look like his mother or would he love you also in the dark. Loretta let's get off the phone. I'm going to tell him. In case he disagrees, I will let you know. See you, and I will leave the door open for you.

"Pachouco, your fiancée is crazy. I wish you could comprehend what she was telling me."

"I comprehend every single answer you gave her. She asked you to remove the light from the room I'm sleeping. For three nights straight, she will be there with me, but I will not be allowed to see her face. To ensure I do not love her because she resembles my mother."

"Good, you understand English very well. Are you ready to stand by your words, Pachouco?"

"Why not? I gave her my word."

"Do not cheat Pachouco. She will be upset. Please take my word for it."

“I heard you, Natacha.”

“Take your shower Pachouco but let me show you which Knob is for hot water, and which one is for the cold. Natacha mixed the water asked him to feel it to see if it was warm enough. In the same token, she added, remove the light from your bedroom and give it to me after your shower. A naïve Pachouco did accordingly. Natacha stood behind the door, telling him not to worry. Loretta will lock the door on her way out. “Natacha wished him a fabulous Night.”

THE ENTICING DEVIL

In the dark, there Pachouco was. Shaky like a cat, trembling like a neuropathy emotionally challenged, yes, he was. He began to listen, knocking at his door, which was an illusion. So far, loneliness was his date for the night. All his nerves were activated and ready to be used. The ambition to touch by Loretta developed in his heart a zealous spirit. I got to have her instantly, and it had become his motto.

A familiar voice unexpectedly rehearsed in his attentive ears, just relax, Pachouco. Allow me the privilege to be your servant for the night, your caretaker. Grant my fingers the opportunity to be your massager. As your Massa 'gist, I promise to make your nerves glad, evenly resurrecting the ones that were dead without your knowledge. Give me the free course sexually over your total being. Then, I'm sure you assign me the right to drawback in a perfect manner, the limb that has mutilated. Suffer me, Pachouco, to caress your head. I pledge again to bring chills on both your body and soul. I still can make it happen in ninety-degree weather. It does not matter how cold it is outside, zero below, and I'm confident I'm willing and able to overheat you with my sensuality. Until Natacha thinks there is an arsonist in this room. Pachouco, when making love to someone you love, love becomes so patient, so musical, and as admirable as fine art. Let my soft hands be your towel and permit my body to be your blanket on this wintry night. Let my body exercise your body together; they can work it out. Our natural insulation has no other purpose but to keep us warm.

Pachouco prohibited entering a word due to an arrangement made previously. He kept the pledge. Loretta left the room feeling heaven was at her fingertips, "the devil is a liar." The expenditure of the night with Pachouco was the biggest mistake Loretta ever made. It was too costly and risky; her love budget could not afford it. She left the room craving more for his body. The remembrance of when was the last time, she had felt this good had evaporated from her mind because it had been a long time, too long to remember. The statement did not mean she was deprived of sex. No, she does have sex often.

Nevertheless, it has been a while since she had the pleasure of enjoying the art of lovemaking. Anyone can engage in sexual activity, but it takes genuine love to activate lovemaking. To have sex just to have it is to take your partner for granted. To have intercourse to prove to your mate how much you love your soul mate is to explain unspeakably the heartfelt condition when in each other arms, and this is the beauty of the scenery. Loretta was singing a song now; "I want more, I want more."

Moreover, she hopes for the memory to sustain her for a minute after everything predestinate becomes chaotic. She has two more nights to gratify

Pachouco, and the covenant will arrive at its expiration date. There are important questions that need answers. Whatever happened to his belief not to have consensual sex before marriage? Was he backsliding? Did Leslie create a monster when she raped him six times? Pachouco's thinking of faith is out of the equation. He has two more days to celebrate Loretta.

Leslie taught him something; otherwise, he would have fought Loretta until his last breath. Anyway, he gave Loretta her gift.

On the next morning, Natacha woke up happy. He handed her the gift. Natacha was impressed by the beauty of it. Pachouco, she said, "I feel like I've known you a long time. For me to enjoy these expensive gifts, please do not tell your brother you gave them to me. He is your brother, but there is a lot to learn from him."

"Is that right?"

"Yes, sir, you are not accustomed to his ways. Time will tell."

"Surely it will, quicker than you think, Pachouco."

"Your honey woke me up this morning. I wondered, what in the world had you done to that girl last night or this morning, whatever? My goodness, you drove Loretta crazy. She wanted me to inform you she will be here tonight at 10:00 pm. Will that be a problem, handsome?"

"Oh, not at all. I'm leaving soon, so I plan to make every opportunity worthwhile, Natacha."

"Will you be able to hang, brother-in-law?"

"Me," Natacha, rephrase the question? "Will Loretta be able to hang out? I'm in good shape," bragged Pachouco.

A laughing Natacha answered "I'm convinced you are. Loretta is pleased."

"You and she are close for real," entered Pachouco.

Natacha changed the conversation by injecting,

"Pachouco, a boy is living in one of the apartments, and he favors you a great deal. He might be eleven or twelve; he stays to himself."

"Dr. Valada's pastor lived here once upon a time, and she tried to get your brother in church. She is a great woman of God. If there were a church that I would join, it would be hers. She has a powerful testimony. Her testimony has drawn many people to accept God. She is a well-put-together preacher."

"I might have the opportunity to meet that woman of God through Dr. Valada before going back to Haiti. Eric, Danielle, and Jeffery, where are they?"

Another lifetime's story, we will postpone this conversation," answered Natacha.

Pachouco, in speaking with Natacha, finds out that his brother is a liar. For example, the apartment he lives in is a rental property, but Pachouco sent him money to avoid foreclosure on his house. Pachouco insinuated the only certainty from his brother is Loretta because she was with him last night. Pachouco, most of the time, regarded information as gossip. The sad part he ignored the signs of danger around him. He received numerous clues from his mother, Dr. Valada, and even Natacha. He chose to bypass every one of them. His belief had not changed, "Let me see it for myself," a motto that could result in shame and deception.

The second night approached too fast. She had reminded Pachouco of the "rendez-vous." It was time for him to wish Natacha a good night. She appeared to be in the best interest of their relationship. Natacha coached him well, unbelievably of the things that displeased Loretta. He was so grateful to his teacher. At exactly 10:00 pm, as an obedient child, Pachouco did accordingly. Another romantic night in the dark, but its pleasure furnished its light. Through the sense of feeling and touching, both knew even in the darkest room where each other's part of the body was situated. In this capacity, Pachouco and Loretta enacted as they graduated in physiognomy. To give credit where credit is due, they made beautiful love. He received the latest message tonight as he had been discharged from the muteness. He could express himself to comment on the task. From the top of his head, after a long talk with himself, he wrote these words in a dark room.

"In a murky cell, there I was, a roommate with solitude. Captive by an oath, I must keep a perfect attitude. Minutes and hours have gone by; still, I have my beatitude.

Waiting for my delivery to come, come to set me free. Love, where are you? Hurrying up helps me be carefree.

To lay next to me, in a particular mood, is to set me free.

Darling, what took you so long to expedite my need? It is so hard to understand that I am a man in need. Loneliness is killing me, but will you lead with you by my side?

Who has the key to my release, not another woman? Under the sun, you are my superadd, my tender woman.

Loretta, you are my woman, the one that brings me on my knees.

I must say goodbye to my solitude; by me, you are now. Squeeze me with a lovely attitude and play on me now.

Set my need free with new kisses. Let us make a baby now."

Loretta arrived in his room with a readiness to begin the art. Pachouco, an overnight lovemaking activist, did not have any objection. He offered her the free hand to conduct this business as she saw fit. She would take charge anyway. She always enjoyed being in control. In the back of his mind, he still had a big question mark concerning Loretta's inability to speak French. He had a good reason for adopting this belief; something fishy is definitely wrong with this picture. In their moment of folly and experiment, she used too many French words and sentimental phrases. Was making love that good to make someone fluent on the spot in a complex language such as French?

Anyone could agree the magical feelings of lovemaking could make one speak some surprising words. Even the speaker has trouble defining the meaning of his own words. The same feelings could bring madness if one partner, during intercourse, instead of calling the other partner's name as an expression to symbolize the goodness and the sweetness of these incredible feelings. However, the expressionist manages to call somebody else's name that is not even near the action physically but thoughtfully indeed. When this occurs, ravenously, it kills all sexual moods. Anxiously, it leaves the victim with a broken heart. The offender tries to dig him or herself out of the mess by accusing the victim of having a temporary hearing problem. The more the offender enters a defense, the more they lie like Satan.

A fight in the middle of intercourse can result in death, especially when one of the couples blabbed out too many lies. Just express your true feelings, and the rest of the confusion will vanish away.

As usual, Pachouco's sister-in-law woke full of energy for the last three days. She fed him well. As a newcomer, he wanted to visit 42nd Street in Manhattan. Back on the Island, he had heard of many crazy things there. Honestly, he was waiting on his brother to take him there. However, Natacha insisted on taking him, and she prevailed. Besides, he enjoyed Natacha's company. Pachouco ranks her as the best sister-in-law in the world. He cannot wait to congratulate his brother on the choice of having her as a wife. Therefore, they went, they walked around and shopped a little bit. He snuck a quarter to watch the performance of a female stripper. He was ashamed to look at something like that in the presence of Natacha. She was the one who encouraged him to view it. She led him to believe that was a request from Loretta as a preview. She planned to be his private stripper tonight to commemorate the final three nights before revealing herself to him physically in the light. They spent the full day out. He was exhausted, but he did not intend to break up the final hours of this agreement. He has a duty to perform, and his tiresome body allowed him a couple of hours of sleep. The next hour will mark the last debut of Loretta hiding her face. Nature had placed a rush on the hour; there it was. This time, Loretta avoids knocking on the door to announce her arrival. Before he realized it, the bed was a part of her. They took pleasure in caressing each other. Pachouco could hardly concentrate. All he

thought about was seeing Faye Esther's twin Loretta in an illuminated place tomorrow Wednesday. Well, he did pull the night off. Strangely,
Loretta, in her enjoyment, spoke only English. In a rage, she became not in rage enough to stop her fun. She was complaining against Serge Gerard, complimenting Pachouco at the same instance. Again, all her comment made in English was to keep him from knowing about what she was fussing about. In that little bit of English, he had discovered she called Serge Gerard's name on numerous occasions. Because of his lack of English, he did not want to jump the gun. He started to pay more attention to her phrases. It seemed to him she said, "Serge Gerard, why are you not as good as Pachouco?"

"What did you say, Loretta?"

Without breaking her move, she whispered slowly in his ears, "When I see Serge Gerard, I am going to ask him why your brother Pachouco is so great?"

"Tell him, baby, tell him," replied Pachouco.

Every good moment must end. Loretta charged him, never voluntarily mentioning to his brother that they spent some romantic times at his house. She left for her house, and he heard her say, "good night to Natacha."

She replied, "You too," Loretta, lock the door behind you.

BAD NEWS

Fascinating Serge Gerard, in the meantime, called Haiti that night to speak to Pachouco. He needed some money. Faye Esther answered out of panic and said, "Serge Gerard, is something wrong?"

"Why would you have said that mother? You know I speak to Pachouco weekly, is he home?"

"Serge Gerard, what is the matter? You are killing me; Pachouco has been at your house since Sunday. He went to visit you and Loretta. Have you been home lately?"

A shocked silence invaded Serge Gerard's end of the phone.

Speechless he became. Faye Esther steadily uttered, "Are you there? Are you okay, Son?"

"Yes, Mother, I'm here. I spoke to my wife Sunday, Monday, and Tuesday, she briefed me not a word that Pachouco was home."

Faye Esther intervened with an alibi that "Natacha had promised to allow this to be a surprise to you and Loretta."

Even in his shocked state, Serge Gerard is still a dangerous man. He will take this opportunity his way out. If he does not, he will be in deep trouble. Faye Esther perceives he is whining.

She questions him about the behavior. “Is there a problem, Serge?”

“Affirmatively” he answered, “But I do not want to bother you with my shameful situation. Right now, I deserve to die. I’m not worthy of calling you Mother Faye Esther nor Pachouco, my brother. I am also a disgrace to the whole family and my wife and children.”

Faye Esther was getting worried about Serge Gerard. Her heart was not at ease. She insisted on knowing the reason his countenance stood out so low. He let out to her; the purpose of his phone call was not necessary to chat with Pachouco. It was for him to confide in her the obstacles that destroyed his life. Besides death, he had no knowledge where or who to turn t, and his last statement emotionally brought tears to her eyes. Attentively, Faye Esther geared up to listen to him, but he decided to talk to her later because he would show his brother the city. Faye Esther also advised him to speak to Pachouco before doing anything stupid.

Again, Serge Gerard is a compulsive liar. He was testing the ground earlier. Eventually, he would chat with Faye Esther.

Serge Gerard was addicted to gambling drugs, and he was an alcoholic. He spoke to Faye Esther earlier from a casino. Serge Gerard tried to recuperate

Pachouco's money, but Serge Gerard lost it all a long time ago. He did not expect Pachouco to be in New York. Besides, Serge Gerard had never filed any papers to bring Pachouco to the United States. How will he break the news to his baby brother, who is so proud of him?

Serge Gerard was a hardhearted man. He coached his baby brother to sell most of his assets, which he did. He sent the money to Serge Gerard to open a savings account in a New York bank. At least seventy-five thousand dollars, he blew every dime of Pachouco's money. Faye Esther and Ema sent him seven thousand dollars to pay an investigator to find Leslie. He was in the casino, gambled with their money, and lost it. How cold can he be? Serge Gerard may have respect for Pachouco, Faye Esther, and Ema. However, he sure does not have any respect for their money.

Natacha went outside a minute. She charged Pachouco to answer the phone if it rang. She stepped out, and it rang. Serge Gerard was on the line. He appeared happy to Pachouco. "Hey, little brother, welcome home. I'm glad you are here. When are you going back?"

"I have seventeen more days left, big brother; I can hardly wait to see you."

"I will be home Friday; we have a lot of ground to cover. The first person I will introduce you to is your lovely Loretta."

"Natacha had already beat you to the punch, man. I spent the last three nights with Loretta. For some reason, she asked me not to tell you."

"I do not understand," applied, Serge Gerard. "You see Loretta in person, Pachouco. Are you sure? I thought you did not know how to lie."

"Serge Gerard, I'm not lying. We made passionate love three nights in a row. She told Natacha she would meet me first in the dark those nights, and Friday, she would allow me to see her face-to-face. Man, she tried to kill your baby brother with good lovemaking. I thank your big brother for giving her to me. The way she makes me feel I would not mind marrying her before I leave. She told me, Serge Gerard, that I'm the best thing ever happened to her. It had been a long time since she felt this good. Loretta prayed last night for a baby from me. Hello, hello, hello, are you there, big Brother?"

"I'm here, man, entered Serge Gerard. Whoever you slept with; she was not Loretta."

He smashed the phone in Pachouco's ears. At that point, Pachouco was no longer any good.

Pachouco would have been deceived either way. After learning from Faye Esther that Pachouco was at his house, Serge Gerard automatically conceived in his heart a mischievous alibi to cover his track. Serge Gerard has arrived to deliver a non-existence Loretta to Pachouco.

Serge Gerard expected his wife to answer the phone that night when he called. He would have told her to start crying inconsolably to reach Pachouco's attention if she did. Then, she would let Pachouco know that it was Serge Gerard; on the phone, he said Loretta had just died in a plane crash near the town of Society Hill in South Carolina. Loretta was on her way to visit her parents.

Pachouco answered the phone, and Serge Gerard lost his train of thoughts. Quite a blessing, there is any way Pachouco could have survived this untruthful tragedy.

Anyway, Pachouco felt so cheap and so confused. He figured his brother was in a bitter mood. He hung the phone up without a goodbye. Pachouco enthused to find some clarity on the last statement made by Serge Gerard, "Whoever you slept with, she was not Loretta." The only person that could enlighten him was Natacha. He hated to accept the fact that he had deceived once more. Life deception followed him wherever he went. The people Pachouco loved always played tricks with his intelligence. He hoped Serge Gerard was kidding. Otherwise, his sister-in-law had a lot of explaining to do. Concerning opinions, Serge Gerard will be the author of this confusion at the end of the day. He will be liable for all consequential damages caused by his deceitfulness. Speaking of deceit, while Pachouco and Natacha were on 42nd Street in Manhattan, Danielle, who had the key to the house, went into

Pachouco's belongings, and she stole all her uncle's money, even her father's gifts took a walk from the house. It was another low blow in store for the naïve Pachouco. As terrible as it might sound, Pachouco will soon be destitute and temporarily homeless because his integrity and character will not agree with this lifestyle.

Pachouco is as good as pure gold. He would give the last penny from his savings account to his family and anyone else in need.

Nevertheless, it is expressly prohibited to steal from him or to play with his intelligence, which would make him angry. Careful is the word of wisdom Pachouco should cherish right now. He is remarkably close to being slandered; why is he well appreciated as an honorable and understandable family-oriented person. Any defamatory remarks from Serge Gerard against him could affect him significantly. Natacha returned home. She had in her possession some green, red, and yellow light bulbs. She put them in the sockets, and pretty the living room became. She was still celebrating Christmas. Natacha glanced at Pachouco and added he had made her season greeting more joyful than ever. He was flattered by her compliment. He announced to her that he had spoken to Serge Gerard. He rehearsed for her the whole conversation between him and his brother. A guilty Natacha suddenly yelled, "I'm a dead woman." Pachouco naively did not comprehend the reason behind the statement. He said to her; he was so confused when Serge Gerard schooled him; the woman he was enthusiastic with the last three nights was not Loretta.

"Natacha, I'm begging you, please tell me what is going on? With all the love I give for my entire life, deceitfulness always seems to be my reward. I have done my best to sow good seeds in the ground of humankind to express my love and my gratitude. Pain, sorrow, and unhappiness are all I ever reap. Please, sister-in-law, set my wandering spirit free. I have a great need to educate on the truth. Whatsoever is done has long gone. However, if it is terrible, we can prevent it from repeating itself shortly. I do not understand the way Serge Gerard ended our conversation. It appeared to me; he was vexed about something I said in rapport to Loretta. Is there anything fishy between Serge Gerard and Loretta that I should be enlightened about? Please, Natacha, for honesty's sake, tell me the truth," "And nothing but the truth." "The fact, to me, has a deeper meaning than the ordinary people would embrace. Truth covers a more extensive territory in my life. It means freedom, happiness, joy, liberty, love, peace, and understanding. There is a great relief in being honest, even though the consequences are costly. Natacha, please do the right thing."

Pachouco went fishing for information that could be too tough to deal with. If there was a moment, he greatly needed his mother, and it would be now. Faye Esther helped him find his way out of many deceptions. The outcome of them dragged him as a patient to a local hospital. Anyway, he relied on Faye Esther too much. The hour is here for him to stand up and fight his own life battle.

Natacha, uncomfortably, gazed at Pachouco to beg him to pardon. Her words departed from her lips. It seemed they were on strike against her thinking. Mute was the mode her mouth was. Her eyes were steadfastly on Pachouco in readiness to shed tears. As the old saying goes, "Confession is good for the soul," its application was miles away from her thinking. She constructed a last minute of nerves, and her lips gave an avenue to her words. Then, she began these shameful testimonies:

"Pachouco, deep inside, I feel I deserve to be hated by you. Not only that, but I also deserve to burn in hell. Your brother Serge Gerard is a jerk. He is an abusive man. He would do anything to support his gambling, alcoholism, and his drug addiction, even it meant selling you out Pachouco."

"Natacha, please. You are lying to my brother. Let us drop this conversation because my ears have had enough already. I would appreciate it if we concentrated on Loretta's story. You try to defame Serge Gerard Casimir in my presence, the only brother that I love and trust. My brother has a profound respect for you. He worships the ground you walk on. He is your ladder to step on whenever you find yourself in the low valley. Yes, Serge Gerard is your life jacket when your boat sinks in the middle of the ocean. He is your parachute when a plane crashes.

He loves you, and I love Loretta with unconditional love. Do not do this to me. Do not criticize him in this fashion. He is someone you need to be proud of; he is a great husband. He is candid, and he holds fast to his character."

An enraged Natacha has heard enough from her brother-in-law, who does not obtain any idea of what he is speaking. Aggressively she declared, "Shut your mouth Pachouco." The truth is knocking at your brain. Show it some hospitality and listen. Serge Gerard loves me, but he does not know how to treat me. He abuses me constantly physically and mentally, especially when I refuse to be a part of his scams." "Pachouco: THERE IS NO LORETTA." "I am sorry. Serge Gerard had threatened to leave me if I declined his proposition to play Loretta. I agreed as a big idiot, pressured by his punching, slapping, and other physical abuse against my will. The finances you sent for Loretta's modeling school was wasted as soon as he received it. The malicious expenditures are drugs, alcohol, and most gambling. These are, in fact, his problems. He is also over jealous."

Pachouco's physical strength left his knees, maybe his whole body. There he was on the floor. Natacha led him to a chair, and he sat down. The only part of his being that seemed to work correctly was his eyes. He was weeping as if one who lost a loving mother. Natacha was not in any condition to continue this testimonial. She inquired from him if he wanted her to stop or not. She left the choice totally up to him.

At his request, he nodded his head to say, “Let us get this over with.”

“I started to enjoy being on the phone with you, Pachouco. Your letters and your poems had captivated my heart. They made me feel like a woman again. Because of these feelings, my heart, soul, and total being were in your control. In love, I found myself with you. Compared to Serge Gerard, you were a different breed. The worse was he took a few pictures of Mother Faye Esther when she was younger. She was in her early thirties. He sent them to you as Loretta to entice you more. He knew how much you loved your mother. He promised to kill me if I ever picked up the phone and spoke to you as Natacha. I am sure he is going to hurt me now. He is a violent man, Pachouco. Take this conversation as my last rites, consider yourself a priest or a preacher, and pray to God, "my soul to keep." The way you expressed yourself to me triggered my sexual desire to be with you, one way or another. He blew away every dime you entrusted him to deposit at the bank. He spent Christmas at the casino because a woman named Ema and your mother wired Serge Gerard at least seven thousand dollars to hire an investigator to find a woman named Leslie and her children. Here is the receipt from the transfer. He cashed it and bragged about how stupid those women were. Unbelievably, he has not given me a penny for me. He told you we were about to lose our home, and you sent him the money for that. He lied to you, Pachouco. We are renters. We have never owned anything. Pachouco, I deceived you the last three nights. The right to hate me is at your mercy. I would do it again if I had a choice. You fulfilled my wants just as you said you would in the writings of your letters. Pachouco, I must skip town before Serge Gerard arrives tomorrow. My life is in danger for being your Loretta and for spilling my gusts to you. I love you, Pachouco; I am sorry, I love you. The only two people I can blame are my husband and me. We should have known never to play with one's feelings in love."

Pachouco was on the verge of fainting. Natacha was looking for the phone to call for the ambulance. However, she decided to use chilly water on his face instead. Pachouco entered strong words.

"Natacha, I would not say I liked the day I met you. You are a disease to me. You made me sin against my brother and against my belief to satisfy your whoredom spirit. Do not ever refer to me as your brother-in-law. You and Serge Gerard are a disgrace to the universe. Furthermore, you blame Serge Gerard for your behavior in pretending you were Loretta. However, he was nowhere around when you tricked me into sleeping with you. You are a low-class traitor. You faked your citizenship to exploit my love. For the last seven years, you were not in a hurry to stop playing me. I thank God for a praying mother who reasoned with me to visit New York. She knew you two were crooks. I was too blind to allow her to show me your true colors. You have crossed the bar of death. You have brought an embarrassment to lovemaking. Unclean, yes, you are. To think of the moments, we had in a room illuminated with deception and delusion. Your deceptive self has contaminated everything in this house. It also destroyed a family structure. How long did you plan to play Loretta? Forever, I guess."

Pachouco, are you finished yelling at me? I am so sorry, and I did you wrong. There is one fact that remains; I am in love with you. Serge Gerard did not intend to bring you to this country. When my passion got stronger for you, I got a passport. Here it is. I decided to visit you secretly in Haiti for three days to explain the situation. You beat me to the punch, and this is my ticket. I was supposed to be there next week, Thursday, January the 2nd. I canceled the reservation Sunday night after Dr. Valada dropped you off."

"Natacha, I'm sorry, I hate you and your husband. I am going to ask Dr. Valada to come to pick me up. It is too filthy for me to spend another night here. I was hoping you could do me a favor, do not tell Serge Gerard; you said to me about the money."

"Pachouco, I will be gone by the time Serge Gerard gets here."

Pachouco walked into the room to find Dr. Valada's number in his little book where he kept his funds. He found the book, but his money was missing. He said to Natacha someone had stolen my belongings. She came into the room and saw where an inside thief had broken into his suitcase. They took everything that appeared to be valuable to him. They cleaned him out. He blessed they left his passport. Natacha acknowledged that it was the act of her daughter. Pachouco repacked his stuff and was ready to go.

Right after Serge Gerard spoke to his brother, he was on his way home. He and Natacha had numerous fights about Pachouco. She used to make him jealous. He knew automatically she tricked Pachouco into sleeping with her. Serge Gerard intended to end her life. Pachouco decisively was going outside to call Dr. Valada. He met Serge Gerard, who greeted him with a cold hello. He jumped on Natacha and knocked her down on the floor. Serge Gerard punched her several times. She steadily yelled for help.

Pachouco, who had never experienced such violence, a man beating on a woman, lost it. He grabbed his oldest brother from her. He told him "If he hit her one more time, you and I would fight. You know Serge Gerard, our father, Fernand Andre, did not raise us to fight a woman or slap her. He taught us to bring her flowers and never scandalize or embarrass her in public, only a punk beat on his wife or girlfriend. Natacha got off the floor; he kicked her again, and Pachouco pushed him and said, Serge Gerard, you only worry about yourself. I heard so many wonderful things about you back in the day. I just met you five minutes ago, and you have flushed all the respect I have for you in the toilette. You wasted my mother's money and mine. You set your wife up to do me evil. The two of you got caught in your evilness. Seventy-five thousand dollars plus is a lot of money. The saddest moment in a thief's life is when he starts to steal his stuff blindly. To steal from your brother is to steal from yourself. To waste your money gambling, shooting drugs, and drinking alcohol is to steal from yourself, your family, and the people who care for you. Look, Serge Gerard, your daughter Danielle broke into my luggage and pinched every penny I have, including valuable items. Where does she get that from? You need to enter a rehabilitation center and be the man you used to be when I came up. You do not owe me any money, big brother. However, you owe me the right to do right. Sign yourself into a rehab Serge Gerard. That much you do owe my mother and me."

Pachouco walked toward the restroom, and a tyrannical Serge Gerard struck at his wife again. This time, she was bleeding, and Pachouco fought his brother to remove him from her. In the meantime, somebody called the police. When they arrived, they questioned Natacha about her bleeding? She told them Serge Gerard spilled some water on the floor, and she slid and fell. "They called us and said there was domestic violence in progress here." She replied, "No, Officer, we are fine." They left the apartment. Serge Gerard took Pachouco's luggage, set it at the door, and put him out in the cold, saying, "Go back to the person's house that brought you here."

It was the coldest night of December. He had just arrived in New York from Haiti. He still had some calories left to fight the cold. Pachouco did not have a dime in his pocket to purchase a piece of candy. Pachouco thought he was getting sick outside because smoke seemed to come out whenever he opened his mouth. “Welcome to New York Pachouco; you have not seen anything yet.” He finally reached Dr. Valada. It was too cold for him to even express himself clearly to her. She understood Serge Gerard put him out on the street. She was one hour and thirty minutes from him. She called her pastor, who lived four doors down and asked her to shelter Pachouco until she got there. The preacher was glad to do so because she was acquainted with the feeling of being homeless. Dr. Valada rang him back and told him to walk over there. He knocked at the door, and a sweet voice answered, “Who is it?” He uttered “Dr. Valada's friend.” She opened the door, and he walked into the house. Goodness, who did Pachouco see?

THE LAST LAUGH

Life is something else; it never pays to treat anybody terribly. Again, it is a blessing to have praying parents. Faye Esther directed Dr. Valada to purchase a phone for him because, in her spirit, she felt he would need one. Everything that occurs in life has a reasonable explanation. Why do people struggle? Do they hold on to things that do not mean them any good? The lousy treatment received from spouses, friends, and family members could begin a brand-new blessing for the victims. The question remained, who did Pachouco see when he entered the house?

Pastor Leslie, his ex-fiancée, the daughter of Ema and Kirk, is whom he saw. Pachouco was dismayed to hear she was a woman of God now. When he saw her in the house, he held his chest and begged for some water. He had trouble digesting it, standing up before Leslie. He said to her, "Am I dreaming?"

"No," answered Leslie, "You are wide awake. You did tell me that" "God is a God of a second chance and a God of favor. He has found favor in me, and He called to preach His word."

Suddenly, her two children ran to the living room unexpectedly. My goodness cried Pachouco. Those two children looked so much like him and his mother. One of the boys asked his mother, “Is he, my father?” Leslie inquired of the boy “What made him think so?” He replied to her, “I look just like him.” Besides, Leslie prophesied to them that they would meet their father early this morning soon. She told the boy she would discuss it later. He insisted on an answer right away. Leslie looked at Pachouco and smiled to say the child was like him. She finally convinced the boy to wait.

Wow! What’s going on here? Pachouco’s doctor secretly did diagnose him sterile. Could he be the father of the boys? How can this be? Well, time again will tell, and God has the last word in any given situation. How can this be again? God knows.

Isn’t that something these children lived almost next door to their uncle and had no idea? Well, this is New York. She named both after his father. One’s name was Andre, and the other one was Fernand. Pachouco questioned Leslie why she did not tell Fernand the truth because they are his sons. Leslie quickly reminded Pachouco with a sense of humor it was still cold outside to be careful. It will not be healthy for him to be put out twice on the coldest night of December. She told him the only way she would discuss the children with him as if he agreed to do a paternity test. He responded she ascertained they belonged to him, and he did too. She made it clear again a paternity test was necessary. She had a reason for that. In the meantime, she wanted him to keep it on the downlow. Whenever he decided to test, she would pick him up. He advised her to make him an appointment to see the doctor in a hurry. He forgot that all his money was stolen. He had to pay for the test; she had already assigned this task to him. She was curious to find out what transpired between them over there. She did not perceive that Serge Gerard was his brother. Pachouco shared with Leslie what had taken place how he was used and abused by his sister-in-law and his brother. Leslie cried; she charged him not to mention this to his mother. If he did, Faye Esther would worry herself to death. She prayed with him and apologized to him again. He uttered that was ten years ago. She realized the situation at hand could be fatal for him. He played cool, but Leslie understood his pride. On the inside, he experienced pain now. He might even take a trip to the hospital behind this mess.

Pastor Leslie was still in love with him. Since the incident, God healed her from being a nymphomaniac. Therefore, she refrained from sexual activities. Her story helped many people that suffered from this sickness. The night was far advanced. Dr. Valada had a last-minute call to the operating room. One of her patients needed emergency surgery. She telephoned Leslie to explain the inconvenience.
Leslie assured her all was well with Pachouco. She will arrange for him to rest. She did not tell Valada

what her plan was. Leslie got off the phone, called a local hotel, and reserved a room for one night not too far from her home. Pachouco fell to sleep on the couch, and Leslie woke him up to carry him to the hotel.

A move he had trouble comprehending. He questioned Leslie's decision; he considered it a waste of money. She replied to his criticism, saying "She would not flirt with the devil. Besides, to let him spend a night at her house tempt Satan. Leslie told Pachouco that principals helped her to arrive at this judgment." He accused her of being afraid of his company. He promised not to let her lower her guard. On that note, she notified him she was confident that nothing would ever betide among them if he and she were to sleep naked in the room. However, why tempt the flesh voluntarily. She was not concerned with Society and what one may say to the fact a single man spent the night in her house. She took conscience of her intense feelings for him, which had never disappeared. She concluded the right idea was to place him in a hotel. She drove him there, and he expressed his understanding to her. Leslie and the boys checked Pachouco in at the Inn. She had to do it because he was lacking in English.

The man at the Inn's front desk named Claude recognized Pastor Leslie and her children. Claude shouted when he saw Pachouco, "My God, Fernand, and Andre look like their father. Sir continued the clerk; you cannot deny them even if you wanted to." Pachouco thanked the clerk for the compliment. She accompanied him in the room. Fernand seemed more outspoken than Andre is. On the spot, he connected with Pachouco. He said to his mother, “Can I stay here tonight with my daddy?” Pachouco's emotions kicked in; tears were dropping all over the place.

Moreover, poor little Fernand sadly said to Pachouco, “Did I offend you? I am sorry I did not mean to, and nevertheless, what did I do to make you cry? If you do not want me to spend the night with you, I will understand.”

“Yes, I want you to, but it is up to your mother. You know I did not receive a Christmas gift from anyone this year. Your mother could give me the greatest gift of a lifetime tonight.”

“What might that be,” said Andre?

Pachouco answered “To let you two special angels spend the night with me. Pastor Leslie follow your heart and see if I deserve a second chance also?”

“No boys, we need to go home. Say goodnight to your father, sorry I mean to Pachouco. They did, and they started to cry.”

On the way home, a spirit of doing right convicted Pastor Leslie of selfishness and inconsiderateness for depriving the children of the right to be around their father and their grandparents.

Fernand continued to bug her about Pachouco. She got home, picked out their pajamas, and drove back to the Inn where Pachouco abided for the night.

Fernand and Andre knocked on the door. “Daddy, open the door, the good Lord had touched and changed mother's heart, and she let us come back.” An exciting and thankful Pachouco joyfully ran to the door widely he opened it. Pachouco kneeled in the middle of the doorway. Graciously and gloriously, he embraced them. Pastor Leslie went inside the room while the three were on a hugging and crying spree. They tried to fill up the ten years void among them. She realized his pillow was wet because of grievous pain. He was authoring a poem, she glared at it, and she read these words:

THURSDAY NIGHT,

Here I'm behind the door, outside of the house.

Here I am behind the door, freezing like a mouse.

The voices of my children are all I want to hear.

My heart cracks as a drain; I do not mean to be here.

I cannot stop crying, but love makes that happen.

I must knock to get in; whatever happens, happen.

The law could control our future, requesting a lousy weekend.

So beautiful creatures, loving you will never have an end.

Fernand and Andre, I will love you in or outside the house.

The boys kissed their mother goodnight. Pastor Leslie requested Pachouco to step outside for a minute while a good cartoon show from the TV occupied Fernand and Andre's interest. He did step out. Pastor Leslie reminded him of her proposition to receive a paternity test from him. Dr. Valada will be more than happy to do so for him and the boys. A leeway spirit fell on Pachouco; he thought he was home free. She perceived a reluctant attitude; then, she clarified that he would not see the boys anymore until he performed the duty. He agreed. She charged Pachouco not to tell his mother anything yet. She would inform him when the time was right. She preferred it to remain a secret from everyone in Haiti. He agreed again, and she left from his presence.

He gave God thanks for turning negative situations into positive ones. He was speaking of the old Leslie who raped him six consecutive times. The old Leslie, she handcuffed him on the bed's post. He was with his legs wide opened bound with rope on his back. That old Leslie hired Yvon to be her sex toy at eleven or so. In other words, the old Leslie was a child molester; she was bad to the bone. A few days before their wedding, with the aid of Yvon, he proved to Pachouco she was unfitted to be his wife. Yvon was also tired of being used and abused by her. There was not a bad word in the dictionary to describe Leslie. She was too bad for herself. Amid all those negativities, two handsome boys were born. The new Pastor Leslie, marvelous and fabulous, is some of the words to describe her. When Pachouco came into her presence before he could question her reformation, the Holy Ghost slapped him on his criticizing mouth with a verse from the book of life King James version: (2nd COR 5:17) THEREFORE IF ANY MAN IS IN CHRIST, HE IS A NEW CREATURE: OLD THINGS ARE PASSED AWAY; BEHOLD, ALL THINGS ARE BECOME NEW.

He got so thirsty afterward, thinking he was dreaming, and begged Leslie for some water to cool his tongue. Pachouco fell right in line like a good little boy, starting to call her Pastor Leslie like everybody else. He became a reformer also because Pachouco did not believe in a woman preacher. As far as he was concerned, there was no room on the pulpit for a woman pastor. The pulpit never intended to entertain such disgrace. The slap from the Holy Ghost instantly changed his stupid and chauvinistic ideas. She did not try to convince him or to argue the fact with him of her redeeming qualities. The God that repaired her did. He thanked God also for everybody that contributed to this night, especially Serge Gerard, Natacha, and Dr. Valada. A night that started very unfair turned out to be the fairest one of his lives.

Pachouco's telephone was bombarded with messages from his sister-in-law Natacha. Serge Gerard and his guilty conscience went up and down the streets searching for his little brother. He asked Natacha to stay home in case Pachouco or Dr. Valada called.

Serge Gerard left him this message “If you come back, Pachouco, I promise to sign myself into a rehabilitation center. I take total blame for everything that has transpired. Little brother, I am a jerk and a loser. You passionately believe I owe you the right to do the right thing. I am paying you now by saying I love you, Pachouco. You have reached way inside of me and pulled out the better man that I could and will be. I will pay you by cutting loose some of my friends who do not mean me any good. In addition, I will be the husband Natacha dreamed of, and I will never put my hands on her again except to caress and to behold her.”

After listening to his messages, Pachouco dialed Serge Gerard and said, "big brother, I'm doing fine; I know you did not mean to put me out. I'm still expecting you to pay me by doing the right thing. See you, brother; I will come to visit you in rehab. I have a surprise for you and the whole family.”

Serge Gerard was about to ask him where he was? Nevertheless, Pachouco meant to hang the phone up to express how serious he was. He also spoke to Natacha and shared with her that “Yesterday was gone and today is a brand-new day, a day to forgive and forget. Let us start as a family again, my sister. Your baby brother is fine and happy. Soon Serge Gerard, and you will discover why. Natacha, my sister, do me a favor, go and kiss his bald head for me. I will talk to you later."

Dr. Valada came to get him early that morning. She inquired of her Pastor where Pachouco was. Pastor Leslie explained that he had lodged in a hotel not too far from here. Dr. Valada was confused; she wondered What triggered her Pastor's decision to place him in an inn just for a few hours? She questioned her Pastor; what did he do? Nothing, responded her preacher. Pachouco is a very respectful man.

"Yes, he is," replied Dr. Valada. "Fernand and Andre, where are they?"

With a classy smile, Pastor Leslie answered, They are with their father, I mean with Pachouco."

"Please wait a minute, let me sit down to get this fact right," injected Dr. Valada. "Pastor, have you known Pachouco before?"

"Known him," here comes another pretty site; he is the man I testified about, which encouraged me to be who I'm today."

Lost for words, Dr. Valada admired her Pastor's bluishness as she retold the story to her. The manner Fernand acted and ascertained that he was his father. Unbelievable was his intuition. Dr.

Valada became more appreciative of her Pastor. Dr. Valada agreed with her the paternity test is necessary. She will perform it for him tomorrow. Pastor Leslie shared with Dr. Valada that Pachouco may not have any money to pay for the test.

"Yes, he does have $2,000.00 in my hand. However, he does not have any idea about it. When I visited Haiti, he gave me $8,000.00 to hand to his oldest brother Serge Gerard. I figured something was wrong. I did my best to warn him of his no good and sorry brother. He did not hear me out. He shut me up before I began. Pachouco was so angry; if Mother Faye Esther were not around that day, he would show me the door.

"Yes, that is him, always choosing to see things for himself, added Pastor Leslie."

Continued Dr. Valada; "I heard a voice telling me to give Serge Gerard $6,000.00 and kept the $2,000.00 because Pachouco will need it someday."

"Pastor, I used to have a crush on him."

"When did the crush expire?" Asked Pastor Leslie.

Dr. Valada died laughing and said, "As we speak, but I have a request when you two get married I want to be the maid of honor."

"Come on, woman of God," uttered Pastor Leslie, "Is that a prophecy?"

"Well, Pachouco's principal and now belief will require him to repurpose in his heart you as his wife."

"We'll see Dr. Valada. In the meantime, keep this away from Faye Esther? I might surprise her with those boys when Pachouco goes back."

"I plan to go back in two weeks; Yvon is getting married to Michelle Casimir and I plan to attend. Lord, what is going on? Is this a test to see if I'm fully delivered? Lord, I'm your humble servant," declared Pastor Leslie.

"You have been around Yvon and Michelle too, Pastor? This is truly a small world."

They were major victims of my craziness. It is time for me to face everyone again, "Just as Jacob faced Esau."

"Pastor, I am confident you can do it. We will surprise everybody, and they will automatically understand that the old Leslie died ten years ago with God on your side."

Dr. Valada enjoyed surprising people. She gave Pachouco his $2,000.00. He counted his blessing from the sky. He understood God has a way of providing for his children. He and the boys underwent the paternity test, and the result was 99.99 %. Pachouco is indeed the father of Fernand and Andre. Pachouco, Dr. Valada, and the boys arrive at church on Sunday morning. The congregation looked at him and perceived he was their father. Furthermore, Pastor Leslie, two Sundays ago, prophesied she saw the father of her boys come to church and sit in the second row and propose marriage to her. Pachouco went in sat on the second row. Then, Dr. Valada remembered her Pastor's prophesy. “So far, she is right.”

Pachouco enjoyed the service. Fernand was on the drums and Andre was on the keyboard. They played to make a statement our dad was watching us. Suddenly, Pachouco experienced a visitation from the dead Minerva, who advised him to marry her sister because she is fit now to be his wife. Minerva told him; “Did I not promise to visit you when it was time to get a wife? Ask my sister now while I’m around.” Pachouco trusted Minerva as his guardian angel and listened to her voice. Pastor Leslie introduced him to the congregation. He stepped out, stood in front of the Church, and asked Leslie to marry him, and that was the end of the order of service. The people glorified God for the wonderful prophecies He has given to their Pastor. It happens just the way she saw it two Sundays ago. Pachouco was still in Haiti when God spoke to her. Pastor Leslie preached a sermon that morning titled: “Don’t settle for anything. Wait, God has a husband or a wife in progress for you.” She opened the doors of the Church, and Natacha came and gave her life to God. Pachouco and Dr. Valada were so proud of her. They congratulated her. Natacha and Dr. Valada said to Pachouco, “they did not know how they failed to recognize that the boys were Casimir." Natacha said, "she could hardly wait to tell Serge Gerard about his nephews."

Pachouco still abided with Dr. Valada. His mother called to remind him of Yvon and Michelle's wedding. He was supposed to be the best man. He had forgotten, and he asked his mother to tell them he would be in Haiti the day before. He would not miss it for anything in the world. Faye Esther charged him not to stand her and Ema up for the wedding because they are the wedding's directresses. In closing, his mother wanted him to ask Serge Gerard had he heard anything new.

Like what mother, answered Pachouco?

"Son, did I ever teach you how to tend to your business and leave mine alone? Comically she added, yes, I did. I remember now."

"I love you, and Mother, recollect this day. I will get you back."

"I love you too, son, and kiss Loretta for me. Pachouco, I dreamed Saturday night you asked Leslie to marry you. The strange thing was she was a real preacher. You and Leslie had two sons."

"Mother dear, let us say good evening, okay. Do not forget to say your prayers, Son."

God strongly uses Faye Esther. Divine forces have already informed her in her dream of Pachouco and Pastor Leslie.

They applied for the marriage license and received it the next day. They planned to get married the following Sunday, right after service. Dr. Valada was the maid of honor, and Pastor Leslie insisted that Serge Gerard be the best man. She talked to him, and he was flattered. Leslie asked a pastor friend named Rosa, the Pastor of Union Baptist Church, to perform the wedding ceremony. She did a splendid job. It was a very private affair. Then Pastor Rosa preached a sermon titled: What is for you? The devil in hell cannot steal it. For the subtopic: Treat your soul mate right. She preached as if it was a private message to Serge Gerard. The message convicted him, and Serge Gerard gave his life to God. Natacha passed out. However, Pachouco still offered him a cold shoulder which he understood why. Pachouco congratulated his oldest brother for giving his life back to God.

Pastor Leslie is an American citizen by naturalization. She filed for her husband the next day. Pachouco, Pastor, and the boys planned to leave for Haiti Friday. Fernand and Andre desired to meet Ema and Faye Esther. Pachouco did not want to spoil the wedding. They decided to be guests in a nearby hotel until Saturday after the ceremony. Serge Gerard and Natacha wanted to surprise Pachouco so that they would leave Thursday along with Dr. Valada. Everyone has been educated not to brief the presence of Pastor Leslie in Haiti. There was a problem the spirit commanded Pastor Leslie to attend the wedding. She shared great feelings with her husband, who agreed with the spirit. Pastor Rosa will oversee

Pastor Leslie's Church while she is gone. Pachouco was convicted for the manner he treated his brother. He stopped by Thursday with the family to tell Serge Gerard they were bound for Haiti tomorrow. He was not home. At this time, Serge Gerard and Natacha had already reached Port-au-Prince, Haiti. Pachouco and his family arrived at the airport early in the morning and flew to Port-au-Prince. He dropped them at the hotel and checked on his mother. He headed to rehearsal. He acted as he was alone. He even slept at home.

Pachouco will never deny a few things. It is hard for him to fool his mother and Ema. They are too powerful in the Lord. After she welcomed him back home, his mother told him, "Son, there was no such person as Loretta, was there? I knew the pictures your brother had sent you as Loretta were my pictures when I was younger. I played the role of a dummy to encourage you to go to New York so you could find out for yourself. You would not have believed me if I had told you the truth. Divinely, I was informed regardless that something good would indeed come out of this incredible deception. However, it turned out to be a blessing. I'm not sure what it is yet, but you reap a blessing from that deceitful love affair and breach of trust. We will finish talking tomorrow after the wedding Pachouco."

Many people were at the wedding the Church was packed. Serge Gerard and his wife Natacha snuck inside the Church. One sat in the middle on the right and the other in the back on the left side. Nobody has an opinion on how Leslie, the children, and the rest of the family would make their presence known, surprisingly.

Faye Esther and Ema dressed alike, white blouse, long skirt, red top and white hat, red and white shoes. These two together could steal the show.

Michelle was a beautiful bride; she made that yellow dress talk. That was how pretty she looked. Yvon was already a handsome young man who wore a black tuxedo, blended with a yellow shirt and a yellow pair of shoes, and Pachouco, a man who can make any woman sin, dressed like Yvon. For the rest of the wedding party, the groom's men wore yellow silk long sleeve shirts with black pants and yellow and black shoes. The bride house cleaners had plain long black dresses, yellow hats, and shoes as if they were contestants in a beauty pageant. It was one hundred and ten degrees outside. Everybody, at this point, was nervous. The ushers started to seat the bride's parents. Yvon did not have anybody for the usher to sit.

Satan was on the ball that day. He was determined to stop the wedding one way or another. Faye Esther and Ema fell behind on time. The wedding was supposed to begin at 2:00 pm. It was already 3:00 pm. What was the hold-up? The preacher and the maid of honor were late. The wedding directresses concluded, letting the party enter, expecting the officiator to arrive before they were through. Pachouco and Yvon walked in; they stood in front of the pulpit. The lights went out; it seemed one of the fuses had blown out. Something like that required the presence of an electrician. Faye Esther, a quick thinker, announced is there was an electrician in the congregation? A voice from the middle of the Church responded, “Yes, Mother Faye Esther, there is one.” Who stood up? Serge Gerard; Pachouco, and his mother were shocked to the point of having a heart attack? He stood up, kissed her, and went toward Pachouco. He whispered in his ears, saying, "I'm your oldest brother, do not make me take off my belt and spank your behind. I come to support the family, man. The right to do right is a part of me now, Pachouco.”

He fixed the light. While he proceeded to his seat, an elderly woman fainted. Many people encircled her. Call an ambulance, somebody cried out, from the back echoed a voice “Not necessarily I'm a nurse, excuse me, please. Natacha kissed Faye Esther in passing” and uttered, “I'm Natacha, Serge Gerard's wife.” She made the woman comfortable. In returning to her seat, she waived at Pachouco, and he was surprised to see her too. “You try to kill me tonight,” said Pachouco's mother. The maid of honor needed to be replaced. Pachouco advised his mother to use that woman in black. When she looked at the woman in black, it was Dr. Valada. His mother's eyes filled with joy, and the tears demonstrated that. It was too hot outside. They asked Michelle, the beautiful bride, to wait in the vestibule. In the meantime, words came to Ema they had carried the officiator Reverend Jeffery Eric Stevenson, the Pastor of the Church, to the hospital. Yvon and Michelle began to lose hope.

The makeup on her face was ripped apart by tears mingled with sweat.

This day was about to become a nightmare for Yvon and Michelle. Suddenly, Pachouco took the floor and said, how many believe “God is a way maker?”

“How many of you believe God always has a ram in the bush?” The Church was fired up emotionally by the pumping up of Pachouco. The people were in the mood to worship. One of Michelle's uncles was an old deacon. His name was Alfonso Stanley. He struck with a song, “The struggle is not yours; it's the Lord.” Pachouco intervened once more and petitioned his mother and Mother Ema to let the bride enter the sanctuary. Nya Enalee, the flower carrier, sowed the flowers, and Michelle walked behind her. It appeared to be the longest walk she had ever taken.

Moreover, her spirit wandered. Uncertain of what to believe and what to expect, she arrived at the tip of the pulpit. No ordained minister was waiting there. All eyes set were on Pachouco, and he took a deep breath, looking joyfully at Yvon and Michelle.

He asked his Mother Faye Esther and Mother Ema to come to stand near them. He said, “Yvon and Michelle, if you two do not have a problem with it, will you grant me the permission of calling on an ordained Pastor and her children from this congregation to come and perform the wedding ceremony for us? She has one of the most influential churches in New York. Siblings let us welcome: he glared at Faye Esther and Ema, he uttered Mothers Dear I'm sorry, let us welcome once again my wife and my children Pastor Leslie Casimir, Fernand, and Andre. Leslie stood up advanced the Church. Kirk, Ema, and Faye Esther were stunned. The three fainted and were carried out to receive treatment by Natacha. Their overwhelmed condition ended. They walked back into the Church to finish assisting with the ceremony. As Ema and Faye Esther sat amazingly in their seat, Fernand and Andre ran and fell in their arms." The boys are innocent, as they could be said to Grandma Ema and Grandma Faye Esther, "We love you. We have been waiting a long time to meet our number one grandma." The two grandmas were no good for the night. They were too excited about those words from their grandsons' mouths.

Grandchildren are familiar with the road that leads to grandparents' sensitive hearts.

Leslie took her time performing the wedding. After Yvon and Michelle exchanged the vows and the

rings, they were pronounced husband and wife the wedding turned into a church service. They received the green light from the chair of the deacon board Jeje to preach to the people. Pastor Leslie preached a sermon titled: We are all guilty." She came from the Gospel according to John, the 8th chapter, verses 1-11. She opened the door of the Church for discipleship. Yvon and Michelle rededicated their lives to Jesus. At the reception, Pachouco and Leslie's family were confused; wondering had they seen each other secretly? Did he go to New York to marry her? They had made a pact not to discuss their reunion. Both Ema and Faye Esther thanked Serge Gerard for finding Leslie. He was frank in his answer. He made it clear that he did not have anything to do with it. Anyway, they chose not to believe Serge Gerard. It was a great wedding, excellent service, great reception, great reunion, and according to Yvon and Michelle great honeymoon all night long. It was too much excitement for one evening. Pastor Leslie intervened with a marvelous idea suitable for the family Fernand and Andre will spend a night with Pachouco's mother and the next night with her father and mother, so forth and so on. Their parents were happy to see them, but those boys had rain on their parade.

Pastor Leslie spent the first night with Faye Esther. Fernand and Andre retired for the night. Faye Esther confronted her son for hiding things from her.

He replied to his mother, can I ask you a question Mother Dear? “Did or did you not teach me how to tend to my own business?”

“You got me back, Pachouco.”

The Pastor of the Church, Jeffrey Eric Stevenson, heard about how God manifested himself through Pastor Leslie. He gave Pastor Leslie a courtesy phone call from the hospital thanking her for filling in for him. Therefore, he asked her whether she could preach for him in the morning. She put him on hold to have a conference with Pachouco. He believed to God is the glory; she needs to bring the word for him. She agreed to do the service for the Pastor. They will televise and broadcast the service on the radio. Faye Esther and Ema became busy calling everybody they could think of, inviting them to Church, including the newlywed. The Church packed to its capacity. Most of the people in the congregation knew Pachouco and the old Leslie. They came just to be nosy. They were the invitees of their wedding previously called off by Pachouco some ten years ago. At that time, everyone agreed she was unfitted to be a wife. Some come to see what kind of crazy pills she is on. She has the nerve to come back into the community, calling herself a preacher.

Others insinuate she is beyond repentance. She considers a joke in the eyes of many except her family members. All her past lovers, most of them come to see if it is true. Leslie, the nymphomaniac, is a gospel preacher. The devotional part of the service was uplifting. It seemed that Jesus himself was the praise team leader. The seconds and the minutes were flying. The time for her to deliver her message had arrived. Her husband introduces her as a new daughter of the community. Those of you that know her, please stand. He pointed at his wife. Most of the congregation stands. I hate to disappoint anyone. You do not have any idea who she is. Her message will introduce her much better than I will. I'm confident after her sermon, you will quickly identify that you have mistaken her identification. She is far from being the old Leslie. She is indeed the daughter of God, my wife, my love forever, the mother of my beautiful two children, Fernand, and Andre. At her request, the choir sang graciously, "Lord I want to go," a song written by her husband, Pachouco. The words of the song go like this:

Lord, I want to go, go, go. Go, where you lead me.

Guide my hands, guide my feet, and use me.

Lord, I want to go, go, go. Go, where you lead me.

Guide my hand, guide my feet, where you lead me, I follow.

Lord, I want to go, go, go. Go, where you lead me.

Guide my hands, guide my feet, and guide my tongue,

Prepare my heart and use me.

Use me, Jesus, Jesus uses me, I need joy, Jesus uses me.

Understanding, Jesus uses me, I need peace my God, use me.

Guide my hand, my God, use me,

Guide my hands, guide my feet, and guide my tongue,

Prepare my heart and use me. Use me, my God.

The choir did wonderfully and beautifully with the song. Some of the people, enthusiastically, were ready for a word from above. Some do not care one way or another. She took her text from the Gospel of John. She uses chapter 4 Verses 4-39 for a thought: AMONG THE MEN, THERE IS A REAL MAN.

She started her message by saying, my brothers and sisters, there is a jungle out there. From the pulpit to the congregation, there is a jungle out there. The Church has forgotten that her purpose was to divinize the world but not judge it. God is the righteous judge that will listen to everyone's case someday with fairness. We are all a wretch undone. The believers that make up the Church as God's children have a missed conception of God's amazing grace. We are deceiving ourselves to believe we are the only one going to heaven, and everybody else in their way is going to hell. We are the only one befitting for the Kingdom's business because we are free from sin. Many have misunderstood the Gospel and its requirements because of this concept, division is what we conceive, and powerless is what we become. "Together we stand, divided we fall." Never intend to be a lip service just to be heard. It is a heartfelt reminder for God's people to stand together to fight Satan and his demons. The Gospel never intends to bring confusion. The Church has forgotten again that it is her purpose to make disciples, not steal disciples through mischievous behavior. Some of our preaching, prayers, and prophecies have driven away potential disciples to the devil's camp. How can this be? Whenever we turn the pulpit into a boxing arena, it's a coward's way to knock out other believers. Even in our prayers, the sick-minded ones sustain their power-hungry attitude. Instead of praying to God, they are tearing up somebody else. Many of us have destroyed the spiritual growth of many by removing them from our churches through malicious prophecies.

Hypocrisies should not be the number one ingredient or the last in fellowshipping with each other. It should have excluded as well as backbiting. I told you there is a jungle out there. When you enter God's family, He equips you with a compassionate heart to refrain from being judgmental. He imputes the agape love in our hearts, and we have no other choice but to be crazy for the well-being of humanity. He places endurance in us so we can run this race patiently without fainting along the way. He gives us listening ears to hear his precious voice instead of gossip. He loves speaking to his children. He provides words of wisdom instead of words of destruction, words of lifting up instead of depressing words. Finally, he equips us, yes indeed, with a spiritual fishing rod encouraging us to be a fisher of man. No matter what we used to do. Let us look at the woman at the well. Rebellious and arrogant seemed to be her trade. Can we blame her for this behavior? I, Pastor Leslie, say no, "why she did not have any spiritual guidance. I am here to tell you whosoever lives without God in their life can act in filthy manners. Speaking from experience, I have been there, and I had my share of trouble.

The church focuses with me on renewing her mind instead of loafing on her whoredom spirit. After talking to Jesus, there comes an automatic change in her life. Could you imagine if Jesus' disciples were around to witness Jesus' private sermon to her? They would try to rebuke Him for preaching to an ungodly woman. In addition, that behavior sounds familiar in our churches. She could have been selfish and refused to share Jesus with others. No, she went back to the town where she was, and I imagine she blew her whistle, and all the men in town came out to meet her, and she preaches the shortest sermon in the history of preaching. It contains one phrase, "COME SEE A MAN, WHICH TOLD ME ALL THINGS THAT EVER I DID: IS NOT THIS CHRIST?" The city men had no problem following her because they recognized she was not the same slut they knew. They wanted to meet "THE REAL MAN," that redeemed her personality, integrity, honor, and self-esteem. That so-called whore was dead the minute she had met Jesus. He swapped her sins for eternal life. I feel like preaching another sermon: WHEN THE WHORE BECOMES A WOMAN OF GOD. WHO CAN STOP HER.? She reminded me of myself when I stole away from my native country to find refuge in a place where my shame was at ease. I thought there was no hope for me in the middle of my mess; THE REAL MAN called me. His name was not Pachouco;

Lord knows I love Pachouco. However, Pachouco honey, you are not, THE REAL MAN. Daddy Kirk, you are not THE REAL MAN. JESUS IS MY REAL MAN. Get out of your seat if you want Him to be your REAL MAN. Run, run, run toward the altar, and give your life to Him then He will be your REAL MAN. He will make you as white as snow. Face your past and defeat it with a right now God knock-out punch. Your-no good history, if you are not careful, could affect your coming to God and take your position with Him. You people reminded me of the day of Pentecost when the disciples were in one accord waiting for the grand arrival of the "Holy Ghost." Keep on coming; the angels are rejoicing over all of you that render your life to Him. People are going to talk about you, that's okay. Nevertheless, I will leave you with a song written by my husband, Pachouco. I know most of you are familiar with the song. "JUST A LITTLE." It goes like this,

Just a little more time, time with Jesus. Just a little,

Just a little more time, time with Jesus.

That's all I need to get my life back on track.

With Jesus, with Jesus on my side,

Everything, everything will be fine-

The more they talk, the more they fuss; hey, hey.

The more they lie, hey, the more I praise my God.

Though they talk about me, hey, scandalize my name, hey, hey.

Lie on me, hey, I love them anyway, oh, oh, oh with Jesus. With Jesus on my side.

Who can touch me, with Jesus on my side?

Who can hurt me, with Jesus on my side?

If God be for me, with Jesus on my side.

The more they talk, hey, the more they fuss,

The more they lie, the more I praise my God.

Though they talk about me, hey, scandalize my name, hey, hey.

Lie on me, hey, I love them anyway, oh, oh, oh with Jesus. With Jesus on my side.

When they call me name, with Jesus on my side.

Is not what they call me, with Jesus on my side.

Is what I answer to, with Jesus on my side.

Just a little more time, times with God.

Just a little more time, time with Jesus.

That's all; I need to get my life back on track.

The people turned the church service to a Gospel concert. Those who came to criticize her or be nosy had repentant hearts and gave their lives back to God.

Pachouco and Leslie's story proved that love is more powerful than ever. The moral of the story is God can use whosoever desires to be used by Him. He specializes in flipping. God can flip anything terrible to good. The God we serve could even convert Satan himself to a great Gospel preacher if he were willing to behave.

The sad part about it is that some pastors will never invite somebody like Pastor Leslie to preach in their pulpit because of her sinful past. Well, not only Leslie, even God, will not be invited in some churches to preach because He did not attend the seminary nor has a divinity degree. Furthermore, God's worship experience would limit for denominational reasons.

Pastor Leslie and the boy's vacation reached an end. They must go back to New York. The boys are unhappy they hate to leave their grandparents. Pachouco had planned to linger behind until his mother got situated. She reasoned with him to go back to New York with his family. She assured him she and Ema would be visiting soon. Pachouco obeyed his mother's voice and traveled along with his family.

As time went by, God called Pachouco to the Gospel Ministry also. Kirk, Ema, and Faye Esther traveled to New York to witness this magnificent event. Yvon and Michelle had already moved near them; they had two daughters, Alissa Michelle, and Irma; they joined Pachouco and Leslie's Church. His sister Barbara Ann was also in Queens on a business trip. All of Faye Esther's children came to support Pachouco. Graciously, God blessed the family. They have ample respect for the ministry that God entrusted in their hands. Serge Gerard was ordained as a deacon and his wife Natacha became the Church treasurer. Dr. Valada was still the superintendent of the Sunday school. Yvon was the minister of music, and Michelle became the president of the Missionary Ministry. Pachouco and Leslie had another set of twins, two girls, Esther Faye, and Ema Emanuella. "To God be the glory."

If God used a Leslie, He could use anyone.

"And we know that all things work together for good to them that love God, to them who are the called according to his purpose." Romans 8:28

Tears of Deception

www.ingramcontent.com/pod-product-compliance
Lightning Source LLC
Chambersburg PA
CBHW070640310726
48982CB00001B/349
9798985720877